THE SKULL RING

Scott Nicholson

Copyright ©2010 Scott Nicholson
Haunted Computer Books

ISBN: 978-1907190902

Haunted Computer Books
P.O. Box 135
Todd, NC 28684 USA

CHAPTER ONE

I locked the door.

Didn't I?

Julia's sweating palm gripped the doorknob, the click of the tumblers still echoing inside her skull. Would he be inside, waiting, his lungs holding a hateful breath? The years fell away, and for a moment, she was a child again. A scared little helpless—

No.

That was Memphis, this was Elkwood. This was the new and improved Julia Stone, the one who was on the path to healing. Imaginary Creeps no longer stalked the alleys of her mind. Thanks to Dr. Forrest.

She glanced behind her at the woods, which seemed to have crept closer to the house since yesterday. The Appalachian Mountain shadows reached out like fingers, and she searched there for movement, any sign that people were watching. That *he* was watching.

Julia let the door swing open and squinted into the dark throat of the house. Nobody home. Nothing to fear, just the bland patterns of her furniture to welcome her. Just another day in her new normal life.

Nonetheless, her hand went into her purse and touched the cool canister of mace. She went inside, not letting herself look back. When you were cured, you didn't care what was behind you. Forward was all that mattered. Coat rack, recliner, sofa, television. Forward, another step, even though something was wrong with the coffee table.

At first she thought they were small boxes of food, maybe

delicate chocolates or caviar, arranged in a line across the table. Something Mitchell would buy her to make up for a slight. But how did the packages get inside?

Her legs carried her closer, her fist clenched around the mace. The row of squares weren't boxes. She touched them in the dimness, let her fingers track over the raised surfaces. A child's wooden blocks.

She picked up the nearest one, her breath catching. Tilted toward the window, the embossed letter caught enough light to show its cruel hook, its sharp teeth.

J.

She placed the block back on the table, casting a look down the shadowed hall. Nothing there but dark and darker.

Her hand trembled as she picked up the next block in line. She lifted it six inches before she dropped it, and the wood clacked against the table's surface and tumbled under the couch like an oversized dice.

She didn't need to read the letter to know what it said. Because the next block was the same, and so was the next.

O.

She slapped the blocks off the table and knelt on the carpet, her heart playing her ribs like a mad xylophonist, the melody broken, the rhythm spastic, the blows landing much too hard.

A noise behind her, louder than her heartbeat. Nothing, she knew. She would be strong, because this was Elkwood, North Carolina, and bad things couldn't follow her here. She wouldn't look, because cured people didn't jump at every imagined sound.

Kurr-chack chack.

Nothing but the wind pushing branches against the house.

Chack.

Only in her head. She couldn't help it. She turned.

The Creep stood on the porch, six-foot-two.

Metal glinted in his fist.

The fish-eye lens of panic both distorted and magnified her vision. Julia tried to scream but had no breath, she rose, glanced frantically for the canister of mace she had dropped, knowing it was too late, it had always been too late, they'd had her since she was four.

The Creep's hulk blocked the doorway, a belt loaded with weapons circling his waist. His eyes were hot and steely, his mouth open in passionate rage.

He had long, long fingers.

The blade flashed, quivered.

Her heart had been set afire and shot from a catapult.

The past had reached her, despite all her running and hiding and pretending. It was here, now, come to towering, fire-breathing life. She would never make it to the bedroom door in time. If she fled, his pleasure would only intensify, and her legs were like stacks of wooden blocks shot through with string.

Why fight any longer?

The Creep was silhouetted against a backdrop of sun and light blue sky, the wild colors of autumn wreathing his head like a halo.

Julia lifted her forearms out of instinct, shut her eyes, and waited for the swift delivery of his decades'-old promise. But first would come the benediction, the words that would cut deeper than any blade.

His voice came, not in the thunder of a murderer, but in a soft, shocked exhalation. "Jesus, lady."

She peeked from behind her arms. The stranger's eyebrows furrowed in concern. His eyes were light green, the color of a murky pond under sunlight. Light green, not red like The Creep's. His arm lowered to his side, and she saw that it was a screwdriver he held loosely in his fist, not a knife.

The man took two steps backward, almost losing his balance at the edge of the porch. "I was sent here to check the windows."

"Windows?" She managed to squeeze the word through her constricted throat.

"With winter coming on and all. The landlord sent me." He paused, squinted, and continued, his vowels stretched by his native Southern Appalachian accent. "This is 102 Buckeye Creek Road, isn't it?"

She forced her head to nod twice. She saw now that the weapons at his waist were only tools, a hammer, tape measure, a couple of screwdrivers, all tucked into his leather belt that had pouches on each hip.

"I was just going to knock when you popped around the corner," he said hurriedly, as embarrassed as she was. He patted his chest with exaggerated force. "Whew. About made my heart jump like an electrified frog."

She nearly grinned in relief, but the muscles of her face were frozen. This was no Creep, after all.

Or was it? Sometimes they were clever, took their enjoyment more from the playing of the game than from the final victory. They'd played their games for years.

But she had asked the landlord two days ago if all the windows could be checked, both the sash locks and the weather stripping. Unless this Creep had tapped the phone line and knew—

No, Dr. Forrest wouldn't like that line of thinking. I'm new and improved, remember?

Looking past the handyman, she saw an old green Jeep parked off the far edge of the road. It was parked under the trees where she wouldn't have seen it while driving up.

A Creep in a Jeep? Sounded too much like Dr. Seuss to be

dangerous. Silly. A coy boy with a toy, bark in the dark, a metal muddle mental puddle. Still, the adrenaline jolt tingled her nerves at a hundred amps and caused her fingers to twitch.

She cleared her throat. One final test. "Did George Wellman send you?"

"Webster," he said, staring at her strangely, as if not sure what to make of someone who didn't know the name of her own landlord. "Mister George Webster from Silver Key Properties. I do a lot of work for him. Name's Walter."

"Of course," she said, gathering her nerve enough to step forward. They were both looking at the red canister of mace on the floor. His forced smile was more like an embarrassed grimace, his cheeks creasing and blushing slightly. She bent and picked up the mace, kicking aside one of the wooden blocks.

"You have kids?" he asked.

She shook her head, avoiding his eyes. How could she explain that the blocks weren't hers without sounding like a lunatic? But the problem was she couldn't be sure the blocks weren't hers or whether or not she was a lunatic.

"Listen, I can come back later," he said. "I'll just pick up a key from Mister Webster and do it while you're at work."

"No, I'm fine. Really." She wiped her hair from her eyes, and her fingers came away moist with sweat. She tried to cover her jumpiness with a lie. "I just ran through the house, I heard the phone ring, and I thought I heard somebody at the door, and—well, look at me, I'm just a babbling mess."

He looked, a few seconds longer this time. Then he cast his gaze down to the porch. "Well, ma'am, I guess I should have hollered when I saw the door was open."

"Don't be silly." Julia hated herself for her panic. "I just wish Mr. Webster had told me you were coming."

"He said he left a message on your answering machine."

She nodded again, feeling as wooden as the blocks that were scattered across the floor. "Why don't you go ahead? I've got to go back to work in a little bit."

"Won't take long." He was around thirty. His hair was brown and just long enough to curl a little at the ends. His muscular hands bore several scars, but the skin on his face was smooth under his short beard. He didn't have the beaten expression worn by many people who worked with their hands, though the shadows of his face harbored a hint of sadness and darkness. He didn't look like the sort who would play pranks with wooden blocks.

Then again, they never did.

"Come on in." She stepped aside so the handyman could enter. His tool belt jangled as he passed. He went to the front windows, flipped back the locks and slid them up. A draft of forest-flavored air wended across the room.

Julia left the door open and crossed to the sofa, sat where she could see him, and pretended to thumb through *Psychology Today*. Her hand gripped the mace tightly. The landlord had seemed overly eager to rent this place. How many keys did Webster have for the house?

"These are fine," the handyman said, sliding the windows closed. "Anderson windows are built good. Double panes. Ought to really help on your heating bill."

"I'll be burning wood," she said, turning the magazine page to an article entitled "Precious Memories: How To Preserve Your Family's Past." She kept looking past the magazine to the blocks on the floor.

"Good for you. Cheaper and you get a little exercise. Where you from?" he asked without turning around, his screwdriver creaking as he tightened a curtain rod hanger.

"Memphis."

"You're in for a treat. We get about eight or ten snows every year. Don't get much down there, I reckon."

"Just once in a while. It melts before you even get to pack a dirty snowball."

"Can't stand to be in the city myself. Breaks me out in a sweat. People piled on top of each other like Japanese beetles on a cherry leaf."

Julia said nothing. She wasn't used to loquacious carpenters. In Memphis, skilled laborers did their work in silence. She was used to her own crowd, other reporters, artists, Mitchell's lawyer friends. In the city, strangers kept to themselves. Unless they wanted flesh, blood, or soul.

"How long you been in Elkwood?" he asked, not pausing in his work.

"Four months," she said.

"That figures," he said. "I did some work here at the start of summer. House had been empty for a couple of years."

"I wonder why. It's a cozy little place."

"Hartley used to live here." The handyman said "Hartley" as if spitting out the name of an old enemy.

"Don't tell me I'm living in a haunted house," she said.

"No ghosts here. Just bad memories."

He gathered his tools and moved into the kitchen. Julia remained where she was, slipping the mace into her pants pocket and browsing the magazine.

After several minutes of the windows sliding up and down and tools rattling, the handyman appeared at the end of the hall.

"Okay if I go in the bedroom?" he asked.

He probably found some embarrassing things in his job. He went into private places, patched things where secrets hid. But Julia had no secrets there, not much to blush about in her bedroom. No ceiling mirrors, no bedside sex toys, no leather straps or chains dangling from the bedposts.

Just a crazy clock that was stuck on 4:06.

"Go ahead," she said. "Can I make you a cup of coffee?"

"No, thanks, ma'am. I don't want to put you to no trouble."

"It's no trouble. I'm going to make some anyway. I only want a cup or two, though."

"Well, in that case, I'd appreciate some to go. I got my thermos out in the Jeep."

Julia busied herself in the kitchen, whistling as she filled the pot. She didn't glance over her shoulder, even though the urge was strong. With the water running in the sink, he could sneak right up behind, reach out his long, long fingers—

She twisted the tap angrily. Tears filled her eyes. Her lip quivered.

It owned her.

Maybe it—the fear, the darkness, The Creep—wouldn't take her this morning, but she knew it was out there.

No, not out there. In *here*.

In her head.

The worst place of all. This was an inside job all the way. The monster rummaged in the rooms of her mind, hid in cramped closets, staked out the shadowed corners of her psyche. What scared her most was the knowledge that she had built that monster herself, bit by bit, sewn it from scraps of memory and the threads of what-if, imagined it to life. The cellar of her head-house was a Frankenstein laboratory for bringing strange creatures to life.

No monster had spread those blocks on her coffee table, had spelled out that name. Because everybody knew that monsters weren't real. Especially Dr. Forrest.

She started the coffee maker. Her therapist in Memphis told her to lay off the caffeine. Dr. Lance Danner. Lance. Freud could have had a field day with that name. Sometimes a cigar was just a cigar and a lance was just a lance.

Dr. Danner also told her that, although they had been progressing in the therapy, a move was probably a good thing for her. He'd encouraged her to take the job in Elkwood, depressurize, embrace a rural lifestyle. Dr. Danner even made a referral to a doctor here that Julia felt comfortable with, touting it as "a continuum of care." Mitchell had been against her leaving, but his possessiveness had only made Julia more determined. If she was ever going to show him she was a big girl, now was the time.

Big girls don't cry, though.

Julia wiped away her tears with the back of her hand. She was glad she didn't wear make-up, because the streaks would show. Not that she cared much what the handyman thought of her. She definitely wasn't out to appear attractive to anyone, especially a potential Creep in a Jeep.

She took her cup of coffee to the living room, picked up the magazine, put it down again. She stared out the window at the red, purple, and yellow of the changing leaves. The mountains were comforting despite their mystery. The ancient ridges of the Appalachians rolled out like soft ocean waves, in a rhythm that promised protection and peace.

The buildings of Memphis had been suffocating, the giant walls looming, dense traffic like a herd of sulfur-spewing demons. The hot jaws of the city nipped at her heels with every step, hounded her, gnashed steel-and-concrete teeth at her. A million Creeps lurked in the alleys, two million eyes followed her every move. Memphis would have chewed her, ground her bones to powder, swallowed her.

The move here had not been a mistake. For the first time in his exalted reign, Mitchell had been wrong, though Mitchell would never admit it.

"All done, ma'am," said the handyman, coming back into

the living room. "The locks are all sound, and you shouldn't get any bad drafts come winter."

"Great." She reached for her purse on the floor beside her. Her foot kicked one of the blocks and it rolled to Walter's feet.

"You a schoolteacher?" he asked.

"No, I write for the *Courier-Times*. How much do I owe you?"

"Nothing," he said. "Mister Webster pays me. Repairs are the landlord's responsibility."

She thought about tipping, decided against it. These mountain folks were proud about such things. Far different from the grabby people in the city. Instead, she said, "Let me get that coffee for you. Soy creamer's all I got. Me and dairy disagree."

"That would be fine, ma'am. I'll go get my thermos. I have to check a couple more things outside first."

He went out the open front door. When he reappeared several minutes later, he was without his tool belt. He gave her the thermos and waited by the door.

"Say, did you know your clock was messed up?" he asked when she returned with the filled thermos.

"My clock?"

"Yeah, in the bedroom. It was stuck on 4:06 the whole time I was in there."

She had unplugged the clock. Hadn't she?

She smiled to disguise the icy rush that shot through her veins. "Thanks for telling me. It's been acting up lately. Guess I'll have to get another one."

"Yeah. Never heard of a digital clock doing that. Usually they just blink or go dark."

"Stuck in time." *Just like me.* The smile felt painted on her face, like a dime-store mannequin's.

"Keeps you young," he said. "Growing old is for people

who give up too soon."

"I'll keep that in mind. Thanks for the work."

"Sure. You need anything else, ask for me. Walter." He smiled again as he reminded her of his name. It wasn't a come-on smile. It was a friendly smile, with slightly crooked teeth, the kind you could trust.

No, that's not true. You can't trust ANY smile. Because every smile has teeth behind it.

She almost gave him her name then decided against it. "Okay, Walter."

"You found a church yet?"

"Pardon me?"

"Church. It can be hard to settle in to a new place." He looked at her with inquisitor's eyes, as if he had a personal stake in her soul. She resented the notion that he saw her as a chance to bank some goodwill and capital in some heavenly coffer.

"I'm set." She smiled, the conditioned reflex of people being mindlessly civil to acquaintances. He'd been kind to her and was probably just extending a small-town politeness. She owed him better than a bland brush-off, and her thoughts were already drifting into the dark cracks of the past.

"Have a good day, Miss Stone." Walter waved and headed for the Jeep, humming a country-tinged tune. Julia closed the door.

Now she was alone.

No, not alone. Inside with the Creep.

The Creep was always in the house, no matter where she lived.

CHAPTER TWO

The phone bleated in a slaughter of electric sheep.

She had two phones, one in the living room, one by the bed. Perhaps overkill for a three-room house, but she liked to have one within reach if she couldn't find the cell. In case of emergencies.

Julia started down the hall so she could lie on the bed while she chatted, remembering the frozen clock. She couldn't face that right now. She picked up the phone on the coffee table and flopped onto the sofa.

"Hello?"

"Hi, Julia." The voice on the end of the line was buoyant and brimming with self-confidence.

"Mitchell," she said, unsure whether she was glad to hear from him or not.

"What's going on, honey?"

She winced at the rote, nearly toneless endearment. "Nothing."

"Great." There was a pause, the quiet hiss of eight hundred miles.

"So . . . what's new?" Julia finally asked.

"The usual."

That was the trouble with Mitchell. The usual was always new to him. "Working on any interesting cases?"

"Yeah, come to think of it. I've got a beaut. This woman owns a piece of land, right? Inherited it from her father, been in the family since Reconstruction. Ugly stretch, half swamp and half hill, forty acres. So this developer makes her an offer so he can build a strip mall."

"Just what Memphis needs," she heard herself saying.

Mitchell didn't catch her sarcasm. "Exactly. This woman wants to keep it, maybe turn it into an organic garden, or heaven forbid, a natural habitat. Jesus, conservation easements are the tool of the Devil. Well, the Board of Adjustment votes to zone the property for commercial use, claiming the area is—let's see . . . ."

Julia heard the rustling of papers. Mitchell must be at his office on General Pickett Avenue, the one with the view of Beale Street. From his window, he could watch the tourists and the busking blues musicians clog the sidewalks. Most of the modern Memphis bluesmasters knew only the blues of a bad day at the stock market.

"Here it is," Mitchell said, his words coming out faster in his excitement. "This is classic. The Board ruled that the property was, quote, 'in an area of urban development of vital interest to the municipality's extraterritorial jurisdiction.' And the property's three miles from the city limits."

"Poor woman. How can she afford to pay you?" Mitchell billed hourly in the high triple figures.

He laughed, that silk-tie, champagne-etched laugh that sometimes made her skin crawl. "She can't afford anybody. She's got the ACLU. We're going to feed them their lunch. The developer is picking up my tab to work as a consultant to the city attorneys."

Of course. Mitchell would be on the side of big business, fat money, legal tender that was more immoral than legal and about as tender as a metal-toed boot. The worst part of it was that his cockiness appealed to her sick, weak nature, an addiction that even distance couldn't break. He was a Leo, through and through, his lion a voracious predator to her moody Gemini.

"But enough about me," he said. "How are you?"

"I'm fine," she said. "Really."

"Really?"

Had a note of concern crept into his voice? She gave him the benefit of a doubt. "Yes. The people at the office are really nice. It's refreshing to cover community issues, the school board and that sort of thing, instead of working the crime beat."

"Good. You know I never wanted you to mess around in all that murder and stuff. I love this city, but it's really gone to hell ever since—"

"How are your parents?" she asked, before he could rant about crime and taxes and the lower class.

"My parents are doing really well. They're up at Martha's Vineyard right now." At one of their four seasonal houses. Christmas in Boca Raton, Easter in Santa Monica, Fourth of July in Boulder, slumming in Yankee country through Halloween.

"Tell them I said hello."

"Sure. You know, they'd love to hear from you. They ask about you all the time. You're practically family, you know."

"Maybe I'll give them a call," she lied. If she called, they'd use the M-word. Every woman needed a diamond for validation, and a gold ring to seal the deal. That was as certain as the rising sun, increasing property taxes, and Mitchell's cologne being made by Jovan.

"So, how's your new doctor?"

"Good. Really good. We're making progress."

Mitchell sighed. "You were making progress four years ago, with Lance what's-his-name."

Mitchell hid his jealousy so poorly. He assumed that any man that got a woman on the couch was automatically on top of her within fifteen minutes.

No, only YOU, Mitchell. Besides, nobody lies down for therapy anymore. That went out with assembly-line frontal lobotomies and Mesmerism.

She said, "I feel like we're close to a breakthrough. I'm feeling much better. I don't . . . ."

—*get the Creeps?*—

" . . . suffer from as much anxiety. I think the mountains are helping me. They make me feel safe."

To his credit, Mitchell didn't laugh. "If you'd let me buy you a gun—"

"Are the leaves changing there?"

"Leaves?"

"On the trees."

"Hold on. Let me look."

"Never mind."

"When are you going to let me come see you?"

"Soon."

"How soon? You said August. It's already football season."

"Soon," she repeated. "I just . . . want to be ready, that's all."

She could almost hear his thoughts, see his handsome eyebrows raised in perplexity. *Women. Why can't they make up their minds? If I have to wait for Julia to get her head together, I'll be old and gray and Mr. Happy won't be able to jump up and do his little dance of joy anymore.*

"You know I love you, Julia."

She nodded at the phone. Her eyes were fixed down the hallway, on the bedroom entrance. The handyman had left the door open, but he must have closed the curtains because the room was dark. She thought again of the clock and those red numerals stuck on 4:06.

The handyman had seen those numerals. But she had unplugged the clock. She was sure, just as she'd been sure she'd locked the door.

The handyman had also seen the blocks lying near her feet. Those weren't imaginary, either.

"Julia?"

"Yeah?" She realized she was still holding the phone.

"I said I love you."

"I know you do."

"Well?"

"Me, too. I . . . love you."

Then it started, at that brief hesitation. The slightly perceptible lift, the higher pitch to his voice. The calm before the storm. Those who dealt with Mitchell Austin in the courtroom knew only the calm, never the storm. "When are you going to start thinking about us again, and not just yourself?"

"I'm making progress. Dr. Forrest is really good. I'm—"

"Please. Spare me the details."

"Mitchell—"

"How about next weekend? I can catch a morning flight to Charlotte, be up in time for lunch. I'll stop at one of the gourmet shops on my way to the airport. Bet they don't have brie or leeks vinaigrette in Elkwood, do they? Or wine that doesn't have an expiration date on the label."

Mitchell was on track now, as if this were a jury civil trial and he had the main witness squirming. Julia felt oddly defensive about this community that she'd only recently joined. "They're good people here. I like this place. I like these mountains."

"When are you going to give in and marry me?"

Said with the same tone as "What flavor of ice cream would you like?" Her own anger rose slightly, a hot snake writhing in her chest. "Mitchell, we've been through this a hundred times—"

"Okay, okay. But, really, I'd love to see you. I need to see you." Voice softer now, trying a different tack. "I miss you."

"I want to see you, too, Mitchell. I just want to be ready, that's all. You deserve me at my best, and I don't think I can give you that right now. Maybe in a few weeks."

"A few weeks, then. I'll hold you to that, honey. Listen, got to go. Another call's coming in."

Wouldn't want you to miss a call. Some savings and loan might need help foreclosing on an orphanage.

"Bye, Mitch—"

He'd already hung up.

Julia held the phone to her chest for a moment. No shadows had crawled from the bedroom. No Creep had tiptoed past her to mess with her clock. Nobody had spelled out strange words on her coffee table.

One good thing about Mitchell, he never failed to make her forget her other worries. He'd driven her crazier than a hundred Creeps could. First by getting her to fall in love and then leaving her wondering if love really existed.

It was nearly noon. She took a sip of cool coffee, carried the cup to the kitchen, and rinsed it. She gobbled an avocado-and-bean-sprouts sandwich and grabbed an apple on the way out the door. Even though the day remained chilly, Julia didn't get her sweater from the bedroom.

The clock might still be stuck on 4:06. Could electronic brains go insane? Or only people?

She wasn't sure she wanted to know the answer.

To warm herself, she balled some newspaper, piled the clumps in the fireplace, and struck a match to them. Then she stacked on the wooden blocks, staring wide-eyed as the tongues of fire licked the wood into a gray pile of ash, erasing the name that had been spelled out on the flat wooden faces.

CHAPTER THREE

"What did you dream last night?"

Julia stared past Dr. Forrest to the painting that dominated the office wall. It was done in shades of orange and brown and red, an abstract piece with jagged edges. Piled triangles, shredded squares, the angles reamed and raped. Art that was disquieting instead of soothing.

Dr. Danner had favored pastorals, not-so-skilled paintings of the sort seen in beginner's art classes. Barns and willows, creeks and fences. No people. No threats. Just plain old boring nature.

"Julia?"

"Oh, sorry." Julia looked at the doctor. Pamela Forrest smiled wisely, her glasses perched on the end of her nose. Fortyish, well-dressed, low heels and short, up-to-date hairstyle. Comfortable in her leather chair, her neat office the external manifestation of an ordered mind.

And here Julia was again, shrinking her shrinks, comparing their defects.

Dr. Forrest nodded, nudging her along. "You're a little distant today. What were you just thinking about?"

She thought about lying. But then she'd *really* be crazy. If you couldn't trust your therapist, who could you trust?

"I had an episode," Julia said. "When I came home this morning. I . . . I thought I had locked my front door, but then I found it open."

"Open?"

"Well, not open, just unlocked."

"And how did that make you feel?"

"Scared."

"Scared of what?"

Julia looked down at her hands. "I don't know."

"I think you do."

"Him. It. The Creep."

"Ah." Dr. Forrest leaned forward in her chair. "You thought the Creep had unlocked the door and was waiting inside."

"Yes."

"Was there a Creep inside?"

"No. But there could have been."

"And what would the Creep have done?"

"I don't know."

"Yes, you do. It's not very hard to imagine."

Julia dreaded imagining it again. The fantasy was almost as painful as the real act would be, had been. But if she acted out the scenario, Dr. Forrest would be pleased with her. Julia needed to please someone.

So she concentrated on what the attack would have been like. The anxiety of that morning came back to her, as fresh as it had been the first time. She gripped the arms of her chair and squeezed until her knuckles were white. *"Please don't hurt me,"* she gasped through clenched teeth, almost feeling the knife thrusting with every word.

"Yes, that's it," said Dr. Forrest, her voice low, intense, urging. "Let it out, live it. Bring out the fear and face it."

"He's got me," Julia said, eyes closed, drenched in the sweat of tension, aching from the hot knife in her chest, seeing her blood spilling on the living room carpet.

"Can you see his face?"

"No."

"Try."

"I'm trying," she said, barely above a whisper. Though the

room was sweetened by the chrysanthemums perched in a vase on the doctor's desk, Julia could have sworn she smelled smoke.

"Try harder. If you can *see* him, it will be a small victory over him."

"I . . . " The Creep's features almost coalesced from the mists of her imagination. The handyman? Mitchell? That college kid who been watching her from across the street yesterday? Or was it older than that, older than her, older than time?

"Who is it? Who has brought this fear into your life?"

Julia exploded from the chair and strode to the window. She paced back and forth, rubbing her upper arms. She was panting, wired from worry yet nearly exhausted at the same time.

Dr. Forrest came to her, put a hand on her shoulder. "It's okay, Julia. I know how much it hurts you to face it. If I thought there was another way to beat it, I'd try it. But you've refused Klonopin and Prozac and—"

"No drugs," Julia said. "I want to beat it with my own head."

"I know, Julia. But we all need help from time to time. At least you're letting me help you." She led Julia back to the chair. "Let's try something different. We've come far enough that I think you're ready for the next stage."

Julia sat meekly and Dr. Forrest leaned the chair back, crossed the room, and lowered the lights. The sky was still overcast, the room nearly dark. Julia closed her eyes and waited for Dr. Forrest's instructions.

"Let's go back," the therapist said.

"I don't want to," said Julia.

"But that's where the problem started, Julia. Everything else, all your troubles, your fears, were born there. Your body knows it, your subconscious knows it. All the rest of you is waiting for you to admit it."

Julia swallowed hard and licked her lips. Darkness. She opened her eyes. Darkness.

"Look up at the ceiling, Julia."

Julia obeyed, but couldn't see the ceiling.

Dr. Forrest's tone softened, but her words kept their even pace. "Look past the ceiling, Julia."

Julia looked. More darkness, a deeper black.

"Look beyond that, Julia. And while you're looking, let your arms and legs relax. Your limbs are like large helium balloons, very light, very relaxed."

Julia floated on that image. For the first time since waking that morning, she felt completely at ease.

Dr. Forrest's soothing voice came from somewhere near her. "Very peaceful, very light. You trust me, don't you, Julia?"

"Yes," she heard herself whispering. It was almost someone else's voice.

"You're free now, Julia. Nothing can hurt you. I won't let anything hurt you."

Julia smiled. Her face felt like a mask of warm taffy.

"You really have to trust me now. We're going to go back. Way back into the past."

Julia mumbled a protest.

Dr. Forrest took her hand. "Shhh. It's okay. This time, I'll be with you. We'll go back together. I won't let anybody hurt you."

Julia waited, looking beyond with eyes closed.

"I won't let *him* hurt you," Dr. Forrest said.

Julia nodded. A few moments more, looking beyond blackness, and she was small again. Four. In her room. Chester Bear against her shoulder. In the middle of the night. Darkness. Darkness. Except . . .

The light spilling through the crack below the door.

"What do you see?" Dr. Forrest said.

"Light." Julia's voice sounded childish even to herself.

"Where are you?"

"My bedroom."

"Which bedroom?"

"In the house. The big house where Daddy lives."

"Daddy? How do you know?"

"I know."

"What's happening now?"

"I get out of bed. I hear voices in the other room. Loud. Like somebody's mad. I'm *scared*."

Dr. Forrest squeezed her hand. "I'm with you this time. Go on."

She went to the door. The floor was cold beneath her bare feet. "I've wet the bed. Daddy doesn't like it when I wet the bed."

Julia went to the door, listened. "The people are mad at Daddy. I hear them. The bad people."

"What does your father say, Julia?"

"I don't know. I can't hear him."

"What do you *think* he says?"

"I don't know."

"Try harder, Julia. Do it for me."

Julia listened. A car horn sounded. Had it come from outside the office, or outside her childhood bedroom?

"No good," she whispered, mouth dry.

Dr. Forrest was quiet for a moment, still holding Julia's hand. "Let's pretend for a little bit. Can you do that?"

"Yes," said Julia eagerly, not wanting Dr. Forrest to get mad like the bad people.

"Let's pretend that the people have come to take your father away."

"No," Julia cried, trying to sit up. Dr. Forrest held her pinned against the chair.

"You're at your bedroom door, Julia," Dr. Forrest continued, holding on as Julia thrashed weakly. "You're four years old, and the bad people are in the living room."

"Bad people," Julia moaned.

"Open the door."

"No. Please don't make me."

"Open the door, Julia."

Her hand was against the wood, pulling, a mixture of horror and excitement racing through her with every ragged leap of her heart. The light made her eyes hurt and she blinked. The door opened only slightly, but she was afraid the bad people had heard the hinges creak.

She blinked and hugged Chester Bear. Daddy stood in the living room. Three people without faces were with him, surrounding him. They wore black robes with hoods.

"Come on, Douglas," said the tallest of the faceless people. "You're either all the way *in*, or all the way *out*."

Daddy shook his head, his face pale and sweating. "I can't do that, Lucius."

"You drank from the cup," the hooded man said. "You made a pledge."

"But that wasn't part of the deal," her father pleaded. He looked around wildly. It was the first time Julia had ever seen him scared. He'd always been so big, so brave, so strong—

"You wear his ring," said the leader of the bad people. The other two closed in on Daddy, one at each arm.

"You're crazy," Daddy said. Julia almost cried out, but fear tightened her throat and froze her tongue.

Then Daddy looked at her bedroom door, saw the light spilling on her face through the crack. And the bad man, Lucius, saw Daddy's eyes widen. The hooded head turned in

Julia's direction.

This time she did cry out, dropping Chester Bear and feeling as if she were going to wet herself again. She cried and shook her head, screamed and screamed against the night.

"Tell me what's happening," came a voice.

Dr. Forrest? What was she doing here?

A hand gripped hers.

And Julia tore herself from the past, remembered the earlier sessions and how they had gone this far into Julia's past, this far and more, and suddenly she didn't want to relive it again, just wanted that night to stay back there in the dim, dark forgotten.

"You know what happened, don't you, Julia?"

She nodded. How could she forget? Her mind had tried, had locked it away in some secret compartment.

"Are you ready to tell me about it?"

"No."

"Julia. I thought we were making progress."

"I can't remember."

"Yes, you can. The body remembers what the mind tries to forget. The memory is in your blood, in your cells. In your heart. Listen to it."

Remember.

No matter how much it hurts.

"They came and got you, didn't they?"

"Got me?"

"The bad people."

"The bad people," Julia echoed.

"And what did they do to you that night?"

Tears rolled down her cheeks, hot on her skin. Her stomach clenched as if expecting a blow from a fist. The muscles of her arms trembled uncontrollably.

"They . . . they *got me.*"

"Yes. And you know what they did next."

Julia shook her head, still denying. *Needing* to deny.

"Let it out," Dr. Forrest said, squeezing Julia's hand so tightly it hurt. "Bring it to the light, so you can defeat it."

It came in a rush. The scraps of images, thoughts like broken glass, a jigsaw-puzzle dream with its pieces spilled in dark water, reflections in fractured mirrors, the splintered bones of memories, fantasies built on smothering air, all clashing together like invisible armies in the night.

Cold stone beneath her naked back. Her legs and arms fastened with rough rope. The candles around her, their orange light flickering off the gray walls and mingling with shadows that slithered like snakes. Above her, ropes dangling from rough wooden beams backed by an endless night. Singing, humming, many voices.

She wanted Daddy. She wanted Chester Bear. Then she saw the bad people. All around her, in their robes, eyes glowing under the dark hoods. Then they were hurting her, even though she screamed and fought against the ropes.

She struggled free, sat up, her lungs on fire. She blinked rapidly.

The office. The impressionist art on the wall, oak paneling, the slight scent of leather and flowers. Dr. Forrest sitting beside her, beaming, her glasses fogged.

"Yes!" said Dr. Forrest triumphantly. "You did it."

Julia looked around, saw the clock on the wall. Her hour was almost up. Good. She didn't think she could stand another minute with the punishing past.

"How do you feel?" Dr. Forrest asked.

"Awful. I've got a headache. My muscles are sore." She rubbed her wrists where the imagined restraints had squeezed her.

"The memory's in the flesh," Dr. Forrest said.

"Psychogenic. The pain's locked away, too. But we can draw it out."

"I wish it didn't have to hurt so much."

Dr. Forrest put her face near, so close that Julia could smell the *fettuccine Alfredo* the woman had eaten for lunch. "You're the victim, Julia. Don't forget that. You didn't ask to be abused."

"Except I *do* keep asking for it, don't I? Isn't that why I fear The Creep so much? It's like I expect bad things to happen to me."

"Yes, but it's not your fault. You're helpless. Those people—*bad people*—have enslaved you. The past has a long reach."

"Then why do I have to keep returning to the past? Can't we just leave it alone?" Julia shook the smoke and sweat and pain from her head.

"Don't you want to be better?"

"Good enough. You know that. That's why I'm here."

"We have a lot of work left to do," the therapist said. "But that's enough for today. I really feel we've made a breakthrough this session."

Julia felt as if the breakthrough had been made from the inside out, that the memory in her meat had slashed and clawed its way to the skin. She stood and gathered her purse, slightly dizzy. Dr. Forrest was behind her desk, thumbing through her calendar.

Julia almost mentioned the wooden blocks, but knew that Dr. Forrest would make her search her purse for the receipt. Because the doctor would say that Julia bought the blocks herself and spread them out on the table to engage in psychological self-torture. A bit of self-indulgent trickery. Julia's diagnosis would change to something meaty like Schizophrenia, Stable Paranoid Type. And Julia would be no closer to being cured.

"Tell me something about your father," the doctor said without looking up. "When you used to play on the floor with him."

No, Julia thought. Dr. Forrest can't read minds. And believing people can read minds will definitely nudge you into the schizophrenic folder.

"I'd spell my name with my wooden blocks. And he'd laugh and say, 'No, honey. It's *Jooolia*.' And he'd take away the second block and put in three O's."

"And what would you do then?"

"I'd say, 'No, it's not,' and then he'd laugh and hug me and rub my hair and lay out the blocks the right way." She glanced at the door, regretting the hour's excursion from her chronic state of denial. "I don't want to talk about it anymore."

"Recovering good memories is just as important to healing as flushing out the bad ones."

"Right now I'm tired of remembering."

"Next week as usual, then."

Julia nodded. Dr. Forrest scribbled down the appointment. "Call me if you need me." Dr. Forrest handed her a reminder card. "And I want you to try something for me."

"Yes?"

"Keep a journal. Jot down some of the things that happen, your dreams, anything. It doesn't have to be formal. In fact, the more stream-of-conscious, the better."

"I'll try," Julia said, knowing she would do more than try. Dr. Forrest was a good therapist. She wouldn't assign Julia busy work. Everything was done with a purpose in mind. Julia knew a little therapeutic theory from her own college psychology class. And she wanted to please her doctor.

We're making progress . . . .

CHAPTER FOUR

Dr. Forrest walked her to the door. Julia went blinking into the parking lot. As always after a session, the world seemed unreal, the pieces of it incoherent and unstable. The asphalt was a separate thing from the ground, as if it floated over ether. The mountains and sky didn't seem to quite meet up on the horizon. Though the clouds still veiled the sun, the flecks of mica in the sidewalk sparkled like tiny stars, forming galaxies beneath her feet. Even the trees that lined the streets seemed to exist in a two-dimensional universe of their own, as flat as colored leaves pressed in a keepsake book.

It was only after she'd started her car and edged out onto the highway that she remembered her bedroom clock. She hadn't told Dr. Forrest about 4:06, either. The oddity wasn't concocted by her imagination. She had the handyman Walter as a corroborating witness. But Julia had unplugged the clock before Walter saw it. She was sure.

Julia had a feeling that Dr. Forrest would be displeased to hear about the clock. The therapist didn't like Julia's focusing on little coincidences. Maybe Julia would casually mention it next time, or scribble it in her journal. Or maybe just forget all about it. Sometimes the past was best left alone.

She skirted the main drag of Elkwood, four blocks of downtown where the highest building was five stories. The town billed itself as "The Gateway to the Mountains," and had originally been a trading outpost for the hunters who tamed the wilderness, displaced the Cherokee, and eradicated the buffalo and even the elk from which the town had derived its name. Now it was a growing tourist destination, nestled in a river basin between the Blue Ridge and the Great Smoky Mountains.

Julia drove across the Amadahee River and the unused railroad tracks that circled Elkwood's small industrial section. Two of the factories were abandoned, their chain-link fences ripped and sagging, the parking lots pocked with grass, stubborn oil stains, and broken bottles. Some of the factories were being torn down and replaced by condominiums and technology parks, the South's New Reconstruction.

Maybe Julia would write a series about it. Her editor had pigeonholed her, though. She was a "soft" writer at the *Elkwood Courier-Times*, even though she'd been a straight news reporter for *The Commercial Appeal*. That was okay, too. She no longer had to sleep with a police scanner, hoping for someone's personal tragedy to supply her day's work.

She made it to the office just in time for her 3:00 writers' meeting. Her assignments for the week included a flower show at the mall, a disease outbreak at the animal shelter, some famous literary writer she'd never heard of speaking at the library, the dedication of a new soccer field, and a crafts festival coming up in three weeks. The crafts festival included a lot of the paper's advertisers, so the editor wanted to give it a big push. Julia could handle it, although glorifying glued beads and poorly-woven baskets was a challenge to her writing skills.

Covering the local school boards and arts committees was also a challenge. She'd learned that the most valuable journalistic skill was making people's quotes sound smarter than they actually were. She was bothered when readers referred to the weekly paper as "The Snooze," but she was thankful for the low-stress job. Pulitzers could wait. She was in Elkwood to get her head together.

As she left the conference room, her co-worker Rick O'Dell caught up with her. "Hey, Julia, what's up?"

"Same old," she said.

Rick smiled, eyes bright behind his 1950's science-teacher glasses. He had a Clark Kent-style curl in the middle of his forehead, the studly tress glistening with *mousse*. His zoot-inspired suit was tailored, a luxury at his salary. His retro style was tarnished by the gold chain around his neck, as if he were Palm Beach by way of Cleveland. "Did you read the opening of my series?"

"I don't get the paper," she deadpanned.

Rick laughed too enthusiastically. He was a hot reporter, on the way up, two North Carolina Press Associations Awards under his belt already. But he wanted other things under his belt, such as every young woman who crossed his blotter. "It's a killer story," he said. "Literally."

"Do tell," she said, continuing to her desk, knowing Rick wouldn't need a nudge. Persistence was important for a good reporter, and Rick's cockiness meant he didn't give up easily.

"Remember in the 1980s, when there was all this buzz about Satanism, the huge underground network, how all these children were disappearing that ended up as human sacrifices?"

Julia's head lifted at the word "Satanism." She stopped walking and turned to Rick. "Yeah. Didn't everyone pretty much agree that the whole business was overblown?"

"Sure. I mean, how do you account for some of those claims that as many as 50,000 people were murdered as human sacrifices? You just can't hide that many bodies without somebody finding a bone here or there."

"Bone?" Last night's dream stirred in its slumbering grave.

"Yeah," Rick said. His angular sideburns lifted as he smiled. "Well, maybe it's coming back. Did you hear about the body they found in the Amadahee?"

"No." Julia avoided the television news, the radio, even the paper when she could. She hadn't been kidding about not subscribing to the newspaper. If ignorance was bliss, she wanted to be as blissful as a meditating Buddha.

"Caucasian male, in his twenties. Nude, hands bound, his abdominal cavity ripped open. Pretty ritualistic."

"Wow," Julia said, her interest piqued. Elkwood didn't have as many murders as Memphis, but was as suspect to that particular sin as any other American community. Still, this one sounded different from the run-of-the-mill Saturday night armed disagreement. Julia hadn't shaken the habits of the crime beat as easily as she had thought. "But what's the link to Satanism? If you've done your research, and I bet you have—"

Rick grinned, showing perfect white teeth that could afford smugness, and nodded at her to continue.

"Then you know that ritualism is usually more to fill a psychological need than a spiritual need. At least when it comes to murder."

"Sure. Serial killers do what they do to fulfill a sexual need. Everybody knows that. They don't make necklaces of women's body parts just because they want to please some higher or lower power. They do it because they like it. They get off on it. And they keep doing it until they're caught or dead."

"So, you took 'Creep 101' in college, too?" Julia asked.

"The home course."

"Then why do the authorities think this was a Satanic killing?"

"They don't. Not yet. But the victim was male. Gutted. And here's the kicker. The guy's pinkie was chopped off."

"Chopped off?" Julia was hooked, despite herself. She loathed the public's unending appetite for atrocity, the hunger for controversy, the prurient fascination for the dark side of humanity. She'd even made it her stock in trade, trafficking in human misery to deliver juicy headlines for her Memphis editors. She was as guilty as anyone for wallowing in bad news, but she could understand it. She had her own built-in dichotomy, the black past that she kept re-entering like a prospector probing a shaky mine shaft.

"Sure. Now, a chopped finger doesn't seem so bad compared to being gut-hauled, but the thing is, the pinkie wound was *healed*. A stump of scar tissue. Meaning the injury had been inflicted years ago."

"So? He could have had an accident, caught it in a textile machine or a car door."

"He could have," Rick agreed, adjusting his already-perfect jet-black curl. "But pinkie amputation is another ritual practiced by the you-know-whos."

"Our old buddies, the Satanists." Julia shook her head. "Rick, you've watched too many 'X-Files' reruns."

"I've got plenty more evidence. Let me buy you a beer at the Whistle Gate and I'll tell you all about it."

"No, thanks," she said, smiling to disarm him. Then she thought about going home, with darkness falling and her house waiting and the clock in her bedroom still stuck on 4:06.

Better the Creep you know, I suppose. At least this one has a face.

"On second thought," she said. "I haven't eaten out for a few weeks. Might do me some good to see what civilization is up to these days."

Rick's chest swelled visibly. "Great. *Great!*"

"I'll meet you there. Six-ish."

He backed down the hall, grinning like a kindergartner who'd put a worm down a girl's dress. "Wonderful. I'll get us a good table."

As Julia went to her desk to put her notes and papers away, she wondered if Dr. Forrest would approve.

CHAPTER FIVE

Julia got home after dark. The Subaru's headlights swept over the house as she drove up. Lights blazed from the neighboring apartments, and Mabel Covington's front porch light was on, a flotilla of moths seeking out its heat. Even though the forest hovered dark and thick, Julia was determined not to be afraid.

Music spilled from one of the bottom apartments, the Rolling Stones' "Sympathy for the Devil." Mick Jagger was the one that needed sympathy. Hobbling out on stage with his cane and hearing aid, but still dressed in Spandex and feather boas. The Devil had obviously not kept his end of the bargain in that deal.

A tan boxer barked at her from the ragged grounds of the apartment. The dog was friendly, but it made a habit of dropping smelly little presents around Julia's door. She was torn between shooing it away and feeding it snacks, and in the end they'd reached an uneasy truce in which Julia gave the dog a pat on the head instead of bacon bits, and Fido kept his poop to the edge of the driveway.

Rick had practically invited himself over to Julia's for a nightcap. Julia had deflected him, casually mentioning her fiancé and all the work she needed to get done. Now, entering the dark, silent house, she almost wished she'd accepted his offer, assuming he could keep his hands in his pockets. Maybe a little platonic companionship would ease her sense of isolation.

But she wanted to beat the fear alone. Even with Dr. Forrest helping, Julia knew that only one person could clean the mental house. Only one person could go into those rooms, sweep away the cobwebs, roll up the shades and let in the light. Only one person held the key.

She flipped on the living room light and closed the door, cutting off the Stones in the midst of their endless "whoo-whoos." No wooden blocks awaited her, spelling a cryptic message. She laid her purse on the coffee table and gave a cursory glance around the room to make sure everything was in its place. So far, so good. No sweat. No problem. *No Creeps here, ma'am.*

But now the real test came. Could she walk down the hall into the bedroom? Could she look at the clock?

Sure you can.

Even though now you know there's at least ONE Creep in Elkwood. A Creep who went to the trouble of binding his victim's hands and feet before eviscerating him. A Creep who knew how to operate the business end of a knife. A Creep who did it slowly, making sure the victim expelled the greatest amount of blood and endured the deepest possible suffering. A Creep who took pride in his work.

Rick had taken great joy in sharing the grisly details over dinner. He knew she'd worked crime for *The Commercial Appeal* and hoped to impress her. She had to give him credit for originality. He was the first man who had ever tried to talk his way into her bed with a Satanic murder theory.

But her bed might already be occupied. That very same murdering Creep might be under her blankets this very moment, his sharp toys carefully resting on the pillow like a lover's flowers. Maybe he had a ring of black candles waiting for the touch of a match. Maybe a red pentagram was painted on the floor, some demon holding its foul breath in anticipation of being summoned.

Like HELL, she thought, laughing, though the sound came

out like the choking of a horse. She accepted the idea of God, something big behind everything. In the house of her head, she could give God a little shelf in the cupboard. But the idea that evil existed beyond the minds of humans, well, that was a wider leap of faith than she could make. She was merely crazy, not bug-brained insane.

But remember what Dr. Forrest said. You're not crazy. You just suffer from a "behavioral disorder." Something with a safe, handy label like "delusional" or "borderline personality" or "non-specific anxiety" or whatever diagnostic bricks the doctor cared to stack.

And, ultimately, she was in control of her own behavior. She could walk right into that bedroom, turn on the light, look at the clock, and then get on with the rest of her life. Conjuring up Satanic cults did little for her peace of mind.

She left the mace in her purse. She could do this alone, just like Dr. Forrest recommended. Down the hall, with every step bringing a slight creak of the floor in the silent house. The bedroom door was open. She reached around the wall, quickly, and flipped the switch.

The room was empty, her bed neatly made. The digital clock said 10:13. She checked it against her wristwatch. Right on time, just like clockwork. She was about to leave when a draft rippled the curtains. Muffled music leaked into the room from across the road.

The window was open. Why hadn't Walter shut the window when he finished checking the locks? These mountain people expected everybody to suck down fresh air all the time, even when the mercury dropped.

Julia frowned and parted the curtains. She didn't have a backyard. The forest grew right up to the rear of the house, the autumn canopy so thick that the distant streetlights couldn't penetrate the trees. The smell of loam and damp wood drifted in the dew. She closed and latched the window. Then she saw the muddy footprint on the floor.

The print showed only the outline of a heel. A small broken oak leaf was stuck in the tread marks. Walter must have left it.

Then why hadn't he left tracks all through the house? And he'd wiped his feet well, she'd seen him.

Julia knelt and touched the print. The dirt was damp.

Electric worms crawled up her spine.

Someone's been in the house.

For real, not for pretend.

And The Creep might still be here.

She grabbed the phone off the bedside table. She punched a nine and a one, and was about to touch the one again when she looked down at her own shoe. Mud ringed the heel.

No, not mud.

Fido had broken the peace treaty. Julia's smelly trail was marked from the living room.

"Oh, poop," she groaned, putting the phone in its cradle. She'd almost made a fool of herself. The cops could have been in here, responding to her breaking-and-entering report.

She could hear them now.

First cop: "You want to run a test on that, Lieutenant?"

Second cop: "Sure. Got the measurements already."

First cop: "Wait a second. This ain't mud."

Second cop: "Shoo. Smells like dog crap. What's that on your shoe, ma'am?"

Julia cleaned up the mess and put on a Natalie Merchant CD. Nothing bad could happen while Natalie Merchant was singing of motherhood and gratitude. She checked her e-mail, spam jokes from co-workers and a few posts from her St. Louis Cardinals newsgroup. The Cardinals were about twenty games out, as usual. But with the season winding down, the hot prospects were up from the minors, getting some playing time.

She deleted the messages because one of the newsgroupies was giving away the events of the day's game. Julia had taped it and wanted to watch it free of spoilers. She sat on the sofa and flipped the remote so that the videotape rewound. She punched the answering machine and stared at the blank TV screen.

The only message on her answering machine was the one from George Webster, telling her that Walter Triplett would be out to check her locks. She reset the machine, wondering if Rick would call.

That wasn't a date, she reminded herself. *That was definitely "hanging out." But I hope he knows that.*

She didn't want to spend all her office time fending off advances, but being noticed was always flattering. Rick was different from Mitchell. Not quite so pushy, respectful of her opinions, interested in more than just making money—

Whoa, girl. Back up a little. If you start down the road to where you compare other men to the one you're marrying, the potholes are going to bounce you out of a happy future. That's as bad as comparing shrinks.

And her future *would* be happy. She'd move into Mitchell's three-story house in Colliersville, join a tennis club, maybe volunteer for a library board. Social evenings with Mitchell's lawyer circle, the men talking shop, the few female lawyers trying to shoehorn into the conversation, the wives comparing vacation packages. She would wear pearls and heels and scan the fashion magazines to find out which perfume maker was conducting the most extravagant ad campaign. She would eventually give in and wear makeup, hiding all the damage done by time and gravity.

Mitchell would let her continue in therapy as long as she didn't take it too seriously. His circle would view it as just one more of the fringe benefits of affluence, a way to pass idle time, the same way one passed time by taking crafts classes. Mitchell would have an affair in his forties, maybe even more than one, when the first gray crept into his hair and he thought he'd missed out on something in his youth. Julia would accept the dalliances, get a facelift and Botox injections, maybe have some plastic surgery to lift her breasts so that Mitchell could still proudly display her.

They would inherit two of the seasonal homes owned by Mitchell's parents, the others going to his sister. He would choose Santa Monica, and would humor Julia by taking Martha's Vineyard as well. Julia would sit on the beach in the fall, sipping margaritas and rum punch. She didn't drink much now, but she would take up the habit in earnest, because everybody drank in Mitchell's circle. She might even become an alcoholic, a solidly fashionable occupation for the wives of overachieving men. The new disorder might even overwhelm her current one.

And would that be so bad? The fear slowly eroding into a great gray fog, the memories growing dimmer and more distant. The past lost in the wash of years instead of being probed, mined, collected, and analyzed. The past as past only, nothing to do with the wobbling, hazy present that ended at arm's reach, in the soft, cold bite of liquor, easy amnesia a swallow away.

A metallic click and whir brought Julia back to the blank TV as the tape finished rewinding. Tears burned in her eyes, refusing to fall. She wiped them away and pressed the remote. The screen flared to life and the tape started. Julia put her thumb on the fast-forward, ready to skip the pre-game analysis.

The game wasn't on the tape. Instead, the screen was filled with a man's smooth-shaven face, his eyes fevered and bright.

The man was pointing at the camera as if chiding both the camera operator and the audience. At high speed, the man looked comical, making wild hand gestures like something out of an old Keystone Kops short.

Julia was positive she had set the tape for ESPN2, the network of choice for also-ran teams like the Cardinals. She double-checked the schedule lying open on the coffee table. There, Cardinals vs. Astros, 4 PM, Channel 27. VCR's were notoriously complicated to program, but she'd taped much of the season without being thrown a single curve.

Unless her memory of setting the VCR had been a tiny little game she had played on herself, another trick to scare herself stupid. And didn't delusional people lie to themselves?

No. I didn't spread the blocks out on the table this morning, and I didn't tape this . . . this WHATEVER.

She stopped the tape and let it play at regular speed.

The man's face crowded the edges of the screen, the close-up so intense that she could see drops of saliva spraying from his mouth as he spoke. The man's manic voice thundered forth as she thumbed up the volume on the remote.

"And Satan has come unto the world, the world that Satan owns, the one that he has stolen from God," the man said. "And Satan spread his wealth, spread his lust disguised as love, spread his greed disguised as need, spread his warfare disguised as righteousness. Satan stretched his fingers out across the world, touching every man, woman, and child."

The man pointed at the camera, at Julia, his voice softening. "Touching *you.*"

Yeah, right. The Devil touched me in the HEAD. Thanks, mister. Now I have an excuse. Here I was, all ready to accept the blame for my little problem, and now you come along and give me the greatest out of all time. I'm only a victim. Of course. Why didn't I see it before now?

The preacher allowed a dramatic pause. "This world belongs to the devil. It's right there in the Book of Luke, set down by God's own hand. 'To you I will give all this power and glory,' the Devil says to Jesus, as they stood on the mountain overlooking the wonders of this world. 'For it's been given over to me to do with as I please.' The Lord could withstand the temptation, but you would snatch it right up, wouldn't you? You'd take it all and still want more.

"And I don't blame you," the wild-eyed man continued, wiping away the sweat that was collecting on his face from the Klieg lights and exertion. "I don't blame you for biting into the apple, into that red, shiny, sweet apple. I've tasted it myself, we *all* have. How can we resist?"

Julia almost clicked the screen off, but something about this televangelist's spiel fascinated her. His hair was slick and perfectly styled, swooped up in a grand swirl that would stand in a hurricane. The man's teeth sparkled, brighter than heavenly pearls, his jaw muscles contorted in the rapture of his delivery. She had no doubt of his utter sincerity.

"How can we resist?" he repeated, and the camera pulled back to reveal the man's outstretched arms, as if he were offering himself up for Christ's welcoming hug or the next UFO. "We are empty vessels, and unless we fill ourselves with the Lord, the devil will wash in"—the man arched his arms as if diving into a lake—"and drown us with sin, drown us with sorrow. He'll steal our breath with his false promises. He'll take us down and we won't even fight it. We'll hug him right back and give him thanks."

The man paced back and forth in front of the plush purple curtain and floral arrangements that served as a stage setting. The Love Offering telephone number was emblazoned on a banner in great golden numerals.

"But the *Lord* will fight," said the man, voice lifting, fist shaking in the air. "The Lord will burn Satan's eyes out, the Lord will take our love and use it as a weapon, a mighty sword that will cleave down into the fire—" He made a slicing motion with his free hand "—and cut Satan's grasping fingers and silence that nasty tongue, the one that whispers such sweet lies to us. Lies of all the pleasures we can have, if we only turn our hearts from God."

Pause. Medium close-up. The man lowered his head in sad reverence. A perfectly scripted moment.

He pointed again. "Satan wants you," he said, almost a caricature of those patriotic Uncle Sam posters. "He *owns* you."

Julia pointed back, her fascination shifting to boredom. "No, he's only borrowing me."

She'd rather watch the Cardinals lose by six. The VCR must have jumped its memory, shut off and lost its programming. First the clock and now this. She'd have to call George Webster and have Walter check out the wiring.

Sure, blame it on mechanical failure, not operator error. Or operator insanity. Talk about God sending messages wrapped in ridiculous packaging.

She clicked the set off, the sound dying, the televangelist's face sinking rapidly to black. After checking the front-door lock, she went to the bathroom and took a shower. She managed to shampoo and rinse without once looking outside the shower stall. No Creeps here, no Anthony Perkins wannabes, no peepholes carved in the walls, nothing but the sweat of mist on the tiles.

Before leaving the bathroom, she glanced at the figure in the full-length mirror on the back of the door. The steamy glass almost disguised the two long scars than ran up her belly and just under the swells of her breasts. Aside from the scars, she was not too bad for an old-timer of twenty-seven. Mitchell certainly found her worthy.

She went to bed and read some Jefferson Spence and was carried away to a land where the protagonists always drew upon inner reserves to overcome evil obstacles. The clock was still behaving itself, so she set it to wake her early. As she turned off the bedside light, she went over a checklist in her head.

Doors locked. Windows locked. Curtains pulled closed. Mace in the living room. Baseball bat under the bed, the commemorative Louisville Slugger her adoptive parents had given her for her sixteenth birthday.

All set.

Nothing but darkness and the quiet settling of the house. The leaves flapped a little on the trees outside, one of them occasionally brushing against the window screen. The neighbors had cut the music. They were pretty considerate about that, except during their weekend parties.

She lay in the dark thinking of the morning's episode of paranoia, the wooden blocks, the session with Dr. Forrest, the Satanic murder, Rick. Dr. Forrest. Something during the hypnosis. A memory, crawling from its slumber, fingers reaching from the damp murk of the cellar. Clawing its way out.

The bad people, around her, touching and hurting her.

No.

That memory was for Dr. Forrest's office, where it could be bound by walls. Not here, not in Julia's house, where it could slither out of her ears and under the bed to lie in the beggar's velvet and wait. Wait for just that right moment when Julia was asleep, tangled in the sheets of nightmare. Then it would grab her ankle, open its slathering jaws and—

She sat up and flicked on the bedside lamp.

The digital clock moved on, counted its way from the past or toward the future, however you wanted to look at it. Julia watched it for a while, and then picked up her book. Julia read until after midnight. By that time she was thoroughly irritated with Spence's too-perfect heroine and his libertarian worldview, not to mention the obligatory dog chuffing here and there among the pages and occasionally bloated, pompous prose. But the book had helped her forget her troubles. Spence was reliable for that, as solid as a dictionary.

She tried the pillow again.

Not so bad this time. She was almost ready to try the dark, but decided to sleep with the light on. Just once more wouldn't hurt.

She thought of the tape, tried to remember setting the VCR. She *could* remember. She could see herself punching the buttons, Channel 27. And she'd gotten the hair-oiled preacher from hell.

Oh, well. Everybody made mistakes.

Her thoughts spilled into nonsense, Rick's face, the lake at the club where she'd met Mitchell, her dead adoptive parents, a teacher she'd had in the sixth grade who had worn green suspenders, Mickey Mouse, images skipping by faster and faster on the preview screen of dreams.

She was nearly asleep when she heard a crack outside the window. The sound of a damp stick breaking.

She held her breath, kept her cheek against the pillow. Listened. Listened.

A scrabbling sound on the outside wall. How close was the baseball bat?

It's nothing, Julia. Probably the neighbor's boxer, leaving you a stinky present for tomorrow. Or a raccoon. You live right by the WOODS. Remember wildlife?

A swashing across the window screen. The boxer couldn't reach six feet off the ground.

It's a Creep.

Should she pretend that she hadn't noticed, turn off the light as if preparing to sleep? In the darkness, she could reach the bat unobserved. She could roll to her feet and wait by the window for the Creep to come through. Then—

What? *Whammo*, like a steroid-stoked Mark McGwire in his prime feasting on a rookie pitcher's fastball?

No. She could call the cops.

The cops.

First cop: "You see anything?"

Second cop (playing his flashlight beam on the ground outside the window): "Hmm. Looks like some kind of animal tracks."

First cop: "What kind of tracks?"

Second cop: "Damn. I just stepped in dog crap."

Sometimes a cigar was just a cigar.

Sometimes noises were only noises.

She reached out, switched off the light without looking at the window.

Swash against the screen.

She couldn't resist looking.

Eyes.

A scarce glint of fire on them from the distant streetlight, weak between the curtains.

But *eyes*.

And a face behind them?

She eased one hand off the bed, tensing, ready to scream, to reach for the Louisville Slugger, the phone, anything.

The eyes were gone.

She lay in her own sweat, trying to convince herself that she'd imagined the eyes, that she was safe as milk. Dr. Forrest warned her about letting her fantasy world intrude on reality. Dr. Forrest wasn't going to like hearing about nonexistent eyes at her bedroom window.

The wooden blocks had been real. But, if she closed her eyes, she could picture herself selecting them off the toy rack, paying the cashier, taking them home and arranging the letters on her table. Then forgetting so she could scare herself later.

That sounded crazy, multiple-personality loopy, and she was not ever going to be crazy. Dr. Forrest wouldn't let her. Better to pretend that the blocks had never existed. No Creep played tricks on her except the one inside her head.

Julia would leave that part out of the journal she would start in the morning. And if she didn't want to imagine eyes at her window, the best thing was to shut her own eyes and watch the imaginary silent movies on the backs of her eyelids.

For a moment, she longed for Mitchell's presence in the bed beside her. *Better the devil you know.*

She lulled herself into a shallow, exhausted sleep by the second reel.

CHAPTER SIX

"*How* many did you say?" Julia asked.

The manager of the animal shelter took a draw on his cigarette, exhaled, and made a futile attempt to brush cat fur from his sweater. "About thirty or so. Might not seem like much, but if you're the pet owner . . . "

Thirty dogs and cats reported missing in the last two weeks. The leathery old man who'd walked her through the shelter and let her take pictures with her digital camera leaned against the fence, flicking his ash to the gravel. Five dogs pressed their noses against the chain links, only one wagging its tail. The rest looked like lifers, fur dull, ears drooping from the boredom of chronic confinement.

"We usually get about three reports a week," the manager said, his voice rough from half a century of smoke. "Most of them are killed by cars, of course. Some just plumb run off, but a dog or a cat is a lot smarter than you think. But, just lately, a hell of a lot of them been lost, if you'll pardon my French."

"I don't speak French," Julia said. "That's a hell of a language."

The man laughed, coughed.

Julia wrote some notes on her pad. "Has this ever happened before?"

"Not since I been here, ten years," he said. "I'd just as soon you leave that part out of the story. The people who did our stories before focused on what important work we do, how much we rely on donations, that sort of thing."

"A warm and fuzzy piece?"

"Yeah." He knocked the fire from his cigarette butt, stomped it out, and put the butt in the pocket of his coveralls. The strong smell of animal waste rose with the shifting of the wind. The man didn't seem to notice. "We got enough problems here, as you can probably imagine."

"Let me guess. The county funds only a tiny portion of your operation, but they impose all kinds of regulations. Not to mention all the state laws you have to follow. Then there are the outbreaks of parvo and feline leukemia and mange and fleas and heartworms. And the only thing you get out of it is, every once in a while, somebody comes by and adopts one of these guys."

She reached her fingers through the fence and rubbed the nose of the nearest dog. It licked her fingers and gazed at her with morose, questioning eyes. She looked away before the guilt could finish its journey from her heart to her brain.

"That's about the size of it," the man said. "A lot of people don't give a second thought to the way animals are treated. I just wish I could take them all home with me."

The manager's eyes misted a little. Julia averted her eyes and scanned the wedge of sparse woods, the river, and the Elkwood wastewater treatment plant on the neighboring property. The mountains rose in the distance, red and gold and orange with the changing of the leaves. The clouds were high and thin in the sky.

"Okay, warm and fuzzy it is," Julia said. "Just a question. Off the record, of course. Why do you think so many animals are missing?"

The man reached into his pocket as if for another cigarette, but brought his hand away empty. "I used to live down in Austin, Texas," he said. "One morning a few farmers on the outskirts woke up to find some of their animals dead. Dogs, cats, a few lambs, even a cow. Had their throats cut. The cops found a little mashed-out place in a mesquite thicket. Whoever done it had themselves a little party."

"Party?"

"They made a ring of blood on the ground and poured out a star shape in the middle of it. Devil worshippers, the cops called it. Never did catch nobody."

"Did it ever happen again?"

"Not on that big a scale. They got reports now and then, dogs mutilated and such as that. Cops said some of them devil worshippers was known to actually *drink* the blood." The man's face wrinkled in revulsion. "Kindly hard to believe, ain't it?"

"Not in this crazy world," Julia said. "Did you ever hear of any mutilations of people?"

"Hell, that was Texas," he said. "People would throw down on each other with knives over which model of pickup was best. Sometimes they'd whittle a fellow right down to the bone."

"Do you think somebody in Elkwood is killing animals?"

He shook his head. "It can't happen here. Not in a town like this. They're good, God-fearing folks who live by the Bible."

"That's what they say everywhere," said Julia.

"Excepting Los Angeles. And maybe New York."

Julia smiled and nodded. "Well, thank you for your time, Mr. Cole. Look for the story next week. It'll be the piece that's so warm and fuzzy that fluff will drift off the pages."

"I sure appreciate it, ma'am."

He called after her as she headed for her car. "Sure you don't want to take one home with you?"

She paused with the car door open. She scanned the entire shelter, the tiny shack that served as the office, a larger shed that housed the cats, the cinder block-and-wire kennels for the dogs. The dogs by the fence were sitting now, except for the little white dog with the furry butt. Its tail whipped back and forth, the dark eyes shining in some secret game.

Don't make me feel guilty, she mentally commanded the dog. *That's all I need is another thing to worry about. I've got enough on my mind. Like my own selfishness. That takes up ALL my time, you little Fido or Fidette.*

"I don't think my lease allows it," she said to the manager.

"Well, you think about it." He waved.

"I will," she said, getting in the car. *I most definitely will.*

As she drove back to town, she thought of what she'd written in her journal this morning, wondered if it was the kind of thing Dr. Forrest wanted. She'd awakened on the first brittle cry of the alarm, the clock having kept time through the night. Even before going to the bathroom and brushing her teeth, she opened a notebook and wrote down her dream.

The same dream.

The one of the bones hidden under the floor.

The floor wasn't the one in her house, or of any house she had lived in. It was of long wooden planks, tongue-in-groove hardwood. For some strange dream-reason, she had to keep the secret of the buried bones from others. She was pretty sure she hadn't buried the bones, hadn't killed anyone, but that part of the dream wasn't very clear.

Maybe Dr. Forrest would know what it meant. Dr. Forrest had helped her decipher an earlier dream, one where Julia was pregnant and a snake was trying to take her baby. According to the Freudian interpretation, the snake was her father, and the fetus was herself as a small child. Therefore, Julia's father had stolen her childhood, and was the one to blame for Julia's current disorder.

She was still thinking about her father when she pulled into the parking lot of the *Courier-Times* office. The afternoon sun was behind her, and she saw her reflection coming to meet her in the glass of the front door. Did she look like her father? She could scarcely remember his true face, only the one she had fashioned out of dim memory. Was he alive? Why had he left her? How much of him still lived on in her? How much should she hate him?

She shivered, even though the day was warm, and went inside. Rick was waiting in the chair beside her desk.

"Hey there," he said. "How are you?"

"I'm fine, thanks. And thanks for last night. I really needed to get out."

"Yeah, I could tell. Maybe you need to get out more?" He leaned toward her, smiling, as she sat.

"Are you asking me?"

"Maybe," he said.

"You know I'm engaged, right?"

He waved his hands as if brushing aside a cobweb. "You've been here four months, and I've not seen any sign of this knight in shining armor. He can't be too big a part of your life."

Julia booted up her computer. Rick finally decided she wasn't going to take the bait. "So, what did you think of my Satanic murder theory?"

"Pretty creative," she said. "I guess you're going to need a little evidence before you run it. Or even get editorial approval to stick with the chase."

Rick sat back and put his hands behind his head, sprawling in the chair, casually accepting her rebuff. "The *Independent* is all over this case. Sometimes I hate being a weekly. They beat us on almost everything. Except they aren't working the Satanic angle."

"They don't have time for the depth of coverage that we get, either."

"The cops identified the victim."

Julia nodded, half-listening, clicking her way through her files. "Poor guy."

"Charles Edward Williams. Age 39. Last known address, Memphis, Tennessee."

Julia froze over her keyboard. "Memphis?"

"Your old stomping grounds. Is it known as a hotbed of Satanism?"

"Well, aside from Elvis selling his soul to the devil and Richard Nixon . . . and we all know how *that* turned out."

"Eternal life on a hundred thousand collector plates and black velvet paintings, but in exchange, he had to die drugged out on the porcelain altar."

"You are so delicate, Rick."

"Yep. Journalism hardens your heart, and that explains everything," he said, shifting into a mocking tone. "How long did you say you've been a reporter?"

"Very funny. Do the police have any new leads?"

"No. They've shipped the body off to the state medical examiner's office. Should be able to tell if the guy was drugged when he died. If the Brotherhood used him as a sacrifice, they probably had to drug him pretty heavily."

"Unless the sacrifice was voluntary. What's this 'Brotherhood' business?"

"One of the names Satanists use for their group."

"Boy, even Satanists are sexist. What's the world coming to?"

Rick's face grew serious. "Are you religious?"

"More spiritual than religious," she said, expecting Rick to ask which church she attended. She considered telling him she was a Scientologist or Moonie, something offbeat that might throw him off the scent. "I believe in a higher power. I just don't think you need an escort to get you there, and you don't have to kiss the Pope's ring, the Buddha's feet, or Pat Robertson's ass."

Rick nodded and smiled. "Sorry to put you on the spot. Some people get touchy about things like that."

Julia almost asked Rick about his spiritual beliefs, but decided against it. What if he'd only taken her out to dinner to try to convert her? She liked the idea of being desirable company better than that of looking like a lost soul. Too many people lately had seemed hell-bent on saving her. "Well, for the sake of intellectual argument, I don't think Satan exists, but I'm willing to believe that other people do, and that they might perform all kinds of crazy acts in the delusion of devotion."

"One thing's strange. There's a case a couple of years ago that never got solved. A little girl was stabbed to death. They found her body out in the woods."

"That's sickening." Julia's heart clenched. "Any suspects?"

"A few names were kicked around. Deacon Hartley's came up the most often."

"Hartley? That's a common local name, isn't it?"

"There's a few dozen of them, been here since the buffalo walked these mountains."

"Any rumors of Satanism with that murder?"

"No. But that's the kind of thing the police like to keep quiet. Especially when they can't solve it. Maybe my series will be called 'The New Satanism.' Catchy, huh?"

"Better get some more evidence first. Otherwise, you'll come off as preachy. Besides, even the Baptists have pretty much given up the idea of Satan."

"If I were the devil, Elkwood would make a fine place to get started on that Armageddon thing. Go where people are the most complacent in their faith."

"You're just stirring up controversy for the sake of that

journalism creed, 'If it bleeds, it leads.'"

"It wins press awards," Rick said. "Satanism's got everything you want in a story. Murder, drugs, bondage, orgies, and the ultimate in good versus evil."

She thought about sharing her tidbit of the disappearing animals, but if he was going to go ahead and run his stories on nothing but rumor, theory, and a handful of spotty research, she wanted to distance herself as much as possible. If Rick would let her. "Well, good luck, but don't take it personally if I hope your story is a dead end. I'd better get back to work. Deadline. You know."

"Yeah." Rick stood and adjusted his glasses. He paused at the door to her tiny office. "Mind if I call you later?"

Whether he was a Christian soldier hell-bent on recruitment or a chronic womanizer, he sure didn't know when to give up. His cheeks wrinkled when he smiled, like a young Robert Redford in "All The President's Men." He'd probably practiced it in the mirror. "I'm pretty busy," she said. "Maybe some other time?"

"Sure. After you're married, maybe."

"It won't be your problem." She smiled at him, hoping he didn't take it as a sign that she was ready to roll back her sheets and let him slide his lithe, fitness-club physique onto her mattress. She wondered if his moral compass allowed him to seduce another man's fiancee, and decided most men only followed one compass, and it was the pointy one in their pants. "Thanks for last night."

Rick straightened up, seeing something in her eyes, the old cockiness back on his face. "We'll do it again sometime. Real soon."

After he left, Julia finished her article, downloaded her digital photographs, and drove home. By the time she'd put away her camera and satchel, dusk was still an hour away.

She decided to take a walk down the little trail that ran through the woods behind the house.

Artificial courage. It works for drunks, so maybe it will work for me.

She locked the door behind her and put the key ring and mace in her pocket. With many of the leaves falling, she'd be able to keep the house in sight along much of the walk. Autumn was her favorite season, and she wasn't going to deny herself the pleasure of it all just because some knife-wielding Creep could be waiting behind a tree.

The trail ran down to a little creek. There, the forest was more welcoming than threatening. Autumn wasn't just a glorious color show. The season had a taste and a smell. Julia relished the sweet decay of leaves in the air, the late-blooming goldenrod and rust-topped Joe Pye weed, rushing water that was silver clean against the rocks. Away from civilization, with only the wild woods and water and sinking sun for company, she felt perfectly normal and worry free. But the sun always set, and darkness always fell, and she was not alone in the world.

The other end of the trail bordered Mabel Covington's back yard. Yellow apples lay on the ground beneath a gnarled tree and two quilts hung on the woman's clothesline, airing out for winter. The grass was thick and nearly blue. The aroma of fried chicken came from the kitchen of the large colonial house.

Mrs. Covington appeared at the door of the screened-in back porch. "Hey there, Julia," she called. "Saw you from the window. How you doing?"

"Fine, Mrs. Covington. Taking a walk. How are you?"

"Just dandy. Won't you come in for a piece of pie? I haven't seen you in a while." A gray cat appeared between Mrs. Covington's ankles, its tail brushing the hem of the woman's dress as it pussyfooted down the wooden steps.

Julia was about to decline the offer, but Mrs. Covington's smile radiated from her ice-blue eyes as well. Julia stepped through the low hedge and started across the yard. "Thanks. That would be nice of you."

"No, just neighborly. With all these outsiders coming in, people don't keep up with their neighbors much anymore. We all got to watch out for each other, especially out here on Buckeye Creek."

Julia braced herself for a lecture that would condemn anyone who dared to be born somewhere besides Amadahee County, but the woman only held the door open until Julia entered the house. They sat at the wobbly, hand-crafted cherry table in the kitchen, though Mrs. Covington had a large dining room with a beautiful walnut table. The whole house was filled with enough rustic antiques to make a scavenger drool.

Mrs. Covington set down plates with thick wedges of cherry pie on them, a scoop of vanilla ice cream to the side leaking white into the red filling. Julia accepted a cup of coffee, waited until Mrs. Covington shooed a black cat out of the kitchen, and then they ate together.

"This is delicious," Julia said.

"Thank you kindly," the woman said, her false teeth stained by the cherries. "Don't have no call to cook much anymore, with my Archibald dead and the boys living out West. It's nice to have somebody I can fuss over."

She patted Julia's hand.

"I only hope this doesn't spoil my appetite for dinner," Julia said, before lifting another forkful.

"A girl your age ought not worry about what she eats. There's a lot of that going on, I hear, girls throwing up and wasting away because they're scared of getting fat. A real man doesn't mind a little meat on the bone."

Julia grinned. She wasn't called a girl very often, not at twenty-seven. "No need to worry. I'm not afraid of a few extra pounds."

Only other things. Lions and tigers and bears and Satanic cults, oh my.

"Mrs. Covington—"

The woman held up a wrinkled hand. "How many times do I got to tell you? Call me 'Mabel.'"

"Okay, Mabel."

"Walter Triplett's been around a right good bit lately."

"He seems like he knows what he's doing."

"A real fix-it man," Mrs. Covington said. "Fixed everything up real nice. Got away with murder, some say."

"Murder?"

"I shouldn't be airing out nobody else's dirty laundry," Mrs. Covington said, as if she didn't get the opportunity as often as she liked. "But a body ought to keep themselves informed. So it ain't gossip, it's more just passing along information."

Julia gripped her purse tighter. The falling dusk suddenly felt like a suffocating blanket, a funeral shroud for the living. The cat jumped into Mrs. Covington's lap, barely visible except for the green glow of its eyes. The woman stroked it and resumed rocking.

"Walter lost his wife about eight years back. When I say 'lost,' that's exactly what I mean. They was out camping on Cracker Knob yonder." The woman waved a trembling arm toward unseen mountains. "And Walter came back the next day and said she had disappeared. Just up and walked off in the middle of the night. Of course, they rounded up a big search team, every man what could walk and even a few women, and went over every square inch of that mountain. Never was no sign of her."

The chair's squeaking was amplified by the silence of the night. Julia noticed for the first time how softly night descended, how it crept up around you, drifted from the trees, rose like smoke while simultaneously descending like dark snow. Insidious, slow, and determined.

"Walter swears up and down she was right next to him in their little tent, sleeping one minute, gone the next. Didn't take her hiking boots or nothing, just whatever clothes she was wearing at the time. And she was a Stamey, old family. Not the sort to do foolish things, raised to know a little bit about the woods."

"Poor Walter," Julia found herself saying. So that was the thing she had seen in his eyes, the bit of gray haunting the brown of his irises. A sadness buried deep.

"Poor Walter, maybe. But poorer for her, I'd say. 'Course, there is all kinds of caves and cliff edges on Cracker Knob where a body could meet the Maker, but a mountain girl would know to watch out for such dangers. And a mountain girl wouldn't wander off in the dead of night no way."

Mrs. Covington spoke as if looking through the mist of years. "Some say Walter kind of helped her along in her disappearing act. That he helped her over a cliff, if you know what I mean. Or maybe strangled her and tucked her in some of those rock crevices on the north slope."

"He seems okay to me. He's polite."

"Well, I hate to speculate on things I don't know for sure, but I hear the Stamey girl was pregnant when she went missing."

The pie felt like a lump of wood in her throat as she imagined a scared young woman wandering lost in the wild mountains, with their granite rock shelves and laurel tangles.

"Of course, that ain't too surprising, since they hung out with Hartley," Mrs. Covington asked.

The name clanged a faint but disturbing bell. "What about Hartley?"

"Deke Hartley lived in that house for five years. A strange old coot. Burned the lights through the night, came and went at all hours, never seemed to settle into a routine. I never trusted nobody who didn't have a routine."

"What's that have to do with weird noises in the woods?"

"All the Hartleys is rough, but Deke managed to stay out of trouble. Some said he was up to funny business, though. I never was one to snoop in other people's affairs, myself, but a body tends to hear gossip."

Despite her unease, Julia hid a grin behind another bite of pie. She suspected she was about to hear everything Mrs. Covington didn't want to talk about.

"I reckon he was into drugs," Mrs. Covington said. "The strangest smells used to come from that house. People would come by to visit in the dead of night, and you'd never get to see their faces. About drove me batty, trying to keep up with the coming and going."

"Mr. Webster told me the former tenant ran out on his lease, and that the house had been sitting empty."

"He ran out on *everything*. Left all his clothes, the television on, food in the fridge, like he just up and walked off the end of the earth. His car was sitting in the driveway for three weeks, never moved, when I finally called the police. I reckon they've still got him down as a missing-persons case. That was about two years back, if I remember right. About the time that little girl got killed."

Julia wondered why Mr. Webster hadn't told her any of this. Maybe he was scared she would have backed out of signing the lease. And the fate of the previous tenant wasn't the type of thing one usually inquired about when house hunting. Julia didn't believe that houses could be haunted, whether the ghosts were dead things or only memories. The house had been a good choice, solid and cheap, despite these revelations. Just enough peace to allow her time to think, and just enough people around to avoid a sense of total isolation. Even if the neighborhood boxer enjoyed spreading little land mines around.

She scooped up the last of her dessert, a bit of crust softened by the ice cream. "You don't think he's missing, do you?"

Mabel Covington's eyes flicked left and right. "I hear things myself, sometimes. When it's dark, people coming through the woods. See, I think they stashed some drugs or money or something, and they want to get it back. Only they don't want to get discovered by having somebody file breaking and entering charges, so they're waiting for the right time. I got a feeling Hartley *likes* to be missing."

And I thought I was paranoid. Maybe SHE could use an hour or two in Dr. Forrest's office.

Julia wiped the corners of her mouth with a napkin. "Thank you for the pie," she said. "That was the best I've ever had."

"You do my heart glad," the old woman said. "I won't even share no credit with the corporation that boxed it up."

Julia made a show of checking her watch. "Well, I'd better run. I've got some work to do."

Plus it will be dark very soon. And even though my house is only fifty yards away . . .

Mrs. Covington walked Julia to the door. "Didn't mean to scare you none. About Hartley and all that. It's just best to be informed."

"Yes, ma'am," Julia said. She reached down and petted the cat that rubbed against her leg.

"You come on back any time."

"Thank you, Mrs. Covington."

"And call me 'Mabel,' hear?"

Julia nodded, waved good-bye, and headed across the grass. The sun was large and golden in the west, just touching the blazing mountainsides. A sudden gust rattled the leaves like paper skeletons. The hint of coming frost rode on the wind.

Julia crossed the woods into her own yard and circled back behind her house, just to set her mind at ease. Not because she really expected to find anything.

Below her bedroom window, on the ground, was a set of footprints.

Her heart crawled into her throat. She ran blindly for the front door, found her key, rammed it home, and burst inside. She slammed the door closed behind her and stood with her back against it, chest heaving, as daylight ebbed inside the house and every creak was like the lifting of a coffin lid.

CHAPTER SEVEN

Call the police?

The phone waited across the room.

Think, think, think.

Julia tried to calm her breathing, tried to slice through the crippling blackness that enwrapped her brain like a sheet shrouded a mortician's meal ticket.

A Creep had walked up to her window. Maybe peeked in. The tracks outside had looked fairly fresh, though a couple of leaves had covered part of one heel print.

But a Creep is the least likely culprit. Because Creeps don't exist, remember?

Who else had business that might have brought him to the rear of the house?

Think, don't panic.

The electric meter was on the side of the house, clearly visible from the drive. Whoever read the meter wouldn't need to look around back. Same with the phone line. The water supply came from a well at the rear of the property, so there was no water meter.

Then she remembered Walter.

The handyman had probably checked the outside of the windows as well. The prints looked as if they were made by boots with a thick tread, someone with a large foot. Walter was well over six feet tall.

That was it. Sure.

She relaxed against the door, her muscles limp.

No Creeps, no calls to the cops.

The Memphis police had responded to her calls four times

in the last year before her moving. All false alarms. They were always patient, except for the fourth call, when the same thin, sneering cop from her first call had shown up.

"What's it this time?" he'd said.

"Someone under my bed," Julia said, already feeling foolish.

The cop had nodded wearily, waited until she unlocked the door, and brushed past her. He went into her bedroom, rummaged around in her closet for a moment, peeked into the bathroom, and waved Julia into the apartment.

"I . . . I swear I heard him. I came in and—"

"All clear." He glared at her. "Same as last time. Did you have the door locked?"

She nodded.

"Then how's a burglar or rapist or whatever going to get *in*?" He flipped the lock on her sliding glass door and removed the security bar, slid the door open on its track, and stepped onto the small balcony. He looked out over the Wolf River four stories below.

"I heard him. I swear."

"Sure you did. I checked on my way over. This is the fourth call since last July. I don't know what you're after. Some like the attention, some are cop groupies"—he'd given her a leer that made Julia want to push him over the railing—"and some just want to screw the system. Whichever reason is yours, filing a false report is a crime."

"I really heard him," Julia said, near tears but not allowing herself to cry in front of that monster.

"Yeah, well, next time, do us a favor and call a private investigator," he said. "We got people out there with *real* problems."

After he left, Julia cried for a half-hour. She never again called the police, even when she was trailed while walking two blocks home one evening, even when she found scratch marks near the lock as if someone had tried to jimmy open her door. And she was determined not to start the same sort of thing in Elkwood. When she called the cops to her new place, she wanted some solid proof to show them.

Except, even in Memphis, you were never really SURE that you heard anything, or that you were followed, or that some Creep had a hot-drool thang going for you. How are you going to convince anyone else when you can't even trust your own mind?

Julia's fear slewed into anger. She slammed into the kitchen, washed the dishes with a great deal of rattling and water-sloshing, and took a shower. She walked nude into her bedroom without bothering to see if the curtains were still closed. She read Spence until he put her to sleep.

She dreamed of bones again.

This time, she was lifting the boards from the floor, prying them up with a long sharp tool. The floor insulation was like yellow cotton candy and had been pushed to the side. She lowered herself between the floor joists to the dirt below. The soil was dark, soft and dry.

Julia dug into the ground with the tool. The first bone was several inches beneath the surface. She cleared it away with her fingers, and held it to the strange, amber dream-light. It was a femur, long and pitted with nicks and cuts, the color of bleached ivory. She placed it on the floor and dug again, coming up with a skull this time.

She picked it up and held it as if she were Hamlet about to reflect on Yorick's demise. She stared into the skull's empty eye sockets. The dark blank eyes had just begun staring back when she awoke.

Lasers of the sun sliced through the trees into her window. Julia blinked against the sudden light, confused, lost in that wasteland between dream and dawn. It was late. Her alarm should have woken her just before the sun crept over the horizon.

Heavy with sleep, she rolled over and reached for the clock. Her hand froze inches away from it.

4:06.

Red digits, simultaneously ice cold and hell hot.

A minute passed, one in which Julia breathed only twice.

Another minute, and still the clock stood at 4:06.

Julia peered over the edge of the bed. The clock was plugged in. She closed her eyes and leaned back against the pillow.

A malfunction, that's all. Something in that idiot digital brain has a hang-up about 4:06. Throw the damned clock out and buy another one instead of worrying about it.

She reached out, found the plug, and jerked it free of the wall socket. She didn't look at the clock as she shoved it into the wastebasket. She was afraid those same numerals might still be glaring, even without electricity.

After she dressed, she called George Webster and told him the wiring had been acting up. She described what had happened with the clock and the VCR. Nothing major, but she just thought he might like to know. Maybe ought to get it checked. Webster said he'd send somebody around to check it that afternoon, and asked if she would be there.

Yes, she would be there, armed and ready if need be.

Before she went to work, she walked around the back of the house. The footprints were still there. Were there more, a fresh set pressed into the dewy grass? She couldn't tell. Leaves had fallen overnight, making a carpet of red and brown. She hoped enough would fall to cover the tracks so that she wouldn't have to see them anymore.

The day passed swiftly as she wrapped up a couple of articles and sat through a staff meeting with the graphics people. Graphics people always complained that they were pushed up against the deadline by slack advertisers who turned in their copy at the last minute. Poor graphics people. They were artists, while writers were only hacks and glorified typists. In the world of modern media, words seemed the least-valuable commodity.

Walter's Jeep was parked in the drive when she got home. A little shiver wended through her belly, and at first she thought it was fright. Then she realized she was glad to see him. She and Walter had already shared a mutually embarrassing moment–after all, it wasn't every guy who came across as a crazed killer on the initial encounter.

Her front door stood open. Walter was in the living room, kneeling by an outlet, a meter in his hands, wire probes sunk into the outlet slots. He looked up and smiled when he saw her.

"Hey there, ma'am."

"Hello, Walter. Have you found anything?"

The room was dark, and she realized he must have switched off the power main. He stood, his face in shadows, his dark eyes glinting. "Nothing so far. What kind of problems are you having?"

"Remember the clock?"

"Yep."

"It got stuck again."

"That's weird. But it's more likely the clock than the wiring."

"It was stuck on the same time. 4:06."

Walter's mouth twisted sideways. He smelled of sawdust and sunshine, honest, warm aromas. "Hmmm. I'd throw that thing in the weeds. It ain't worth the cost of fixing it."

She told him about the VCR problem. She showed him that the programming was still set to record the game. Only, instead of taping the game, she had taped God's greatest snake-oil salesman.

"You like baseball?" Walter asked.

"I love the Cardinals. Ozzie Smith was my favorite player. Just watching him turn backflips made me happy."

"I played a little baseball in high school. I could hit like crazy, but I couldn't catch water in a thunderstorm. Anyway, it looks to me like the VCR is set up okay. I tested all the electric lines, and I ain't found any short circuits."

"Darn. I was hoping it would be something obvious."

"Maybe it's just a stretch of bad luck. Sometimes it happens that way. They make machines smarter than people these days." Walter put his tools back in his belt.

Julia looked at his boots, sizing them up. Walter caught her staring.

"I wiped my feet good," he said. "I noticed you had dogs around the neighborhood."

"Oh, sorry," she said. "Did you by chance go around back when you were here the other day?"

"Yeah. I checked the windows inside and out."

Julia hoped her relief wasn't too visible. "I just saw some footprints around back, and it made me wonder."

"Don't blame you," he said. "Lots of bums and Creeps in the world nowadays. Too many outsiders. You ought to keep your bedroom window locked, though, if you're so worried about it."

"Locked?" She *had* locked it, almost always kept it locked except when she wanted to air out the house.

"I put the screen back up, too. One of those Tennessee winds must have blowed it off."

Screen off, window unlocked. Clock stuck on 4:06.

Suddenly she wanted Walter out of the house, wanted to bar the door, the windows, and never ever ever open them again. But that was stupid. If Walter wanted her in any of a number of Creepy ways, he'd passed up plenty of opportunities. So far, he'd been a tiny island of sanity in this strange sea of uncertainty.

But he did have several sharp tools in his belt. And Mabel Covington had reacted strangely at the mention of his name.

"Thanks, Walter," she said. "I appreciate your checking the wiring."

"Glad to," he said, pushing back his cap. "Sorry I didn't find nothing wrong. Usually its something simple."

"Nothing's ever simple in my life." She followed him to the door.

"I'll turn your power back on," he said. "Reckon I'll see you later. Lots of things seem to go wrong in this house."

"I reckon so," she found herself saying. She waited until he drove away. Then she locked the door and went to the bedroom. The window was closed. The clock was still in the wastebasket.

Julia was tempted to plug it in again, to see if those same haunting numerals were still frozen on the display. But what if they were? Or, almost as bad, what if they weren't?

Had someone taken her screen down, perhaps crawled in through the window she had somehow forgotten to lock? Or had the wind really blown off the screen while she was at work?

Or had she opened the window and forced herself to forget?

Julia sat on the bed and picked up her cell phone, punching the top number in her book.

"Hello?" came that comforting voice.

"Hi, Dr. Forrest?"

A pause. "Yes."

"It's me, Julia Stone. Sorry to bother you at home."

"That's quite all right, Julia. That's why I gave you my number." Someone else's voice, a man's, was in the background. Julia couldn't make out the words. "Is there a problem?"

Of course there's a problem, Julia wanted to scream. *After four months of therapy, you've probably figured that out by now.*

But that was misplaced rage, the kind of thing that didn't bring awareness and healing. That was abdicating responsibility, as Dr. Forrest had so carefully explained. She took a deep breath, closed her eyes, and said, "I . . . I think I'm having another episode."

"Worse than the last one?"

"Not as intense, but longer in duration. I'm imagining things." Julia tried to sound matter-of-fact, almost bored. She related the stories of the clock, the VCR, and the footprints at the window.

"Hmm. Have you been keeping the journal like you promised?"

Julia nodded before remembering that Dr. Forrest couldn't see her. "Yes."

"Did you write down those incidents?"

"No."

"Julia, it's very important that you keep track of everything out of the ordinary, each thought or idea, each fear. I'm very disappointed in you."

"I . . . I'll try harder from now on."

"You do want to get better, don't you?"

"Yes."

"You know that you have to work hard at it. You have to fight. I can help, but only if you let me. Will you let me, Julia?"

"Yes."

"Can you come by the office tomorrow?"

"Sure. But tomorrow's Saturday."

"We'll just squeeze in a little extra session. The problems are very close to the surface. You just have to let them go, bring them into the light."

"What time should I come by?"

"Eleven in the morning."

"Okay. What should I do tonight?"

"Try not to worry. Think about the things we've worked on. The truth is locked inside you. The body remembers what the mind tries to forget. Pay attention to your dreams."

"Thanks, I'll do that. See you in the morning."

"Bye. And Julia?"

"Yes?"

"We'll beat this thing."

Dr. Forrest hung up. Julia slid the cell back on the nightstand. She wrote the clock incident in her journal and added the part about the VCR. Lastly, she wrote down her dream of bones. Then she drifted into an uneasy sleep.

Bones.

Rattling at the window, hanging dry and dusty in her closet, tumbling around on the floor of her childhood bedroom like so many Barbies and wooden blocks.

The bones stitched themselves into a skeleton.

Julia was four. She got up from the bed. Chester Bear had fallen behind the headboard, but she didn't retrieve him. Instead, she went to the door, listened to the voices in the next room, turned the knob.

The skeleton stood before her, its skull grinning like a jack-in-the-box puppet.

She tried to cry out, but then its hard clattering fingers were on her, dirty-white, squeezing, sharp, insistent. The skeleton pulled her from the room, dragged her into the living room. Daddy was gone. The bad people in the robes stood around, watching her. She opened her mouth to scream but a blanket was thrown over her. The wool scratched her skin.

She was carried from the house into the cool dark night. A long time later, maybe hours, the blanket was pulled from her. Two of the people in robes held her. Others stood watching in the darkness. They took her clothes and tied her. Someone stuck a needle in her arm.

She was laid on a stone, its hard chill sinking into her flesh. The bad people circled around her. She wanted to yell for help, but she was so tired, so sleepy.

Candles burned near the stone, along with other things in clay pots. Trees loomed overhead under the bright, full face of the moon. A sweetish, heavy smoke filled the air. The bad people began swaying, singing slow songs that made her blood freeze in her veins.

One of the bad people stood over her and held out his hands. A large ring, of a silver skull with tiny red jewels for eyes, flashed on one finger. The hand with the ring went inside the fold of his robe. He brought out a long knife, its blade gleaming in the moonlight.

The bad people gathered near, the stench of their sweat making her want to throw up. The skull ring flashed a gleaming grin. She struggled against her bonds. Why couldn't she scream?

The bad man with the knife leaned forward and raised the blade high. He lifted his head as if to gaze imploringly into the night sky and his hood slipped backward. Four-year-old Julia looked up at the lower portion of his face revealed beneath the wedge of shadow. That mouth, that chin—

No.

Not him.

Pleeezzzzzzzzzz–

At last she could scream, and she awoke in her bed, the darkness thick around her, the sheets entwined in her limbs.

She sat up, a clammy sweat on her skin.

For a horrible moment, that face was still frozen in her mind. She fought for breath. It was all a dream, only a stupid, strange nightmare.

Then why did two rivers of pain sluice down her abdomen?

She ran her hands under the sheets and touched the scars.

They were moist.

She fumbled for the bedside lamp, nearly knocked it over before she found the switch. The light burst to life. Julia looked at her fingers.

Only sweat.

Not blood.

Julia glanced instinctively at the clock then remembered it was in the trash. She lay back down and thought of soft, sunny things, the lake shore at the country club where Mitchell had taken her virginity, the little beach house at Cape Hatteras that her adoptive parents had owned, the playground at Denton Elementary where she'd been a diminutive kickball star.

Soon she was breathing evenly. She pulled out her journal and wrote down the dream. The images of the fire and smoke and skull ring sliced into her willful focus on mundane things. She thrust all memories aside and calculated the Cardinals' chances of moving up in the division standings the next year and their perennial search for a decent closer, centerfielder, and left-handed starting pitcher.

Julia turned out the light. As much as she feared the dark, and the things it could harbor, she hated the thought that something outside could see her more easily than she could see it.

Darkness won't win. Please, God, if you're up there, don't let it get me.

She couldn't fix an image of God in her head. The pasty, stringy-haired old man with the shimmering aura that was popular in children's Bible books was the first to emerge from the mists of drowsiness.

That stern, paternal visage was no comfort, so she let it shift to a woman. She had no model for a female godhead, except the popular depictions of Venus, Athena, and other mythological goddesses, and their beautiful faces came off as haughty and vain instead of generous. She killed the formative image before it could sneer down at Julia in disdain. She recalled something she'd read once, probably by Nietzsche or Heidegger or one of the other renowned existentialists, that posited the theory that if God were dead, he'd have to be replaced.

Sounds like something Dr. Forrest would say.

The therapist's face took over the spot that had been occupied by the gods. Dr. Forrest's smile was benevolent, patient, and understanding. Existentialism gave no comfort in the night, but human kindness was a snug lover.

Finally, sleep crept over her, mercifully blank, the fingers of the past receding into shadow.

The next morning, the first thing Dr. Forrest said was, "You look exhausted."

"Thanks, I've been working at it." Julia forced a smile. She felt rumpled, like a silk shirt in a sock drawer. Dr. Forrest had just started a pot of coffee. Her receptionist wasn't in, and neither was the other psychiatrist who shared the small office building.

"Do you mind if we lock the door?" Julia asked when they were in the office.

"I don't really think that's necessary. It's good that you are recognizing your fear, that you're not lying to yourself. But let's just risk leaving the door unlocked. Then, when we're finished and no crazed stranger has burst in, you can claim a small victory."

Julia nodded. Dr. Forrest had elicited a lot of small victories. But Julia was ready for a big victory. The dark place inside her head felt as if it were growing, like a cold black fire that was consuming her from the inside out.

Julia settled in her chair as Dr. Forrest closed the blinds. As she dimmed the lights, Julia said, "Do we have to be in the dark?"

"Trust me," Dr. Forestt said. "You want to become whole, don't you?"

"Yes," Julia said, reciting the mantra Dr. Forrest had given her. "The whole Julia Stone."

"Where shall we start?" the therapist asked, sitting across from her.

Julia wondered if she should mention her imagining of Dr. Forrest on the high throne of heaven and decided sharing such a thing would be as disturbing as having had a lesbian fantasy about the older woman. Both were silly when laid on the harsh examining table of daylight, since Julia was heterosexual and secular. As far as she knew. "Maybe I should tell you about my dream."

"Ah. Did you bring your journal?"

Julia fished the notebook out of her purse. Dr. Forrest perused the recent entries and looked up with excited eyes. "I think we're onto something here. Are you willing to face it now?"

"Whatever you think is best."

"Okay. I'm going to hypnotize you, and this time, we're going to go all the way."

Julia's breath caught. "All the way?"

"Let's find out what happened to little Julia Stone. I think I know, but what's important is that *you* know."

Julia dug her fingers into the arm of the chair, but listened as Dr. Forrest gave the relaxation instructions and then began counting down slowly from ten, leading Julia more deeply beneath the surface of the world like Persephone making her annual descent into Hades. Her eyes were open, and she could still recognize her thoughts as her own, but she floated on a soft, insistent current. She was carried through the shadowed past, twenty-three years back.

"The hooded man is standing over you," came Dr. Forrest's voice, as if from behind a wall of water. "The man with the skull ring."

"Help me," Julia said, scared, her hands tight in the knotted rope, the stone hard beneath her bare back.

"The bad people are around you, Julia. They're chanting, belladonna and incense are burning in the crucibles. At the end of the stone is an inverted cross, a decapitated goat's head speared on its tip. Its eyes are open and black, and flies circle the rotting flesh."

Julia squirmed in her chair. She couldn't remember giving Dr. Forrest all those details. But Dr. Forrest had taken her deeply into her subconscious, had mapped and mined it, perhaps knew the territory more intimately than Julia herself did.

And Julia was so forgetful, wasn't she?

"What's the hooded man doing, Julia?"

"He—he's putting his hand inside his robe. He pulls out—"

"A knife. He pulls out a long sharp knife, doesn't he, Julia?"

She nodded, a lump in her throat, sweating even in the chill of the imagined night air.

"What happens next?"

"He . . . he's raising the knife. He shouts something."

"You remember, don't you? Tell me what he says."

"He says 'Lord Master Satan, we offer you this blood in your sacred name, that you may smile upon . . . that you may smile upon—"

"You recognize the voice, don't you, Julia?"

Julia moaned, writhing on the granite slab under the bright eye of the moon.

"Whose voice is it, Julia?"

Julia whispered, her mouth dry.

"Tell me, Julia. Who did this to you? Who is to blame for all your fear and pain and sorrow?"

Julia looked up at the man whose hood had fallen back, his face revealed. She struggled to sit up against invisible bonds.

The name tore itself from her lips. "Daddy."

And the response, drifting from the corners of the world and the cracks in her mind, insinuated in a whisper:

Jooolia . . . .

CHAPTER EIGHT

Julia ripped free of the dream altar, broke the hypnotic trance.

Dr. Forrest held her as she cried.

"You're not alone, Julia," the therapist repeated over and over.

Julia wept herself dry, trying to forget the face beneath the hood, the man who held the knife, the man who had given his daughter to the bad people.

"It's always hard to accept a truth that's so awful, but it's the only way to let the healing begin," said Dr. Forrest. She opened the blinds and let light spill into the room, and then sat across from Julia in her usual chair.

"Daddy," Julia whispered to herself, blinking against the harsh glare of reality. She shook her head. "No. He couldn't have done that. He loved me."

She could remember his arms around her, hugging her, dressing her, holding her hand and walking her through the park. Taking her to the Pink Palace outside Memphis, showing her all the strange animals that stood stiff and still in the museum's glass cases. She remembered his smiles, his blue eyes as warm as August sky, the way his stubble tickled her cheek when he kissed her. She told Dr. Forrest these things, evidence against this cruel, freshly conjured memory.

"All that may be true as well, Julia," Dr. Forrest said. "The mind tries to protect us. One of the ways it does that is by burying the bad memories deep in the basement, way down there where they're hard to dig up. It's natural that the mind lets you retrieve only the happy memories. A survival mechanism."

"He loved me."

"The body remembers what the mind wants you to forget. Don't you feel the pain in your stomach and chest? In all the places the bad people touched you?"

Julia nodded. Her muscles were sore, her stomach felt as if someone had punched it with a fistful of nails, and the place between her legs—

"I know it's hard for you, Julia," said Dr. Forrest. "But we have to do this all the way. We have to be honest. What else do you remember about your father?"

"He . . . he told me bedtime stories when he tucked me in at night."

"Would this take place in your bedroom, or in his?"

"In mine."

"Are you sure?"

"Yes. Chester Bear was always beside me. There was an oak tree out the window, and a streetlight on the other side of it. My room almost always had stripes of shadows across it. We lived next to a farm, you could smell the chickens."

"When he tucked you in, how did he do it?"

"What do you mean?"

"Did he help you put your pajamas on?"

"Sometimes."

"Were you ever naked when he tucked you in?"

"Maybe."

"Did he ever touch you in ways that felt wrong?"

Julia thought of that creased face, those clenched features beneath the hood, the strange light in the eyes of the man who was going to cut her. Her father. She shuddered and looked down at her hands fidgeting in her lap. His blood was in her. Or maybe he thought of her flesh and blood as his possessions, free to give and take.

"It's very important, Julia." Dr. Forrest leaned forward and touched her knee. "Other women have gone through the same experience. Do it for all of them." A pause and a whisper. "For all of *us*."

Julia looked at the therapist, trying to read those somber gray eyes behind the glasses. Not her, too? Had this wise and supportive woman suffered through a similar experience? Was her compassion constructed on determination, perhaps seeking to resolve her own psychic wounds by applying salve to others?

But Dr. Forrest had survived, had conquered the past and shed all its baggage. Dr. Forrest had not let abuse destroy her present and future life. The doctor was whole and healed.

A surge of anger swept through Julia. Her life was being stolen from her. She was being raped and tortured more viciously today, by her fear and doubt, than she had been as a child. In this instance, the scar was worse than the wound, because at least wounds brought pain. Even pain was preferable to numbness.

"Did he ever touch you, Julia?" The woman's voice had slipped from its calm professionalism into a sharp, firm tone.

"I don't remember," Julia said, her eyes welling even though she thought she had drained her reservoir of tears.

Dr. Forrest squeezed her wrist as tightly as the bad people's ropes had. "He touched you, didn't he?"

Dr. Forrest should know. Dr. Forrest had learned things about Julia that Julia herself hadn't accepted yet. But she wasn't going to take this last terrible step, she wasn't willing to throw open the cellar door and shed light on those bones. She couldn't force herself to face a memory that made her entire life a lie.

"Okay, let's pretend for a moment," Dr. Forrest said softly, releasing her wrist. "It's safer to play make-believe at first.

Suppose he had touched you?"

Julia said nothing.

"How would that make you feel?"

Julia looked at the clock. The session had lasted nearly two hours. The televangelist that had hijacked her VCR had threatened an eternity of fire and brimstone for sinners, and Julia wasn't sure such a punishment could be worse than a life sentence inside her own skull.

"I'm sorry," Julia said, rubbing her temples. "I think we'd better stop. My head's splitting."

Dr. Forrest sat back and pursed her lips. "It's always hard to admit. Perhaps the hardest thing in the world. That a father's love could go so wrong—"

Julia gathered her purse and headed for the door.

"You're not alone, Julia," Dr. Forrest called after her. "You're never alone."

Julia drove home, her thoughts jumbled. The world outside the car windows seemed unreal, a strange movie set onto which she had been dropped. The faces in the passing cars showed no signs of comprehending the conflict of this particular scene. And the script, well, apparently the script could be rewritten at any time, to alter the opening scenes and therefore change the meaning of everything that came after. Even though the later scenes contained the exact same sequences and dialogue as before.

As she left the office district and came to the outskirts of Elkwood, some of the tension fell away. Fewer cars closed her in, fewer traffic lights ordered her to stop. The trees were more numerous, and the colorful leaves provided momentary distractions from her rage and pain. By the time she pulled onto Buckeye Creek Road, she had almost convinced herself that the session had never happened, that the vision of her father's face beneath the hood was just one more misleading memory.

She went straight to the phone.

"Hello?"

Good. He was home, probably watching golf on television, a Chivas Regal and coke sweating cold in his hand.

"Hi, Mitchell, it's me."

"Julia!" He sounded pleased to hear from her. She very rarely called him, and she felt a brief shiver of shame at her diffidence. After all, this man had stood by her through her adoptive parents' death, through her reluctance to offer her heart fully, through her budding disorder and relocation.

"How are you doing?"

"Fine, fine. Is something wrong? Your voice sounds strange."

"I've just been busy. Absentminded. What's new with you?"

"Nothing since the last time we talked, what, two days ago?"

"The reason I called is . . . I'm coming down."

"*Here*? Hey, that's really great! I can't wait to see you," he added. "When are you coming?"

"I hope I can get an afternoon flight."

"Wow. That's short notice. You want me that badly, huh?"

She couldn't tell if he were joking. "No, it's not like that, Mitchell. I'll be getting a room."

Petulance entered his voice. "You should stay with me, honey. It's been months."

She wondered if he'd managed to resist temptation in her absence. He was handsome and wealthy, the kind of big catch a lot of women were trolling for. But he sincerely seemed to be willing to wait to marry her. Predictable. She didn't deserve him. Perhaps no one did.

"I need a favor from you," she said.

"I can't figure you out."

Neither can I. "Will you check with some of your contacts in the police department and the D.A.'s office?"

"Look here, Julia. My friends are starting to think I'm weird, turning down dates with sweet, young, *interested* women so that I can save myself for you. And I'm starting to get tired of waiting. I mean, I love you, but—"

"When you love somebody, you don't impose conditions," Julia said.

"Where did you get that little nugget of wisdom? From one of your shrinks? As if *you* know the first thing about love."

"Mitchell—"

"Have you ever loved anybody, Julia? Besides yourself, I mean? And the little voices in your head?"

"Mitchell, please don't get mad." Her voice cracked. "I'm trying—"

"Jeez," he said, exasperated at her tears. Surrendering. "Okay. What do you want me to do?"

Say you're sorry, for one thing.

But she knew he wouldn't. Mitchell was never sorry. "Could you check around, see whatever happened with the investigation into my father's disappearance?"

"Julia, we've been through that a hundred times. The case is dead. No leads. He just walked off the face of the earth. Why can't you let it go and get on with your life? Sometimes I think you wouldn't be so crazy if you left the past alone. Hooded men and all that crap."

She squeezed the phone until her knuckles were white. Eight years. She'd known him nearly a third of her life. In those early years, they had made passionate love often, and she had unfolded like a flower beneath the sun of his affection. Then her problems had started, tiny paranoid thoughts, a nervous stomach, a sense that she had forgotten something important. Soon came the little surprises, the bad dreams, and the blame.

Mitchell had encouraged her when she first started seeing Dr. Danner. He had already elaborately planned their future and saw therapy as only a minor detour on the road to their eternal bliss. Over the years, though, as he became more mercenary in his law practice, he'd grown stubborn and possessive, angry at her both for her weakness and for her refusal to marry him. He'd given her an obscenely large engagement ring that she kept in a safe-deposit box. What was scary was that she couldn't let him go, couldn't grant both of them their freedom. This was love held hostage, love with a gun to its head, love in a straitjacket.

"Will you do it for me?" Julia asked when she had regained control of herself. She didn't want to prostitute herself by tempting him with her flesh when her heart and mind wasn't fully ready, but she could appeal to his ego. "You know how to get things done. People jump when you call, Mitchell."

"Well, I'll give it a try." He sounded mildly assuaged. "No promises, though."

"Thanks, Mitchell. I'll call when I get in to Memphis International."

"Can we at least have dinner together?"

"I'd like that," she said. And she realized she *did* look forward to seeing him. Mitchell had helped her get through the car-crash death of her adoptive parents, providing moral support in his own domineering, Leonine way. Sometimes she wished she could adopt more of his philosophy, just give in and be his country club ornament, the one who completed his image of the successful young professional.

"See you in a few hours," she said. "Bye."

She made flight reservations and took a shower. Her suitcase was nearly packed when she heard a knock on the front door. She tightened her bathrobe and went to the living room, peering through the crack in the curtains. Walter's Jeep was parked at the curb.

She hadn't called Mr. Webster about any repairs. What was the handyman doing here?

"Hello?" she called from behind the closed front door. Perhaps she should have waited to see what he would do first. If he were a Creep, he might try to break in one of the windows. Then she remembered that he probably still had the key to her house, the one he had gotten from Mister Webster.

"Hello, Miss Stone?"

He could come right in if he wanted, and she couldn't do a thing about it. She considered what Mabel Covington had said about Walter's wife.

She glanced at the phone. The cops might need fifteen or twenty minutes to respond to a call this far from town. Plenty of time for Walter to do whatever he had in mind, unless he was one of those meticulous Creeps, the kind who liked to slowly peel his victims like ripe peaches—

She pressed her fist to her forehead.

"Miss Stone?" Walter repeated.

"What is it?" she asked, careful to control her voice, trying to sound unconcerned.

"I was just on my way into town, and I had something I thought you might like."

A knife to the throat, maybe? Or a screwdriver punching me a third eye socket? Or whatever you did to your wife when you took her to the woods on Cracker Knob?

In jurisprudence, suspects were innocent until proven guilty.

Julia remembered the kindness with which he'd treated her.

"Hold on a second," she called.

She glanced at the phone, decided against it, went to the bedroom and slipped off the robe. As she slid into a T-shirt and jumper, she thought she heard something bump against the window. The glass was misted from the shower's steam, so she saw nothing. She collected the mace from her purse and held it behind her back, and then returned to the door and opened it.

Walter stood off the edge of the stoop, by the snowball bush. He looked ill at ease, without his baseball cap and wearing a short-sleeved knit shirt instead of his usual flannel. Like a starched golfer instead of a carpenter.

"Sorry to drop by unexpected," he said, his cheeks crinkling as he tried to smile.

Julia pushed her wet hair behind her shoulders. "Is something broken that I don't know about?"

"Uh, no. I was just passing by, and I thought of you."

"The electricity has been fine," she said. Did Elkwood handymen drop by to check up on their work? Was that another of the maddening unwritten rules of mountain pride, along with extending invitations to church?

"Good. Wouldn't want the house to catch on fire."

"Thanks for checking," she said. "But I'm afraid I'm in a hurry. I've got to make a flight."

Walter nodded, the smile frozen on his face, squinting in the day's brightness. "Where you fixing to go?"

"Memphis."

"Oh. Old friends, I guess."

"Something like that."

"I won't keep you, then. I brought something I thought you might like." He pulled an envelope from the rear pocket of his jeans and gave it to her.

Julia looked across the street to the apartments, and then shifted her gaze to Mrs. Covington's house. She peeled back the flap and peered inside the envelope, expecting one of those cartoonish Bible tracts that showed the car-crash victim wandering through the flaming tunnels of hell and eventually realizing he was dead and it was far too late for the salvation offered by John 3:16.

Her first peek, however, suggested photographs.

She pulled them out. Not photographs, but baseball cards.

Ozzie Smith. Jack Clark. Willie McGee. Ted Simmons. A few scrub pitchers and utility infielders, the Julian Javiers of the world. And some older cards, Bob Gibson, Lou Brock, Ken Boyer. And the last . . . probably the greatest Cardinal ever. Stan Musial. The Man.

"Do you like them?" he asked, his eyes wide and serious.

"Yes, they're wonderful!" she said. "My father used to give me baseball cards when I was little."

Walter grinned at her happiness, his slightly crooked teeth making him look innocent and young. "One of my buddies gave them to me a long time ago. They were tucked away in a drawer. I got some others, too, but they ain't Cardinals."

"That's really thoughtful of you," she said. "But I can't take these. They must be valuable."

"Some of the old ones might be worth a little bit of money, but value is from what you care about them," Walter said. "I don't care that much. I bet you could care about them more."

That made sense, in a strange kind of way. She studied the cards. Pieces of the past. But not a bad past, because in the photographs the outfield grass was green, the players smiled, and baseball was just a game.

"Well, I'll let you go," Walter said. "Hope you have a good trip."

"Thank you, Walter," was all she could think of to say. "This is the best thing to happen to me since I've been to Elkwood."

He waved as he drove away, the cloth top off his Jeep, his hair ruffled by the wind.

Julia sat on the couch and looked at the cards for a few minutes, read the statistics on the backs, spread them out on the coffee table. She arranged them into a lineup, setting the batting order by position. The smile felt good and rare on her face. She'd almost forgotten such simple, childish delights existed.

She set the VCR to tape the evening's doubleheader, finished dressing, and drove to Charlotte-Douglas Airport, where she caught a jet. As the plane lifted off the runway, she embraced the freedom of flight and vowed to leave her mental baggage behind, even though she wasn't sure what memories were tucked inside it.

CHAPTER NINE

On the approach to Memphis, Julia marveled at the lights of the big city, a million stars spread against a dark backdrop, the Mississippi like a galactic rift. After the months in the rural Blue Ridge Mountains, the crush of people at the airport seemed senseless, like a stampede of cattle into the slaughterhouse.

Mitchell met her as she debarked. He wore his unbreakable lawyer's smile, a Rolex, a tailor-cut pinstriped suit, shoes so gleaming that he could check his dark, curly hair in them. Perfect Mitchell. Still perfectly, utterly the same as when she had last seen him, as when she had first seen him. He didn't age, only accumulated thicker layers of sameness.

As he headed toward her at the luggage conveyor, she wondered why she couldn't be grateful for the stability he offered. All she had to do was say "Yes," and she could be Mrs. Austin by April. Sure, he would irk her from time to time, would grant only the perfunctory four minutes of intercourse before rolling over to call his stock broker, would pat her on the hand and call her his "Little Woman," would smother her with boring endeavors like tennis dates and new window treatments. But he would never, ever create a bad memory for her. In fact, she was quite sure that, after a lifetime with him, she would have very few memories at all.

And that might not be such a bad thing.

They hugged stiffly, him looming over her, trying to press her breasts against him. He kissed her cheek before finding her lips. No tongue, and she didn't offer hers. His cologne was musky and sweet.

"You're looking great," he said, letting his eyes roam over her figure. If he noticed the weight she'd put on, he didn't say anything, but he might have been calculating its effect beside the country club's pool, and how a small bulge around the bikini lines might affect that complex formula of social standing. Arm candy couldn't eat candy, at least not too much of it.

"You're looking perfect, as usual," she said.

"I work at it," he said. Truer words never spoken. Another thing about Mitchell, he was pretty honest for a lawyer.

"Did you find out anything about my dad's case?" she asked.

"A little, but can't it wait? I got us reservations at The Blue Note, and it wasn't easy, let me tell you. Even Mitchell Austin has to grease a few palms to get a good seat in this town."

Now he was referring to himself in third person. How the mighty had risen in her absence.

He pointed to her hand. "Hey, where's the rock?"

She mulled the short list of lies and came up with a tired one. "I was cleaning the stove before I left and didn't want to tarnish it. I was in such a rush packing, I forgot to put it back on."

"Jesus, Julia, do you know how much that cost?"

She supposed in the five-figure range, but she merely said, "Don't worry, I left it in a safe place."

"You're not waffling, are you?"

Lying got easier with practice, and she served it up with one of Mitchell's pet phrases. "No, Mitchell. I'm sticking with the game plan."

He smiled but the gesture didn't reach his eyes. He took her hand and dragged her toward baggage claim.

They caught a cab downtown, Julia gawking at the skyscrapers like a tourist as Mitchell possessively put his arm around her. He helped her out when the cab pulled to the curb. The muggy air on the sidewalk settled around Julia like a second skin. The car exhaust, the noise of traffic and evening commerce, the kaleidoscopic neon and flashing lights all kept her off balance. How had she survived this sensory overload for so long?

They had a cucumber salad for openers, Mitchell ordering wine, Julia sticking with lemonade. "So, tell me what you found out about my father," she said.

Mitchell arranged his napkin with a flourish. "Later. This meal is costing a small fortune. You can pay me back by gazing into my eyes and melting."

She gazed, but didn't melt. She hoped someday soon she would be able to melt again, but not tonight. "It's important, Mitchell."

He sighed and drained his glass, tapped it until the waiter brought more. "It's like I told you, not much new. I got hold of the detective who worked the case, a Lieutenant James Whitmore, he's retired now, but I served on a Chamber of Commerce committee with his sister, so he was easy to track."

Mitchell fumbled in his jacket pocket, brought out a small sheaf of papers. "Got these at the records division. The case is still officially open, of course, but several hundred people have disappeared since then. Yesterday's news."

Julia scanned the documents. The basic details were unchanged: Douglas Arthur Stone, age thirty-six, reported missing on the morning of September 28th. He'd called the police to his house for an emergency. Stone's four-year-old daughter was found outside the house, confused, bleeding from cuts on her belly, and asking when her father would be back. The front door was unlocked, none of Stone's clothes appeared to be missing, his car still in the driveway. Credit-card and financial records had gone unchanged. The few distant relatives lived on the West Coast, and had heard nothing from him. And that was that.

Strange that, for years, all she could remember of that night was standing barefoot in the grass. Now, Dr. Forrest had led her to the memories that had been lost for so long.

"What did Whitmore say?" Julia asked, after reading the neighbor's unrevealing statements.

"Said he remembers following up leads at the school where your father taught. All dead ends. The case got buried pretty fast." Mitchell leaned over the table and held her hand. "Why don't you just let it go?"

She pulled her hand away. "I can't."

If only she could tell him about the image of the Black Mass, the recovered memory, the only piece to this puzzle that she had. However elusive that memory was, at least it was something. But part of her was afraid that Mitchell would be shocked, view her as damaged goods, and once and for all decide that her "behavioral disorder" was no longer just a cute little quirk and decide to cut his losses. Though she was unsure what place she had in Mitchell's life, she couldn't bear the thought of being without him and the secure future he offered. The other part of her was afraid that Mitchell would laugh in her face.

Dinner came, and they ate over small talk of Mitchell's legal cases, local politics, how Julia should re-invest the small inheritance that her adoptive parents had left. It was easy for her to fall into the role of sympathetic listener, nodding and affirming Mitchell's rightness in all matters.

Mitchell walked her to a downtown hotel and rode the elevator with her. "Your skin smells sweet," he said at her door, his breath on the soft nape of her neck.

"You feel good," she said, her arms embracing his familiar and comforting form. He took that as an invitation and dug his fingers into her shoulders. She dodged his next maneuver, a nuzzle under the ear. He hadn't changed his repertoire in her absence.

He would follow his instructional manual by rote until Tab A was inserted into Slot B. Part of her wanted to surrender, through the genetic instinct that needed a mate and provider, but her head was swirling so much she wouldn't have been able to derive any pleasure. And though Mitchell was certainly not afraid to indulge himself irrespective of her response, she wasn't up for a game of false enthusiasm.

She kissed his cheek and danced away from his grasp. "Not tonight, honey. But soon."

His face darkened. "As soon as you're better?"

"You've always said you don't want half a woman."

"I don't want half, but I could at least get a piece."

"Mitchell."

"If I didn't have so much invested in you . . . "

"If you really love me, it's worth the wait."

"I can't wait forever," he said, anger flushing his cheeks red, portraying emotion he would never let loose in a court of law. "I'm under a lot of pressure. I'm out on the gangplank with some creditors, and these people play for keeps. Once we're legal, I can get your money for you. For *us.*"

"My inheritance wouldn't even cover the down payment on a house, much less bail you out of big trouble. And I'd give that to you right now if you ask."

"Never mind," he said. "I've got people to see."

He gave her a kiss and pressed a slip of paper in her hand. He hurried down the hall, giving her a terse wave as the elevator swallowed him. She put her fingers to her lips, about to blow him a kiss, but he was gone before she could float the gesture his way.

She looked down at the paper. It was James Whitmore's

phone number. Beneath it, in Mitchell's neat, obsessive-compulsive writing, was written: "Sweet dreams, Jooolia."

CHAPTER TEN

Julia met James Whitmore at the hotel bar. She picked him out immediately. He'd told her to look for the man who didn't belong, and that would be him. Whitmore sat on a stool, three hundred pounds, his bald head reflecting the neon beer signs. His face was wrinkled with great folds of ebony skin, but his eyes were clear. He was drinking milk, and a milk mustache contrasted with his broad lips. He nodded at her in the bar mirror as she sat beside him.

"Mr. Whitmore?"

"My, haven't you grown up," he said.

She realized he must be comparing her to the four-year-old Julia, the one whose father disappeared one autumn night long ago.

"Thank you for coming down. I know you don't owe me anything, and you probably had plans for the evening."

"A drink with a pretty lady? Sounds like a plan to me."

The bartender came, and she ordered a gin gimlet. The strong bite of the alcohol kicked away some of the day's accumulated weariness. "I know Mitchell Austin talked to you about my father's case, but I was hoping you might remember something he overlooked."

"Doubtful," Whitmore said. "Lots of people owe him favors. If he asks for something, he usually gets it. You with him?"

"Excuse me?"

"You his girlfriend? Wife? Or, what do they call it now, significant other?"

"We're engaged," she said, taking a second, larger swallow

of the gimlet. "Could you please go over the case for me? Just one more time, and I promise I'll leave you alone."

"Not much to add. I wasn't the lead, that was Lieutenant Snead. I was just part of the investigating team. You've seen the case files and the incident report. We put out an APB, sent photos to the FBI and the state agencies, dug into his background to see if anybody had a grudge."

He looked down at her. "We talked to you, too, of course. But you were so confused, you didn't know what happened. My, you were cute. We felt so sorry for you, losing your Dad like that. And the deep cuts on your belly, from the broken window in your room. You must have tried to crawl out."

"The reports said that, besides the broken window, there was no evidence of forced entry and nothing was taken."

"As far as we can tell. Of course, he might have had a million dollars in a paper sack, for all we know."

"He was a high school teacher."

Whitmore looked at her over his glass of milk. "Some people don't like to hear bad stuff about people they thought they knew. What about you?"

"Try me," she said. "I've probably imagined worse things than you can come up with."

He smiled, eliminating the fierceness that would otherwise show in his bold features. "I suppose you have. Well, he could have been into drugs, maybe he was dealing. Couldn't find anybody who dealt with him, but it's not exactly the kind of information you volunteer to the police just to be a good citizen."

The night's band was setting up on the stage at one end of the room. A stringy-haired teenager plugged in a guitar, one of the legion of fast-fingered guitarists that wandered through Memphis on their way to nowhere. Julia had watched them all her life, marveled at the endless power that dreams held on people, dreams that let them lie to themselves about the odds of making it. Or of being happy.

Whitmore's bulbous eyes took in the scene. "Your father was pretty white-bread plain, as far as we could tell. Could be that he tried real hard to make it look that way. Wouldn't be the first."

"No plane tickets, no cab calls, car sitting in the driveway. Anything turn up on his driver's license or credit cards?"

"Nothing. In a missing person case, you retrace the victim's steps over and over, trying to find the point where the trail veers off. The day he disappeared, Douglas Stone taught class, dropped you off and picked you up at daycare, took you to the library and the park, fed you at McDonald's. Apparently tucked you in that night. Then just up and walked off the face of the earth."

The teen played a blues lick, not bad but nothing special, and began helping the drummer put her kit together. A tall man with a bass guitar strapped across his shoulder began running cables. It would probably take another half-hour before sound check, and Julia wanted to be far away before the first out-of-tune chord screamed.

Julia finished her drink, closed her eyes, and tried to summon details from her dreams and hypnotism sessions. What would Dr. Forrest ask her to look for? "What happened to his personal effects?"

"They were held in the evidence locker for two years then sold at public auction. The money went to the foster home where you were staying."

"Any valuables or personal effects?"

"Men didn't wear much jewelry back then, not like they do now. But I remember something that I thought was strange. Didn't Mitchell tell you about the ring?"

"The ring?"

"Yeah. Big silver thing, shaped like a skull. Had two tiny rubies set in the eye sockets."

The ring. The one on the hand that held the knife. Julia's stomach tensed, and a shiver of remembered pain ran up the twin scars on her abdomen.

"That's kind of how we figured the disappearance wasn't in connection with a larceny," Whitmore continued, studying her face. "That ring was probably worth a few grand."

"Did that get auctioned off, too?"

"Yeah, as far as I know."

"Any records of sale from the auction?"

"Probably someplace, yeah. That was more than twenty years ago, before computer databases, and paper records have a way of falling through the cracks sometimes. But you might go down to the Records Division and take a look. They'll probably put up with you for fifteen minutes before they run you off."

He finished his milk. A man at the end of the bar lit a cigarette. Whitmore glared at the smoker, who promptly picked up his drink and ashtray and went to find a booth.

The bartender came by, Julia ordered a second gimlet, Whitmore passed on more milk. "Can I ask you something, Mr. Whitmore? And you don't have to answer, because you don't owe me anything and, as you said, some people don't want to hear bad stuff about people they thought they knew."

"Ask away," he said, glancing at his watch, and then at the band in the corner.

"Were there any reports of Satanic activity in Memphis around that time?"

The corners of Whitmore's lips lifted a little as if he were about to laugh, but realized she was serious. He must have seen his reflection in the bar mirror. He covered his mouth, wiping away the milk mustache. "There's always talk of that kind of thing," he said. "And, no, I don't believe the devil popped up and dragged your daddy down to hell through the bathtub drain."

"I don't, either. But some people apparently take it deadly seriously."

"We've had our share of mutilated animals," he said. "Most of it was just high school kids with too much time on their hands and too many people to impress. As for an organized effort, we don't have any Church of Satan branches here or anything. Who was that guy that started that mess out in San Francisco?"

"Anton LaVey? The guy who wrote the Satanic Bible?"

"You really *did* study up, didn't you?"

"Even better. I work with a guy who did. He's either the world's leading expert on Satanic ritual or else he ought to be writing horror novels. But LaVey was nothing but a glorified carnival barker. I'm talking about the real thing, people who are into it so deeply that they're willing to kill to protect their secrets."

"Well, there was a lot of talk a few years back, claims of Black Masses and that sort of thing. Mostly came out of psychiatrist's reports. You know, ritual child rape, child sacrifice, chronic abuse. Cops watch the news and read the papers, just like everybody else. Sometimes we'd see things that made us wonder, but there was one big problem with all those reports."

"Let me guess." Julia took a large gulp of her drink. "Same as with my father. No hard evidence."

"If even a dozen kids were sacrificed every year, they would have been noticed. Sure, Memphis has a lot of runaways just like everywhere else, and probably more kids run *to* here than away from here." Whitmore nodded his head toward the girl sitting beside the sound board, a pale, trembling fifteen-year-old blond. "It's either music or go into the trade. Sometimes both."

"So you don't think it's possible for a huge, organized, underground cult to exist without being discovered?"

Whitmore shrugged. "Hey, I was a cop for thirty-five years. I know anything's possible. But, you'd think at least one or two of the cult members would eventually become . . . now, what's that word I'm looking for? Disillusioned, maybe?"

"'Disenchanted' might be more appropriate."

He laughed. "Maybe you ought to be a writer or something."

"Or a reporter, maybe. So nobody ever came forward?"

"Not in my experience. But looking back, there's maybe a handful of unsolved cases that still give me the Creeps. The Mississippi floats up something ugly once in a while."

"Like an eviscerated corpse?" She told him about the Elkwood victim, and Whitmore's eyes opened wider.

"We had a couple of cases like that," Whitmore said, his voice soft. Julia had to lean forward to hear him over the noise of the gathering crowd and clinking glass. "Cut up just as you described," he said. "Come to think of it, one of them turned up a month or so before your father disappeared. Of course, there was no connection between the two, and no reason to think there might be."

"You've got a good memory."

He looked down at the bar, at the streaks of light in the polished oak. "A detective never forgets the cases he doesn't solve. Because, deep down inside, he never stops trying to solve them."

The guitarist had cranked his amplifier and strummed an ominous minor chord. The audience hooted, whistled, and drank. The drummer played a fill, checking the angles of the drum heads and cymbals. Ten years ago, the anticipation would have Julia electrified and ready to dance all night. Now, she preferred a radio so she could control the volume.

Whitmore looked similarly pained. "That's my cue," he said, heaving himself from the stool.

Julia gathered her purse, finished the last sip of her drink, and paid her tab. She walked Whitmore to the sidewalk and thanked him again.

"Doubt if I helped you any," he said. "Probably just made you more troubled than you already were."

"Trouble is only what you make of it," Julia said, reciting one of Mrs. Covington's mountain sayings. It sounded alien in that world of concrete and steel.

"I won't tell you that you'd be better off just letting the past alone, and getting on with your life," he said. "I'll bet you hear that enough already."

She smiled. "A detective never stops trying to solve them, right?"

His teeth gleamed in the streetlights. "Keep my number and give me a call if anything turns up."

She shook his hand and went up to her room, slightly woozy from the drinks. She lay on the bed and listened to the steady throb of traffic, the city's blood pumping through its monstrous asphalt veins.

Why hadn't Mitchell told her about the ring? Surely he knew that James Whitmore would mention such an unusual item. But he could have easily withheld Whitmore's number from her, he could have failed to mention the detective at all. She may or may not have found Whitmore through her own efforts.

By the time she fell asleep, fully clothed, she had convinced herself that Mitchell had only been trying to protect her. Mitchell didn't want her bothered by the past because he wanted a perfect future for her. As she drifted into a haze of jumbled imagery, she tried to pray but no words came, and neither did a response to her seeking.

CHAPTER ELEVEN

Julia hadn't dreamed at all, at least as far as she remembered in the morning. She had a mild hangover, and she gave her reflection a hard time in the bathroom mirror.

"All it takes for you to avoid nightmares about bones is to slug down some eighty proof," she said, looking into her own red eyes. "You could be onto something there, girl. Something that doesn't sound like it leads to a happy ending. I believe I'd just as soon be crazy as turn into a lush."

Then she realized that probably only crazy people talked to themselves in the mirror, so she showered away the muscle aches and then dove into the Memphis phone book. She got the answering machine of her friend Sue McAllister, who had been a fellow reporter with *The Commercial Appeal*. Julia left a message that she was in town and wondered if they could get together tomorrow.

Mitchell called, and they met downtown for lunch. Julia glossed over her meeting with James Whitmore and didn't mention the skull ring. Mitchell had been a patient ally so far, and she didn't want him to turn on her. She concentrated on being pleasant, the kind of woman she thought he craved. But her mind strayed back to Elkwood, and halfway through dessert of lime Italian ice, Julia found herself thinking of the baseball cards Walter had brought her.

Mitchell's cellular phone interrupted his eating, and as he spoke into the mouthpiece, Julia studied his features. He was tan, with a strong jaw and cheeks that could raise a shadow by three o'clock. His hair was carefully trimmed, his sideburns cut even with his ears. Dark eyes, a nice mouth. Movie-star handsome, really. He could play the lawyer in a Grisham thriller.

She found herself comparing him to Walter, and she shuddered inwardly. She went after the dessert with renewed enthusiasm. Mitchell was her past, present, and future. Walter was the man who fixed her windows. End of reverie.

Mitchell closed his phone and gave that "tax-exempt status" grin that worked so well on civil-suit jurors.

"Will you drive me out to my father's old place?" she asked.

"The old place? What do you want to go out there for?"

"I haven't been there in seven years." She thought up a quick lie. "Dr. Forrest said it would be good for me, help me gain a sense of closure."

"What does this Dr. Forrest know? You've only been seeing her for a few months."

"Dr. Forrest is helping me. She understands me."

Mitchell pushed his plate away and looked out into the street. "And I don't, is that it? I suppose I should be grateful that at least you aren't seeing Lance Danner." He said the name in a mocking, effeminate manner. "Or are you on his calendar for this afternoon?"

"Will you take me or not? I can afford a cab."

Mitchell sighed, the exhalation of a tireless martyr. "Okay. Let's go. We can talk about the wedding on the way."

The house where Julia had lived was in Frayser, fifteen miles from downtown. The area was a bit run down, old industrial meeting up with the urban push of the outskirts, with working class families caught in between. They had a little difficulty finding the house because the area had changed so much, with new construction and the leveling of the giant maples that had once lined the road. The house still stood, its clapboard siding grayed by weather, a section of the gutter missing, grass high around the crumbled walk. A "For Sale" sign leaned in the front yard.

They walked around back, Mitchell carefully watching his step so his shoes didn't get scuffed. The fence along the back yard was missing some of its pickets and looked like a retired boxer's smile. The farm that had once stretched beyond the row of houses had been carved into lots, though a pasture and the warped barn remained.

"I used to play there," Julia said, looking out over the hayfield that was September-yellow. "Daddy wouldn't let me go in the barn, though."

"No wonder," Mitchell said, standing behind her and swatting at bugs. "The cow manure is probably six feet deep. Why in the world would anybody want to have animals wandering outside his house?"

Julia studied the barn. Something was odd about it, there in the stark light cast by the sun's zenith, the tin roof rusted, gray siding boards askew and pocked with knotholes. The image tickled the back of her mind. But that wasn't quite right. Her memory of the scene was nearly a negative, of the barn in a colder light. The barn against the darkness.

"Jeez, you'd think they'd buy a lawn mower," Mitchell said.

Julia bit her thumbnail.

"Now that's what I call progress," Mitchell said. He pointed off in the distance, through a gap in the red-leafed maples. Bulldozers and trucks were parked on a large leveled plain of dirt. "The city needs to expand the tax base out this way. They're running sewer and water at a few hundred a foot, but these crappy houses provide zilch for valuation."

Julia stared into the black throat of the barn. *What? What?*

If only Dr. Forrest were here.

"Well, honey, look on the bright side," Mitchell said,

walking away from her to the edge of the lot. "I mean, I know it's terrible what happened to your father, but at least you were lucky enough to be adopted by wealthy people. If you had grown up here, we probably never would have met."

The barn. Something from that night, the night of the skull ring and altar.

"Honey?"

The barn, stone, chanting, hoods. Bad people.

A hand touched her shoulder, and she yelped and turned.

Mitchell stood with his hands out, mouth open, as startled as she. "Huh?"

Julia put her hands over her face.

"Jeez, honey, why are you so jumpy? I knew we shouldn't have come out here." He stepped toward her. She moved away to the fence.

"Why can't you leave the goddamned past alone?" he shouted. "It's no good, and it never has been."

He adjusted his tie below his red face. "Why in the hell do you do this to yourself? Why do you do it to *me*?"

She looked away from him, out across the pasture. The barn's shape blurred with her tears. She felt on the edge of a great rift, her balance thrown, as if one of the earth's plates were breaking off and carrying her away. She gripped the fence, wanting to hang on to this world. Even with all its pain and troubles, it was the world to which she belonged.

If Mitchell came to her now, hugged her, she would let him. She would hug him back. She would leave this place and its memories, accept the safe life Mitchell offered, give up the senseless fleeing to Elkwood. She would go back to Lance Danner, no, she would get another therapist of Mitchell's choosing. And with the new therapist, she would only work on the present problems, the day-to-day ones that led forward to the future.

She would never look back. As much as she could avoid it.

"Maybe someday I'll understand," she said hollowly. "And someday I can make you understand."

"Someday," Mitchell mocked. "Well, we don't have a lot of 'somedays' left, so you'd better make up your mind."

She started to turn to him, to let him see the tears, but she knew that would weaken him and make him ashamed. Which Mitchell was real, the one that shouted at her or the one that caressed her tears away?

She continued staring across the pasture, at the golden-seeded grass that rippled in the breeze. It was a soft sea, a place that drowned memories. For only a moment. Because the barn floated like a dark ship on its surface.

She heard Mitchell stalk away and slam the door of his Lexus. She gave him a chance to drive away, knowing he wouldn't. She waited until the continents drifted back together, until the ground was stable under her feet. Then, without looking back at Mitchell, she stepped over the fence and headed across the pasture.

CHAPTER TWELVE

The interior of the barn was dim, even with the door open and the siding planks warped enough to admit slices of light. The support posts and boards were gray with age, and the hayloft floor sagged overhead. The place smelled of moldy hay and the dust from dried manure. Beneath that lay the odor of animal fur, even though the stalls had stood empty for years.

As she entered, the shadowy corners crawled toward her like legless things, dragging memories as if they were sacks of dead animals. Her feet moving across the dirt floor made a sound like the slithering of serpents' tongues. She shivered even though the air was humid and still. Julia hugged her arms to her chest, afraid to go forward but unable to stop herself.

She had been here before.

The scars on her stomach throbbed.

She knelt, light-headed, as if she were going to vomit. Her ears rang with a high, piercing whine. Her heartbeat doubled its pace.

Panic.

The panic she had fought so hard to overcome. The panic that she'd managed to hide from Mitchell and her coworkers and even, while they were still alive, her foster parents. The panic that rose up and swallowed her on nights when the past drew too near, when the awful fingers came clattering and clutching.

The panic that Dr. Forrest insisted Julia could conquer.

But Dr. Forrest was in Elkwood, eight hundred miles

away, and Julia was here, alone, on her knees in the dry crumbling hay. Julia closed her eyes and pressed her forehead to the ground.

The cloak of panic descended, swift and suffocating.

Deep breaths, she told herself, but the thought was only one of many, crowded by death and a hot knife and the man with the skull ring and the cold stone and the bad people around her, the bad people touching her, laughing and chanting, the bad people, watching the blade touch her stomach and the silver slipping into flesh and red drops welling around its tip and the hand with the skull ring and the man with the hood and the face beneath the hood and —

She clawed forward, hands meeting a partition. A splinter penetrated her palm, but she kept her grip and pulled herself up, forced herself to her feet. The tears on her cheeks gathered the dust she had stirred. She sucked in a lungful of dirty air, trying to ignore her rapid pulse.

Panic is only in the mind, came her mental tape recording of Dr. Forrest.

Julia looked wildly about, the square light from the barn door like a great gate to a promised land. She thought of yelling for Mitchell, but she wasn't sure she could summon enough air, and he likely couldn't hear her from the car anyway. She pressed her back against the wall and raised her arms, resting them on the top of the half-wall to support herself. She sprawled there like a reluctant martyr awaiting nails to flesh.

Panic is only in the mind, Dr. Forrest repeated.

Julia unclenched her fingers. She willed her hands to be warm balloons, balloons in the sun, balloons the colors of jelly beans. It was working, she was in a park, lying on her back in the grass, she could breathe, the air tasted of sky and life and clouds, except she coughed from the choking dust, crazy, she was in the barn, *the barn*, *THE BARN*.

She closed her eyes again.

The bad people circled, the candles flickered, the thick smoke from the crucibles insinuated like gray dragons under the moonlight, and her body was as cold and deadened as the stone beneath her. The man with the skull ring, the High Priest, raised the knife and addressed the rotted goat's head that hung from the inverted cross.

"Highness of Darkness, Satan, Master of the World, accept this offering from your humble and loyal slaves, that you may continue to give us your blessings," the deep voice intoned, filling the hollow of the barn. "So mote it be."

The knife came down, Julia screamed, her breath rushed from her lungs, her body went limp.

CHAPTER THIRTEEN

When she awoke, she didn't know where she was. She turned her head and bits of old hay fell from her hair. The floor smelled of dirt. She looked up, saw the old locust beams of the barn, the square slots cut in the hayloft, the aged tin of the roof in the dim shadows above.

Her heart was beating steadily, only slightly accelerated. Her limbs felt as if they were filled with wet cement. She was sticky from dried sweat.

How long had she lain there?

She checked her watch. Even the act of raising her wrist was a great effort. 3:37. She'd been in the barn nearly twenty minutes.

She blinked away the last wisps of memory and dragged herself to a kneeling position. The panic attacks always roared in like tidal waves and ebbed away in a slow wash, leaving her battered and drenched. This hadn't been the longest attack, but it had been among the most intense.

She gathered her strength and stood on wobbling legs. The panic could sweep in, could crash down on her, but she wouldn't let it carry her out to the mad, gray sea. She clung to the tether of Dr. Forrest's encouragement and experience.

"Panic is only in your mind," Julia said to herself. The whisper died away among the wooden stalls.

Mitchell.

Hadn't he wondered where she went? Was he still waiting in the driveway, tapping the steering wheel with his manicured fingers? Or had he driven away, muttering under his breath?

Julia hoped he had gone away. She didn't want him to see her like this, filthy and unkempt and shaken. A trophy-to-be had to remain nearly perfect at all times, as cool as a drink at the Nineteenth Hole, as unruffled as a damask tablecloth.

But far worse than his dismay at her physical appearance would be his clumsy attempts at pity. Sure, he would brush her hair away from her face, even hug her, probably kiss her forehead, but he wouldn't invite himself inside her. He wouldn't caress her where she needed it most, in her spirit or soul or heart, the name and place of it as unknown to her as to anyone.

But it wasn't Mitchell's fault. She didn't allow an opening, wouldn't let anyone in the secret place where she might be healed with a touch. Dr. Danner and Dr. Forrest came close; they had softened her. But stubbornness or pride or merely the delusions caused by her disorder kept her always alone, always holding part of herself away from the world. Even knowing that ugly truth about herself didn't allow her to alter it.

She stumbled toward the door, squinting against the afternoon's brightness. The meadow was like fire, yellow against the backdrop of blazing red trees and the houses that clustered along the fence line. A train whistle sounded, an iron giant rumbling along distant tracks over in Frayser's industrial zone. The scant breeze shifted, carrying the river-mud smell of the Mississippi.

Julia waded through the tall grass to the fence. Through the trees at the back of the yard, she saw the Lexus still in the driveway. The driver's seat was reclined. Mitchell was either napping or steeped in a deep sulk.

She glanced at the sky, drawing on the reserves hidden behind clouds.

God, I suppose it's selfish to beg for a little help when I don't really believe in you. But maybe just push me a little farther along the path. At least let me walk.

The clouds appeared unchanged, and no shafts of golden light bathed her in benevolent warmth. No calm voice whispered comforting words in her ear, and no squad of angels winged down to rescue her. Yet she felt better from the simple task of reaching out, and the sense of isolation eased.

Okay, if you're not going to help, at least stay out of the way.

Julia brushed the hay and dust from her clothes, pushed her hair back, and climbed over the fence. She went to the rear of the house and opened the sagging screen door. She tried the knob to the back door, but it was locked. Just as she had expected.

She went to a rear window and looked through the smeared glass. Her old room. An electric buzz raced along the back of her neck as memories came rushing back. Not the bad memories of people in robes, but memories of a child at play, a child who had crawled on that wooden floor, who had sat in the sun with dolls and Chester Bear and alphabet blocks and books she couldn't yet read.

The room was bare and the closet door was missing. The walls had been painted, were now dirty off-white instead of the sky blue they had been when she lived here. One pane of the window had a piece of duct tape covering a crack. The top half of the window latch was lying twisted on the ledge.

Julia took a barrette from her purse, fastened her hair back, and banged on the pane to loosen the chipped paint. She worked her fingers under the window and lifted. A shower of dust drifted down as the window slid open. She glanced at the barren houses on each side before climbing headfirst through the opening. Her feet kicked wildly in the air for a moment. Then she wriggled through and stood on the floor she hadn't touched in more than twenty years, letting the window slide closed behind her.

She was inside the room she had been stolen from 23 years before.

CHAPTER FOURTEEN

Despite her shakiness, Julia felt almost giddy from the exhaustion that came after the crippling anxiety attack. What would Mitchell think if he saw that she had broken into the house? Mitchell worked mostly in property law and knew how to bend the rules in favor of his clients. However, he was very straight-laced about property rights. Visiting a vacant house that was up for sale was one thing, but crawling through a window was quite another.

The floor creaked under her feet. The door was the same, only the knob wasn't at eye level to her anymore. She put her hand on the knob—

The voices.

In the living room, Daddy and the man that Daddy called Lucius were talking.

Her breath caught, just as it had done when she was four. She pushed the door ajar with a groan of hinges, fully expecting to see the hooded people gathering around Daddy. But this time she saw only the dull glare of the sun on the worn beige carpet.

Julia went down the hall, past the dark bathroom, and turned to the other room. Daddy's bedroom.

She couldn't rid herself of Dr. Forrest's suggestions that Daddy had taken her in there as a child, had made her do naughty things, had touched her in ways that Daddies weren't supposed to touch. But Julia felt no dread, none of that suffocating shame that she'd suffered while reliving those suggested scenes in the therapist's office. Still, a mild shiver raced across her skin as she entered the room.

It was as bare as her own former room, the cover plates off the wall sockets, strips torn in the Sheetrock walls. The light fixture dangled from two wires, and the curtain rod had been ripped down and leaned in one corner.

Julia approached the small walk-in closet, much of it in a darkness as thick as night. Shelves lined each side of the closet, and the rod held three rusty hangers.

No skeletons here.

She was about to leave the room when she accidentally kicked a bottom shelf. It rattled on its wooden braces. Julia tucked the toe of her shoe under the shelf board and lifted. It flipped away easily, and Julia saw a small crack in the floorboards underneath. Something, a memory or *deja vu* or dream fragment, made her pause.

She got on her knees and ran her fingertips along the rough cut in the boards. The flooring was loose. A hollow sound answered her tap on the wood. She took the barrette from her hair and used it like a small crowbar to jimmy one of the boards up high enough so she could slide her fingers underneath. A cool rush of air came from the gap in the floor.

She removed more boards, three segments less than a foot long. The insulation had been pushed away. Her heart hammering, she reached into the crawl space, hoping that no spiders were waiting in the dark. She inserted her arm past the elbow before she touched dry dirt.

Julia worked her fingers around and scraped the block wall of the foundation. Then she raked the powdery dirt with her fingernails. Behind her, in her old bedroom, came the sound of the window sliding open.

"Julia?" Mitchell called, his voice reverberating in the empty house.

She quickly scrabbled in the dirt, cobwebs clinging to her forearm. Her palm brushed across a sharp edge. She dug around it, glancing behind her as her fingers freed the object. It was a tiny box. She brought it up and wiped the grit from its lid.

The box was carved from soft cedar. A strange shape was imbedded on its top. Julia traced the symbol with her finger. A star?

"Julia!" Mitchell called louder. "Are you in there?"

She didn't think he would crawl through the window, not with his dogged views on trespassing and his love of his power suit. But Mitchell would keep after her. He must have seen her go to the rear of the house. She wasn't sure she could disguise her excitement about her find. What if the box had belonged to her father?

"What do you think you're doing?" Mitchell shouted.

Julia glanced into the dark crawl space, wondering what other secrets might be lying under the soil. She thought of her dream of bones. Did the body really remember what the mind tried to forget?

She stood and went back into the living room, tucking the box into the front pocket of her slacks. She kept her hands in her pockets to disguise the bulge. Mitchell probably would accuse her of stealing if he saw the box, and if she tried to explain it belonged to her, she would have to delve into the past with him. Far easier to act crazy. She hunched her back and tried to look beaten, tired, and disoriented. It wasn't a difficult role.

Mitchell was holding up the window, his mouth set in a hard line, when she entered her old bedroom. "Have you gone nuts?" he said, with no hint of affection in his voice. "Do you want me to be a party to trespassing? Just think what that would do to my reputation."

Your reputation is stainless steel, Mitchell. Cold and shiny and beyond tarnish. Just like your heart.

She smiled weakly and looked at the floor. "I just wanted to see the house."

Mitchell sighed. "Come on, get out of there before somebody sees you."

She crawled out the window as Mitchell held it open. The box worked its way to the top of her pocket, but she managed to shove it back out of sight.

"Your hair's a mess," Mitchell said, letting the window slide shut and then wiping his hands. "Hope they don't check for fingerprints."

"I left it the way it was," she said, walking toward the Lexus, hoping Mitchell wouldn't stare at her and see the box. She needn't have worried. Mitchell hadn't really looked at her in a long time, not at the way she really was. Mitchell must have seen only the Julia he wanted to see, the perfect match for his perfection, a mirror that positively reflected his own self-image.

She got in the car and, before he reached the driver's side, slipped the box into her purse. She took a last look at the barn in the distance, trembled at the memory of panic, and closed her eyes as Mitchell backed out of the drive. Neither spoke on the trip back in. They were entering the city when Mitchell turned on the radio, a middle-of-the-road pop station. The earnestly bland emoting of the singers was almost as interminable as Mitchell's stoic silence.

Carrie Underwood was serving up a dish of love as if it were a slice of frozen pizza when Julia finally spoke. "I'm sorry I was strange back there. But you didn't have to yell at me, Mitchell. I needed you."

Mitchell was in heavy traffic now, and spared her only a cold glance before refocusing on the bumper ahead. "Need. Well, what about my needs?"

"What about them?"

"You call and tell me you're flying in from North Carolina, and what's the first thing I think about? How we're going to have a great time together, get close, reaffirm the wonderful thing we share. God forbid, even spend the night together. And you barely give me the time of day. It's always about you, isn't it?"

Julia had no answer. Though she was burning inside, she couldn't help but admit the truth of it. If only Mitchell could see she needed an ally more than she needed a lover. She hated herself for not being able to reach him, for having so very little to offer. Even God had no use for her.

"You think it's easy to go six months without sex?" Mitchell continued, his grip tightening on the steering wheel. "I mean, if you were holding out on religious grounds, maybe I could respect you. But I can't help thinking you're teasing me on purpose. Your tap runs so hot and cold, I sometimes wonder if you're trying to make me crazy, too."

"I'm not crazy." She stared straight ahead, at the spires of the tall buildings looming in the thick of Memphis. "They call it 'panic disorder.' Or 'personality disorder not otherwise specified, with schizotypal traits,' depending on whom you ask."

"That's what Lance Danner says. But I'm sure he had his own reasons for keeping you on a short leash." The traffic had jammed and slowed to a crawl. Mitchell turned to look at her. "I don't care if these screwballs get their jollies by turning you on a spit and roasting you over the flames of your own juices, but I wish they'd leave a little meat on the bone for me."

"Let me out at the next corner." The hotel was three blocks away. Even though Creeps filled the sidewalks and lurked in the alleys, they were a safer risk than Mitchell.

"Don't be ridiculous, Julia." Mitchell's tone changed, became patronizing. "Let's have dinner."

The traffic backed up to a stop, and Julia opened her door.

"What do you think you're doing?" Mitchell shouted. But Julia was already out of her seat, her purse under her arm, dodging between two parked cars and heading down the sidewalk. Mitchell called her name once more, but a blaring car horn forced him to close the passenger door and move with the traffic.

Julia tried to avoid looking at the strangers who passed her, the people who lurked in doorways, those who hid behind newspapers or peered out from windows. A police siren sliced into her like a laser, its frenzy echoing off the concrete facades. Car exhaust hung heavy in her throat and in her nose. The city's humid stink pressed against her like a second skin, and she suddenly longed for the clean, fresh smell of the Blue Ridge forest.

She kept her eyes on the sidewalk, concentrating on making it to the next crack, and the next, trying to ignore the hundreds of moving shoes. She hugged her purse close to her chest. To have it snatched now, when she finally had a clue to her past that might be more valuable than money, would be the final joke played by this cruel city.

Someone bumped into her, she gasped and glanced up despite herself—

A bad man, face hidden by a hood—

She gave a small scream, and the man backed away, his hands spread in innocence.

"Sorry, lady," he said, sweat beading his balding head. He wasn't one of the bad people, just an overstressed, overweight jogger who was in a hurry for a date with a heart attack. He tugged the hoodie of his Tennessee Titans sweats and continued on. Julia staggered away and the sea of flesh swept on.

The hotel lobby was cool and sparsely crowded. Julia

controlled her breathing during the solo elevator ride and was finally in her hotel room, the door safely locked. She sprawled on the bed, the image of a million bad people painted inside her eyelids, an entire Memphis filled with hooded Creeps. She lay there until she was as back to normal as Julia Stone could get.

Then she sat up, carried her purse to the desk, closed the curtains, and took out the box.

CHAPTER FIFTEEN

It was the first time Julia had ever used the fingernail file she carried in her purse. She scraped the blunt, hooked edge against the lid to clean the accumulated grime and wiped the lid with tissues moistened by her saliva. She turned the box around and saw that the star was actually a pentagram. Carefully etched into the points of the star were the features of a goat's head, with curling horns and broad nose and evil, slanted eyes.

Two words were carved beneath the symbol: *Judas Stone.*

She had hoped that her memories were faulty, that her father had no connection to the bad people despite what Dr. Forrest said. But here was damning evidence that blew a spark of memory into a bonfire of unavoidable truth. Here was a solid piece of the past, hellish and strange and as disturbing as a dozen Creeps. She realized with a spasm of fear that she would no longer be able to lie to herself.

Daddy had been one of *them.*

Her fingers trembled so much she could hardly hold the file steady. She inserted the blade into the crack and pried open the lid. An aroma of aged mold rose from the box. Inside was a tiny piece of rumpled cloth, stained a dark shade of reddish-brown.

She carefully lifted the cloth and placed it on the desk. She sat before her tableau of grit and soiled tissues and old wood spread across the brightly shellacked surface of the desk. She had to look away for a moment, to reaffirm that the sane, sterile hotel room still existed, that order and not chaos still held sway. The telephone, the television set, and the crisply made bed provided a cold comfort.

The cloth tore as she opened it, bits of thread crumbling away from dry rot. At last she reached the final fold, and sat staring incomprehensibly as sunlight bathed the object.

A skull ring.

Just like the ring from her dream and the same one that Whitmore had described, with one difference. The eye sockets of the skull were empty, not set with rubies. Julia studied the silver expanse of forehead, the cruel mockery of a grin. Inside the band were engraved those same two horrifying words. *Judas Stone*, done in an elegant script.

She knew she shouldn't touch it, that the police would want to dust it for fingerprints. But the police should have noticed the loose boards in her father's closet. True, her discovery of it was accidental, but people trained in investigative techniques would have discovered the box in fifteen minutes.

Unless they already knew the box was there. And overlooked it on purpose. Maybe Satan had gotten to the cops . . . .

No, Julia, that is crazy thinking, and Dr. Forrest says you are not crazy. You are NOT going to start spinning conspiracy theories. Who cares if the Bush family plotted 9/11 and if Rick O'Dell says that Satanism reaches into all levels of government, law enforcement, military, and society? I mean, if it were that widespread, it wouldn't exactly be considered "underground," now, would it?

Satanists had surrendered, joined other more popular and lucrative movements. As counterculture, devil worship had lost favor and was hardly more provocative than Islam beliefs. So far as she knew, no political candidate had ever successfully run on a Satanic ticket. And it wasn't the type of thing one put on a job application. In truth, the orthodox were the only ones who even cared that Satanists had unorthodox practices. And Satan had probably sold more Bibles than Jesus ever had, because fear was the world's greatest sales pitch. Julia knew all about how motivating fear could be. After all, it had pretty much pulled her puppet strings for a couple of decades.

And though her stomach clenched like a hot fist, though electric sweat sluiced from her pores, though she shook so much that her chair squeaked, she reached out and touched the ring.

Nothing.

She didn't know what she had expected, black clouds rolling in, thunder shaking the building, the earth opening up and swallowing Memphis, or merely a puff of sulfurous smoke from which would step a red-faced, goatish creature complete with pointy pitchfork.

Just as God had failed to appear when summoned, Satan had also missed a chance to shock and awe.

So much for vanity over the worth of my soul.

Almost giggling with relief, she lifted the ring and held it close to her face.

"Hello, ugly," she said to the engraved skull.

Did talking to a hunk of silver qualify one for the loony bin? People of many religions addressed gods they couldn't see, and seemed better off for it. Julia figured a good rule of thumb to follow was, "You're only crazy if the inanimate object in question talks back."

Or maybe you weren't crazy, merely one of those privileged few to whom gods deigned to dispense wisdom. Modern prophets were likely misdiagnosed as schizophrenics, and if Jesus really did return to Earth and start spouting messages of eternal rewards and miracles, he'd be strapped to a crash cart, pumped full of Thorazine, and wheeled into a rubber room to wait out the rest of his second coming.

The ring wasn't evil. It was only a lump of mineral, heated and cast and polished by human hands. Except this ring had been her father's, if she believed the engraved words.

The ring was the only relic she had left of the man who had helped bring her to life, a man whose face would have faded like an old photograph except for the recovered memories that kept him always on her mind. And though the memories weren't always comforting, she was grateful to Dr. Forrest, and, before her, Dr. Danner. They had linked her with her own past, shown her how the symptoms of the present came from that bewildering period of her childhood, and now Dr. Forrest was finishing the work of teaching Julia to heal.

Now it was no longer theory. Maybe with this final evidence of the truth, Julia could begin to bury the past.

As Julia held the ring to the light, the twin scars on her stomach tickled and itched. She almost wished the ring *had* spoken, because she still had too many unanswered questions.

Had her father been one of the bad people?

Was he one of those who had chained her to the stone, who danced around her in robes, who touched her, who drank from that strange silver chalice?

Was her father really one of the Creeps?

Recovered memories were one thing, something she knew could be manufactured and then accepted as fact. But the ring was solid, substantial, real. The ring bore the name of Stone. The ring threaded reality into the weavework of an imagined past sewn from dreams, suggestions, and fear.

Julia knew she would do it. It was almost as if the skull moved itself, guided its silver smirk toward her left hand. Then to the tip of her ring finger, the one that should have worn Mitchell's engagement diamond. And then the metal band eased itself over her fingernail, past her knuckle, and settled on the flesh above the pad of her palm.

A warm glow expanded out from the ring, radiated up her arm in waves, spread through her body and made her light-headed. The heat turned into electricity and Julia no longer felt weak. She stared into the skull, and it smiled back at her, as if understanding her need to surrender.

"It's been a long time," the smile seemed to say. "But you're finally ready to become Judas Stone."

No, no, NO.

She yanked off the ring and flung it away. She ran to the far corner of the room as if fleeing a feral animal.

She huddled against the closet, fists over her ears, shrugging off the descending cloak of panic. She forced herself to take deep breaths.

Only a ring, only a ring, only a ring, INHALE . . .

The air tasted of crypts and incense.

Only a ring, only a ring, only a ring, EXHALE . . .

Her heart twitched in her chest like a sack of rats.

The panic settled over her, coal black and blood thick.

Her thoughts spun, wheels without tracks, wire unraveling, stones tumbling in an avalanche. The ring on the hand, the hand that held the knife, that brought the knife down to her belly, that made the incision, a slick hot trail on her abdomen, why was the bad man hurting her, *why*?

And the knife lifting again, blood dripping from the bright blade, the candlelight glinting in its rich redness, the bad people leaning over her, the knife descending again, slicing deftly across the other side of her tummy, and she was aware of the injury, only she didn't feel any pain.

The smoke from the crucibles hung in the air like wool as the bad man held the bloody knife to the sky. Then he raised his other fist, and the skull ring shone pale in the night. The bad man touched the knife to the ring, as if allowing the skull to drink, and the red ruby eyes glowed, pulsed in rhythm to little Julia's frantic heartbeat.

And, beneath the hood, the bad man's eyes glowed with that same red intensity.

He reached into his robe and leaned over her, his breath like old goat cheese, and whispered, "Oh Satan, Master of the World, take as thy bride this whore Judas Stone."

This whore Judas Stone.

She was Judas Stone, too.

The words rang in her ears, ripped through her like a death knell, ripped the fabric of her soul, even as that dream-image bad man raised her limp hand and slipped the ring home.

The ring was hers.

Oh, Christ almighty, the ring was *hers*.

But that made no sense. A ring sized for a four-year-old wouldn't fit now. Had it expanded as she touched it, had it widened itself to accommodate her finger?

The ring is yours, the ring is yours, INHALE . . . .

Rings didn't shrink and grow. Satan was not real, and had no power. The only thing that held power over her was panic. She tried to relax the way Dr. Forrest had taught her.

But Dr. Forrest was miles and miles away, and Julia was alone with the ring.

Inhale. INHALE —

She crawled across the floor, and the dark cloak of panic became a noose, clamping tightly around her neck. Tears trailed down her cheeks.

Julia reached the bedside table, her lungs on fire from the lack of air. Her heartbeat was thin and rapid. She found the phone, pulled it to her lap, punched the numbers.

She managed a shallow gasp as the connection was made and the earpiece gave its electronic purr. By the third ring, she had exhaled.

Please be there.

The phone clicked, and the voice spoke on the other end of the line. "Hello?"

Julia could breathe now. The air was sweet again, air-conditioned and cool and relaxing. "Dr. Forrest, it's me."

"Julia?"

"Yeah."

"What's wrong?"

"I—I'm having an episode."

"Where are you?" Dr. Forrest sounded almost angry.

"Memphis. I flew in yesterday."

"*Memphis*? Without my approval?" No denying the anger now. "Something like this could set us back months."

"I had to find out—"

"What could you possibly find out?"

"I went to the old house," Julia said.

Dr. Forrest said nothing. Julia looked around for the ring as she continued. "I saw the barn behind my house. That's where it happened. I know that's where it happened. And my father . . . "

"Say it, Julia. Say it so that you can make yourself believe it."

"My father was one of them."

"One of the bad people. One of the Creeps. You finally believe."

Julia thought about telling Dr. Forrest about the ring, but she was afraid. If Dr. Forrest was this angry over Julia going to Memphis without permission, the therapist might have a panic attack of her own. Julia needed to make sense of the discovery before she shared it.

"Yes," Julia said. "I remember it now. He was there at the ceremony. My father wed me to Satan."

"Just as you dreamed. Just the way you shared while under hypnosis." Dr. Forrest was slightly calmer.

"It's all true."

"I wouldn't let you lie to yourself, would I, Julia?"

"No, Dr. Forrest."

"When are you coming back?"

"Tomorrow."

"Good. I'll schedule you for a Tuesday session."

"That . . . that would be good."

"So, what set off your panic attack?"

Anything besides the ring and the electric power that surged through my skin at its contact. "I was just thinking about it all. How terrible it was. What a monster my father was."

"I understand, Julia." She sounded excited now. "You know what this means, don't you?"

Julia now saw the ring, lying on the floor where the edge of the bedspread brushed the carpet.

"This means that we're approaching healing," Dr. Forrest said. "We've assessed the damage and we've pictured the effects of the ritual abuse. Now it's time for the final step."

"The final step?" Julia watched the ring as if expecting it to turn molten and slither across the floor toward her.

"Preparing for change. Now you're ready to embrace the past, to become whole. To become the whore Judas Stone."

Julia's breath leaped away. "*WHAT?*"

"I said it's time for you to become the whole Julia Stone."

Julia shook her head. If she were going to start twisting the words of her therapist, she would lose herself to the oily sea of fear and float adrift. She couldn't afford to break this last lifeline of trust. "I talked to one of the officers who worked my father's case."

"Who was it?" Dr. Forrest asked, sounding angry again. Why should she care which one Julia talked to?

"James Whitmore. He's retired now."

"Have they learned anything new?"

"Nothing new," Julia said. "In fact, the case is pretty much buried."

Just like the box had been.

Julia felt well enough to drag herself onto the bed. She twirled the phone cord and waited for Dr. Forrest to speak.

"You're not going to see Dr. Danner while you're there, are you?" the doctor finally said.

"No. Why should I?"

"Well, some patients develop an addiction to their therapists. I've been friends with Lance for many years. But I think you need to sever those ties to Memphis. They're not doing you any good."

"I don't want to go backwards," Julia said. "I'm grateful for the help he gave me, but I really feel like you understand me better. I believe you'll help me heal."

"Of course I will, Julia. You just have to trust me."

"I trust you."

"Then listen to me. Practice the visualization exercises we've been working on. Take a deep breath, a belly breath." The doctor's voice became, soothing and even. "Your hands are inflating. Your fingers are swelling with light, warm heat. They are feathers, they are little clouds, they are fish sunning in a pool."

"Mmm," Julia said, the memory of the treatment as effective as her practice of it. Dr. Forrest took her through the rest of the exercise, until she was lying flat on the bed. By that time, the bed was a magic carpet floating high under the sun.

"Are you relaxed now?" Dr. Forrest whispered.

"Mm-hmm." Julia was so relaxed she wasn't even aware of her pulse rate. She remembered something had been bothering her, but somehow only the lightness seemed important at the moment.

"I'll see you on Tuesday. Have a good evening, Julia."

"Bye, Dr. Forrest," she said softly. "And thanks."

She hung up the phone and was very nearly asleep when she remembered the ring.

She rolled out of bed, clinging to the peaceful images that Dr. Forrest had suggested. She took the old stained cloth from the desk and picked up the ring without making skin contact with the metal. She sealed it inside the box and tucked the box back in her purse for safekeeping.

Outside, darkness was falling, and pricks of light appeared in the buildings as the city changed shifts. Julia undressed, slipped into a thin nightgown, and climbed into bed. She fell asleep wondering if Mitchell would call.

She awoke refreshed, unburdened by the lingering images of any dreams. She scarcely thought of the ring in her purse. After a shower, she dressed and went down to the lobby for a cup of coffee. Caffeine was bad for her, made it harder for her to remain calm, but the habit was old. Maybe someday, after Dr. Forrest healed her, she'd be able to give up all her little crutches.

When Julia got back to her room, she dialed the offices of *The Commercial Appeal* and reached her old friend Sue.

"Well, looky what the cat dragged in," Sue said in her slow drawl. The sounds of a busy newsroom spilled from the background.

"Did you get my message?" Julia asked.

"Just got it this morning. I figured you'd call me here, and I didn't want to call back in case Mitchell was with you."

"There was nothing to interrupt, unfortunately."

"That's a shame, girl. Damn, that man is a hunk." Sue McAllister had never been shy about poking into other people's bedrooms or closets. That was why she was such a successful reporter. "Well, if you're not in Memphis to rumple the sheets with Mitchell Austin, what the heck are you doing here?"

"Just doing a little digging," Julia said. "And I was hoping you could help."

"Honey, we've been through all the files in the morgue. You've got every scrap of information on your father's case that was ever printed. Hell, you know more about the case than the cops do."

You can say that again, Julia thought, and almost told Sue about finding the ring. But it was her one little secret, the one thing that provided a solid link to that long-ago night. Julia knew she was being paranoid, but she decided that the secret was worth keeping for now. "I'd like to get a list of the detectives who worked on the disappearance."

"I thought you already did that."

"Well, I wasn't paying attention to the names."

"Hey, I can tell you're onto something. You going to let old Susie Q in on the deal?" Sue used Julia's nickname for her, a reference to the Credence Clearwater Revival song.

"You'll get the scoop if something turns up. I know solving a twenty-year-old missing-persons case isn't Page One stuff, but at least you'll have my gratitude."

"Great. That and a quarter will let me throw a coin in a street musician's hat."

"Is it okay if I come down around eleven? Then I'll take you out to lunch."

"Okay. I'll have to run, though. They're releasing the autopsy report of a suspected drug dealer. Five bullet holes in him, what do you think was the cause of death?"

"Let me guess. No matter what the medical examiner's ruling, the D.A.'s office will go, 'No evidence, no case.'"

"Saves taxpayer money."

Julia took a cab across town. The *Appeal* had changed very little in four months, and Julia grew a little wistful seeing her old desk. The newsroom was just as busy as before, her column inches in the first four pages filled by younger, hungrier writers. A few former coworkers seemed glad to see her, but afforded her only a couple of minutes before turning back to the day's breaking stories.

Sue McCallister was vibrant in a red skirt and jacket, her curly brown hair tied back with a scarf. Julia hugged her, glad for some human contact after enduring Mitchell's mood swings. They spent a couple of minutes catching up on the last few months and Julia's new job, and then Sue said, "You got your 'bloodhound' face on. Let's get to the clippings."

They went to a small cubicle and sat at a table covered with press releases and Styrofoam coffee cups. Sue had already made copies of all the stories on Douglas Stone's disappearance, and the pages protruded from a manila folder. Julia was familiar with most; she had clippings of the case tucked into her filing cabinet in Elkwood. This time, though, she jotted notes from each.

"Ah, what are we looking for?" Sue said, her smile bright with lipstick.

"Cops. I'm tracking the trackers."

"Well, T.L. Snead headed that case, at least early on. It got dropped pretty quick."

"Snead. Why does that sound familiar?"

"Probably because you've read it a hundred times. He's the one who made all the media statements."

They went deeper into the pile. Other officers listed were Whitmore, a Sgt. J.T. Redding, and Sgt. W.R. Ussery. Julia scanned the copy she almost knew by heart, hoping to catch something she had missed the first time. No mention of Satanic connections had ever been made.

One article was accompanied by a photograph of little Julia, her eyes wide and her mouth relaxed in shock. Some unidentified Social Services worker was leading her into an office building. The cut-line copy downplayed the "abandoned girl" theme, but it was impossible to avoid sensationalism totally. Julia had been front-page news for nearly a week, slipped to the crime briefs, and finally was gone, fading into the gray wasteland of dead stories.

Snead was quoted in several of the early articles. He used copspeak such as "We're following up on every lead" and "We're hopeful that Mr. Stone will be found." Snead was photographed at the front of the house, directing the investigation, his hooked nose and dark eyes making him look like a great bird of prey. Far in the background, barely visible in the murky ink of the fence line, the barn stood in the meadow.

Julia's heart raced for a moment, but she turned her mind back to business.

"T.L. Snead, T.L. Snead," Julia murmured. "I wonder what his initials stand for?"

Sue wiggled two of her fingers. "Let your fingers do the walking, girl."

Sue turned to her computer and mouse-clicked her way to a database of public records that included municipal police reports. A separate database listed the members of the police force, their salaries, and career highlights. Sue made a dirty joke about "police briefs" as she browsed the files.

T.L. Snead was not on the current roster. A search revealed that Snead had transferred from the force four months ago, though he was nearing retirement. The lieutenant had resigned to accept a position in Elkwood, North Carolina.

CHAPTER SIXTEEN

"Weird," said Sue. "How many people move from Memphis to Elkwood every year?"

"Do you believe in coincidences?" Julia asked.

"I don't believe anything unless I read it in the paper. You know the first rule of journalism: Consider the source."

Julia's mind raced with this new information. T.L. Snead had led the investigation into her father's disappearance, an investigation that seemed to have been haphazard at best. Was Snead the one who had searched her father's closet and failed to see the loose boards? Or had he deliberately ignored what he saw?

Or maybe—and this was the leap Julia kept to herself, lest Sue believe she was paranoid and delusional—Snead had planted the ring.

And the barn. The barn was part of the area that should have been searched. If Julia had been violated and abused there, some evidence might have remained, spots of blood or footprints or crushed grass marking a trail across the meadow. The police should have canvassed the entire neighborhood. Could Snead have taken responsibility for searching the barn, knowing that any stray evidence would stay secret if he filed a negative report?

No, this is stupid. Rick O'Dell is wrong. The police are not owned by Satan. They haven't sold their souls and aren't covertly working for capital-E 'Evil' under the guise of law and order.

If people were able to sell their souls, and Satan truly was the Master of the World, a cop would probably ask for a job that was better-paid and less dangerous. But if a man were deluded enough to believe that Satan existed, maybe such a willing slave would let the "master" determine the task. Religious fanatics throughout history had done stranger things, such as flog themselves with whips, wear sackcloth and rub themselves with ashes, and perform suicide attacks on so-called infidels.

Then again, if Satan wanted to work dark miracles in the world, why not first corrupt law and order?

"What are you thinking about?" Sue asked, leaning away from the computer.

"How many unsolved murders have you covered since you've been working here?"

"Hmm. In twelve years, maybe eight or ten. Murder is one of the easiest crimes to solve. The idiots almost always have an obvious motive, whether they realize it or not. It's a matter of putting the pieces together."

"And the eight or ten?"

"Give me a minute." Sue left the cubicle and waded through the journalistic storm of the newsroom. While she was gone, a man with graying hair and glasses scowled at Julia sitting at the computer. She looked away and he left.

Sue returned in a few minutes with another manila folder. "Even with computers, sometimes you can't beat good old black and white."

"I've seen your filing system. How did you ever manage to find that?"

"Job security. If you scramble everything around until you're the only person who knows where the good stuff is, they can't afford to fire you. Even in the age of Google and the Internet, sometimes you need a piece of paper."

"Ah-hah. That might come in handy when you write your true crime book."

"'True crime' nothing. I'm going to make it all up. Same as

I do with Page One stories."

Julia laughed, glad to be around someone she was comfortable with. She was hit with a wave of warm nostalgia. Despite her diffuse and fractured memories, she'd had a routine here, along with friends and a fiancé. But Elkwood was more soothing somehow, as if its rounded, ancient mountains were shoulders to lean on in troubled times. She already missed the smell of the hardwoods and the splendor of the autumn forest. It seemed like weeks had passed since she'd arrived in Memphis.

Sue opened the folder, glanced at the incident reports, and passed them to Julia. Sue's original notes on the case were attached to the reports with paper clips.

"Caucasian male, aged approximately 30, found on the shore of the Mississippi by some kids," Julia paraphrased aloud. "Decapitated. Disemboweled. Fingerprint check came up empty."

"Ooh, that was a good one," Sue said, affecting a wistful sigh. "I got two weeks of front page out of that one. I followed up on it about six months later. Nothing ever came of it, but I suppose the case officially is still open."

Julia read through the next case. White female, early twenties, multiple stab wounds to the chest. Wrists slashed. Exsanguinated. The M.E. unable to determine if the blood had been drained before or after the victim's death. Possible sexual assault. Missing the tip of the right pinkie.

Three other victims were found in various stages of mutilation. In one instance, the M.E. had determined that some sort of symbol had been carved into a ruined section of flesh. None of the investigators speculated on the possibility of ritual murder. A couple were more mundane cases that appeared to be drug-related violence. The cases were spaced one or two years apart, and no connection had ever been made between them.

"Did you ever try to connect the dots?" Julia asked. "These murders have several things in common."

"Yeah, once I asked old Budgie if I could spend a few weeks running with it. You know what she said?"

Budgie was the less-than-fond nickname for the *Appeal's* news editor, Bridget Lawrence. She had a reputation for having greater concern for the paper's budget than for her reporters' pay rates. Plus, when Lawrence made up her mind, she wouldn't budge from her opinion, hence the nickname.

Julia drooped her jaws in imitation of Budgie's sour bulldog face. "What are we going to run in the meantime, press releases?" Julia said in a high-pitched, cigarette-scarred voice. They shared another laugh.

For a wild instant, Julia thought of moving back to Memphis and taking up her old life here where she had left off. She could probably get her job back and work on these clues in her spare time. She could get right back to normal, or the closest thing that passed for normal for someone with panic disorder.

Except such straight roads from the past and future didn't exist. Everything had changed. Julia was losing touch with Mitchell, but she had found Dr. Forrest. And being healed was more important than anything else right now.

To be healed, she needed to be in Elkwood with her therapist. Sobered, Julia studied the notes again.

"Well, two things jump out at me," said Julia. "First, all the victims were killed with knives or sharp instruments."

"Yeah, one M.E. says an ax was used to hack open the chest cavity. Other than that, everything from serrated edges to surgical blades. None of them were shot or bludgeoned first, so we assume the victims were carved up while still alive. So, what's the other connection?"

"You're slipping a little, Susie Q. You'll never get your Pulitzer at this rate."

"Sacrilege. What do you see?"

"The chief investigating officer. The same for each case."

Sue snatched the papers away and shuffled through them. "I'll be doggoned. Our old friend Lt. Snead."

"I guess he moved up to Homicide. He headed all these cases and then happened to move to Elkwood right after I did. What are the odds when you cross several one-in-a-million coincidences?"

"I never was good at math. That's why I went into journalism."

"Let's just call it 'right next to impossible.'"

"Works for me. Sounds like we need to do a little digging on Mr. Snead."

Julia stood, stretched, and rubbed her eyes. Her stomach muscles had clenched without her realizing it. She was on edge, wound tighter than the strings inside a baseball. She wanted to keep moving so the panic didn't have a chance to swoop down over her.

"We'll have to leave that job for later. I owe you a lunch, remember," Julia said, though she herself wasn't hungry.

"A reporter never turns down a free meal," Sue said. "It's a long and honorable tradition."

Julia smiled at her friend, though their closeness had waned through the geographic distance. Julia would be back in Elkwood this evening, in that strange land of mountains and forests and cold water running over boulders. How different this city was, with its plate glass and steel and asphalt, its teeming strangers. She longed for a breath of the sweet mountain air she'd quickly come to love.

They ate at The E-String, as elegant a lunch counter as Memphis could offer. Sue agreed to do a little background on

T.L. Snead, and then asked when Julia and Mitchell were "gettin' hitched."

"I don't know anymore," Julia said. "He was so supportive for so many years, but lately he's been acting strange."

"Honey, I hate to say it, but you haven't exactly been jumping into his arms every chance you get. Can you really blame him? If guys aren't getting their pipes cleaned out often enough, they get a little cranky."

Julia pushed her plate away, her chicken salad half-finished. "I know. I feel awful about it. Six months ago, I couldn't imagine life without him. He was so kind and supportive. But lately he's been impatient, trying to rush me into marriage. I just wish he'd understand that once I'm better, I'll be able to give him all of me."

"Probably in the meantime, all he wants is a piece of you." Sue leered and wiggled her eyebrows.

Julia looked outside at the crowded street and the bumper-to-bumper traffic. "He's too desperate. He wants to own me."

"A lot of women would kill to have Mitchell own them."

"That's one thing that worries me. The more possessive he gets, the more the little warning bells go off in my mind. It's almost Creepy. Why is he so afraid of letting me get away when he can have any woman he wants? And he said something yesterday that made it sound like I'm important to his financial stability, which is odd since you know how lousy reporters' salaries are."

"Maybe Mitchell is more complicated than you think. I hope it works out, though. You deserve to be happy." Sue glanced at her watch. "Hate to eat and run, but I got to get back to the office."

Julia had a momentary urge to tell Sue about the ring she had found, but decided against it. She felt as if she was deceiving her friend, but she promised herself that she would tell Sue just as soon as Dr. Forrest found out. The safest place to share secrets was Dr. Forrest's office, not over a lunch table.

They hugged good-bye on the sidewalk, with Julia promising to e-mail more often. Then Julia caught a cab back to the hotel. She rode the elevator up, distracted by the thoughts of packing for her flight. The hallway was empty and quiet, the business travelers already checked out. As was her habit, she glanced around to ensure she was safe before swiping her key card in the door lock and entering.

The door didn't close behind her, even though she had given it a shove. Confused, she started to turn.

A whisper at her back.

Movement of shadow.

CREEP.

Ohgodohgodohgod, a Creep for REAL.

Then a hand was over her mouth, encased in a glove that tasted of bitter leather. An arm snaked around her waist, pinning her right arm to her side and knocking her purse to the floor. The door slammed shut.

CHAPTER SEVENTEEN

She tried to scream, but the glove mashed her lips against her teeth.

The arm around her waist tightened like a boa trying to squeeze the life from a rodent.

Her attacker loomed over her, a powerful stack of darkness. Leg muscles tensed against her, his erection pressed hot against her back.

Not a Creep, a rapist. A goddamned RAPIST.

Julia folded her leg backwards, hoping to kick the attacker in the groin, but he was too fast. Her heel struck harmlessly on the side of his calf. The attacker shoved her toward the bed.

God, right here in the hotel room. Not in the damned alley or shadows or dark parking garage. Right here on clean pressed sheets.

Her eyes bulged, dimmed by tears, as she fought to break free, to stand upright and not let the Creep on top of her. He grabbed the front of her shirt, jerked, and two buttons popped to the floor. One of the buttons rolled across the carpet and disappeared under the desk.

This wasn't happening.

This was *not* happening.

Not to her.

Someone else, not her.

She nearly collapsed as the panic swelled in her throat and joined the gloved hand in suffocating her. The darkness was so tempting. She wanted to grab the edges of those mental shadows and pull them over her head until the rapist was finished. She wanted to disappear like the button had, to be swallowed by the cold, soothing blackness.

God, where are you? If you're up there, why do you let things like this happen?

No answer.

The rapist drew his hand across the bare skin of her belly, and the glove raked across one of the scars. The pain of memory brought Julia back, fueled a fury that had been building since she was four years old. She couldn't fight then, not against ropes and two dozen hooded bad people, but she could fight now.

She drove her elbow into the side of the attacker. He grunted but kept his grip around her waist.

He wrapped a leg around hers, trying to force her onto the bed. Her shirt was now fully open, the flesh goose-pimpled by fear. The man grabbed one of her breasts and squeezed roughly. She screamed against the glove, but all that came out was a soft, agonized wheeze.

Julia twisted, evading that horrible, insistent heat. She reached her left hand to grab at his hair, but the man wore a covering of some kind.

A HOOD.

The man's breath was hot on her ear, rasping in a ragged rhythm. His lips trailed wetly across her neck. A shiver of disgust raced up her spine.

The man pressed her closer to the bed. Her knees bumped against the mattress. She braced her legs as he grabbed for the waist of her skirt.

When his hand was occupied, she attacked. She bent her neck down and suddenly drove the back of her head into his face. Due to his height, she only managed to hit his chin, but the blow gave off a satisfying crack.

The man groaned and his grip eased slightly. Julia took the opportunity to spin, nearly breaking free. Then the arm was around her, crushing more cruelly than before.

As they shifted, Julia saw their reflections in the dresser mirror. Her own pale, frightened face glared back through her tears, the black glove gagging her.

Behind her grappled the man in the hood. It was the gray hood of a jogging pullover, not a hood from her dreams. He wasn't one of the bad people from the past.

Just a miserable, pathetic, run-of-the-mill Creep.

Maybe that's your answer, God.

Julia relaxed her legs, letting him hold her full weight for a moment. Then she snapped upright and tried to squirm away. He held her firmly, though, and used the momentum to flop her onto the bed.

He pulled his hand from her mouth, but before she could draw in enough air to scream, he cupped his other hand over her lips. He rolled her onto her side, pinning her between his knees.

Julia flailed her legs as he sat on her thighs, his elbow digging into her chest. She could smell him, sweat and a raw animal scent, and beneath that, a faint, familiar, sweet aroma.

She looked at his face, but saw only the bright glint of eyes through the hood's opening. He wore some sort of ski mask beneath the hood.

Her free fist pounded his back. She may as well have been punching a sack of mud.

The Creep hissed under his breath, a harsh, evil sound. "Bitch!"

He wrenched her shoulder until she was flat on her back, his palm crushing her lips. The elbow on her chest pressed harder, and Julia thought her ribs would crack. Then the pressure eased and the arm moved away and Julia heard the sound of a zipper.

She wedged her knee toward his crotch. No good. She couldn't even turn her head away. All she could do was close her eyes, run for the long darkness inside.

Surrender.

Just like always.

The Creep forced her dress up, exposing her panties. Gloved fingers tugged at the elastic.

No. Surrender isn't an option this time.

She wriggled, grappling for the edge of the mattress, the headboard, even a pillow. His odor came again, the offal of his lurid excitement. Pungent sweat and–

And cologne.

Jovan Musk.

The brand she'd bought him for Christmas.

Mitchell?

She glanced at the gap of skin between glove and sleeve and saw the Rolex.

Oh my God, it's MITCHELL.

Mitchell, who could have his pick of smartly dressed, curvaceous beauties, who could go down to his country club in Colliersville and have a woman undressing within the hour. Mitchell, who could afford the highest class of call girl if he wanted to get his rocks off.

Mitchell.

A Creep.

Mitchell must have seen the recognition dawning on her face. She couldn't disguise the horror, no matter how deeply she fled into the inner darkness. And her anger fueled her, allowed her to twist beneath him, get one knee planted, and simultaneously drive up and away from him.

He bellowed in rage as she slipped from his grasp, her blouse ripping and a button popping free. The slack gained by the torn cloth allowed her to reach the nightstand and grab the neck of the heavy wooden lamp.

Betrayed.

Always goddamned betrayed.

What had she ever done to deserve betrayal?

Easy. She'd opened the door and let someone into her heart. Trust was a sucker's game.

But her heart was cold now, and so was her nerve.

She slammed the lamp against him, the awkward swing knocking the lampshade against his head and swiping back his hood. The blow stunned him more than hurt him, but Julia seized the opening and spun to her feet, the lamp raised like a club.

You're throwing a curveball but I'm knocking this bastard out of the park.

This seemed like the absurd but logical conclusion to their eight-year relationship. The final swing in the bottom of the ninth. Bases loaded. And the game was over.

Not from blushing, fumbling first kiss to cold, uncaring abandonment. Rather, the end would be a farewell of malice, a last touch that left scars.

A good-bye that bled.

Mitchell shoved himself to the far side of the bed, perhaps recalling the power of her tennis stroke, or maybe just considering how a bruised face might look in the courtroom next week. She stared into those specks of light that marked his eyes.

Julia worked her jaw sideways, scraping her tongue against her teeth to remove the bitter taste of leather.

"Why?" she asked, not allowing the lamp to dip an inch though it quivered in her anger.

He batted the gray hood back and jerked the ski mask off his head. His always-perfect hair now stood like a shock of dark cornstalks in a field. He rubbed his face in his hands.

"Is that all you ever wanted, you bastard?" she said.

A tremor ran through Mitchell's muscular shoulders, and

she was afraid he was going to renew his attack. Julia thumped the base of the lamp against the mattress, her force punctuating the pain she was ready to deliver. The wood was heavy enough to break bone. She grinned at the thought, and perhaps that scared Mitchell more than the weapon.

When he finally spoke, it was as if he were addressing someone outside the room, some all-hearing ear, though his words were cat quick and mouse quiet. "I just . . . I can't afford to lose you."

Julia made no attempt to cover herself. "You'd rather keep me broken?"

"I'm sorry," Mitchell said, keeping his gaze on his feet. "After yesterday . . . "

Julia glanced at the floor. The contents of her purse had spilled across the carpet. The wooden box was plainly visible, the carving of the pentagram delivering a hundred and ten volts to the chest.

The skull ring.

Mitchell's voice rose, the quick mood shift catching Julia by surprise. "Why did you have to go out there? Why the hell can't you just forget it all? You're *mine*, Julia. You belong to me, not the past and those damned hooded people."

He lifted his face. Tears welled in the corners of his eyes. But Julia felt no sympathy, only a shudder of revulsion that she had ever let this pathetic specimen of the male gender hold and kiss her. To think that she had nearly married this creature and spent a life with him.

"I'll never be yours," Julia said, surprised by the chilly strength of her words. "Do you want to know why?"

Mitchell looked like his own evil twin, hair wild, fly open, eyes red. Or was this the *real* Mitchell Austin? The one that hid inside the power suits and lurked behind the smug mask of self-righteousness, a control freak who couldn't even control himself?

His lips moved like those of a hooked fish gasping on a riverbank. Finally, he managed to answer. "Why not?"

"Because there's no *room* inside your house, Mitchell."

His mouth fell open. He didn't speak, but his eyes said, "What the hell?"

Julia got to her feet, pulled her blouse closed and smoothed down her skirt. "You've got your house stuffed so full of yourself, there's no room for anyone else. And I'm not going to live in anybody's basement."

Except my own. In that place where bones are buried. But that has nothing to do with this jerk.

Mitchell backed away as if she were the Creep. He zipped himself and tried to gather his slick judicial composure. "Listen, you're not to going to press charges, are you? I've got a lot of friends in the D.A.'s office. You'll be smeared until you won't even be able to recognize yourself in the mirror."

Julia pictured herself filing a report, talking to the police. Sure, she had physical evidence of an assault. Bruises, torn clothing, maybe some DNA evidence under her fingernails. But assault cases where the rapist was engaged to the victim, where the pair had a long sexual history together, were practically impossible to prosecute.

Her word against his.

Mitchell looked her fully in the eyes and gave a smile that would chill a cobra's blood.

Because they both knew the truth. Julia's behavioral disorder would end up on trial, not Mitchell. He could afford the best in criminal defense, and in the end, Mitchell would walk out of the courtroom laughing while Julia dripped into a black puddle of miserable self-loathing. The defense would have its psychological "experts" prod and poke her brain until she finally convinced herself that the attack was her fault, that she'd staged the whole thing because everybody knew that crazy people did crazy things.

Of course. What jury would convict an upstanding, respectable citizen solely on the wild accusations of a person known to be unstable? She could picture the defense attorney now, giving a sermon during closing arguments, the High Church of Reason against the damned and doomed who had the temerity to be less than perfect, those oddities who "saw psychologists," who "received therapy," who "had been diagnosed."

Oh, yes. She would be crucified, her own fears used as the nails, her own frail attempts at recovery serving as the wood.

And Mitchell would be not only her Judas and her Pilate, he would also be the Roman soldier with the hammer.

She brushed past him, stooped, and gathered the box and her purse. "Get the hell out," she said, dead inside.

"If it weren't for the money, I'd have been out of here years ago," he said, cocky again, untouchable.

"The money?" she asked his retreating back.

"We could have done it the easy way," he said, brushing his hair back into place. "Now it's going to get messy."

The door to the hotel room closed with a whisper, but the door to the house in her head closed with a great groaning of hinges, the rattling of chains, the rusty screams of deadbolts being driven forever home.

CHAPTER EIGHTEEN

The sun was sinking when Julia reached Elkwood. The mountain ridges glowed with autumn, as if capped by molten gold. The sienna and ochre of the changing leaves covered the slopes, the darker greens of balsam and spruce dotted the higher elevations. Shadows filled the long valley where the Amadahee River ran through the center of town, carrying its rich September smells of salamanders and mud.

By the time Julia had turned her Subaru up the hill toward Buckeye Creek Road, the anxiety that had nearly consumed her on the flight home was all but forgotten. The tall trees comforted her, and she was relieved to see again the pastures with their leaning locust poles and rusted barbed wire, the farmhouses set well away from the road, the cows attacking the grass with dull persistence. Here and there the tips of granite slabs protruded through the soil like great rocket ships preparing to blast into the heavens.

Though she had only lived in Elkwood for four months, this place had become home. When she'd first moved, it had been a desperate escape. Mitchell had simultaneously driven her away while demanding that she stay in Memphis. Dr. Danner had suggested this mountain town as a nice place to meet the future, and the referral to Dr. Forrest had been like a shipwreck victim pushed by waves onto the saving shore of an island.

Now the future was clearer even though the past was stranger and scarier than ever.

Now her future didn't revolve around Mitchell and the caged security he had offered. Funny that he had turned out to be more unstable than she. Tomorrow she would return his two-carat diamond via registered mail. The memory of the assault was buried inside, waiting, a nest of snakes. She didn't dare deal with it alone. The breakdown would have to wait for the chair in Dr. Forrest's office.

Julia hadn't yet decided when to tell Dr. Forrest about the skull ring. Perhaps next week. Right now, she had plenty enough memories and emotions to sort out. The immediate past left the freshest bruises. The healing would have to begin from the outside in.

Mrs. Covington's house was dark as Julia drove past, the windows like slate. The apartments stood quiet across the road, spears of light cutting between drawn curtains. The Subaru's headlights swept over Julia's house as she pulled up, and she felt a rush of ownership. Despite its disreputable history, she felt comfort behind its walls. She decided she would talk to George Webster about purchasing it.

The door was solid, the windows cold and empty. Behind that door were her computer, her clothes, her books, Mr. Ned the stuffed turtle. She thought of the baseball cards Walter had given her, left spread across the coffee table, and smiled. Such a small kindness became magnified by the comparative horror of her visit to Memphis.

This was a new past she was building, and the realization warmed her heart despite all the nasty mental baggage she had yet to unpack. She thought of that gospel song, "One Day at a Time, Sweet Jesus," and figured the past need only extend to that morning's awakening and the future was no more than the remaining hours until dark. She eagerly went up the walk, her purse clutched in front of her. She was so glad to be home that she barely glanced at the shadowy spaces between the trees, at the vast forest where crickets chirped and the nocturnal animals began their nightly scrabbling. What formerly had filled her with shivers of dread now seemed to offer more comfort than threat.

She drew a deep lungful of the Blue Ridge air that was moist and tangy with pine. She fumbled in her purse for the key, silently cursing herself for not leaving on the porch light. Her fingers brushed across the wooden box in her purse. She had carried a piece of the past here, a piece of Memphis. Maybe that had been a mistake. But she could worry about that tomorrow.

One day at a time . . .

As she searched for the key, out of habit she tried the knob.

It turned easily in her hand.

The latch clicked back like the hammer of a gun, like the final beat of a heart.

Had she forgotten to lock the door, even after that first scare with Walter?

Impossible.

One thing Julia Stone never failed to do was to lock the door. That was Rule Number One for keeping Creeps out of the house. Unless, of course, they snuck in behind you, as Mitchell had.

Or were already inside.

Julia stood, frozen with her hand on the doorknob.

She replayed the scene in her mind of leaving for the trip. *Suitcase at your feet, slam door, insert key, turn, click. Check to make sure.*

Yes, she had locked it.

Walter could be inside, doing some kind of repair.

Or it could be The Creep. The one who may have left a row of wooden blocks across the coffee table a few days ago.

Because you KNOW you didn't put them there, don't you?

Don't you?

The autumn wind rattled the undergrowth. The branches that had been comforting moments before were now like the gnarled arms of wooden witches. Julia fumbled for the mace on her key ring, fingered the spray nozzle. If a rapist were waiting inside, she would give it to him full in the eyes, give him all the punishment she should have dished out to Mitchell. If it happened in the bedroom, she had the Louisville Slugger under the bed.

Or . . .

She glanced longingly at her car. She could get in, drive away, call the cops from the safety of a gas station.

And maybe Lieutenant T.L. Snead would get the dispatcher's call. The Snead of unsolved cases, the Snead of coincidence.

No. She would not run this time. She would not let someone invade her house. Or mind.

She pushed the door a few inches, and it creaked like the lid of a wooden coffin. Fine hairs twitched like electric wires on the back of her neck. She tried to inhale but couldn't concentrate on a relaxing breath.

Sweating in the chill night, Julia peered through the narrow crack.

Nothing but dark inside. Deep and endless dark, the kind of dark that jumped out and sank its claws into you, sharp dark, the kind that—

Stop it, Julia.

Her hands trembled.

A phone rang in one of the neighboring apartments. It purred faintly six times and stopped. Someone revved a car engine in the housing development that stood behind the wall of woods. A dog's bark echoed across the black hills. The sounds of normal life.

She gripped the mace and shoved the door open with her

shoulder, half-expecting the flash of an arcing blade. With her left hand, she reached across her body and raked her fingers across the wall switch. The lights burst to life like exploding stars.

The room was empty.

Julia went around the hall, her purse against her side, one hand holding the spray can of mace, the other clenched into a fist. Nobody in the kitchen. She kicked open the bathroom door.

Movement erupted along one wall. Julia's forefinger tightened on the mace nozzle. A grunt died against her teeth before it became a scream.

Just her reflection, in the mirror above the sink.

Julia flipped on the light, eyed the shower curtain. No Creep would be that unimaginative, would he?

She reached out, touched the plastic, yanked it across the rod, mace poised. Nothing but the fiberglass stall.

Heart racing, Julia spun and returned to the hall. Only one room left to check.

Of course. Her bedroom.

The ultimate violation, that of the inner sanctum.

The door opened with a whisper. A breeze blew across the room. The window was open.

Go back now, girl. It's okay. No one can blame you for being scared. This isn't just your disorder speaking. It's ME.

Sure, she could flee. She could surrender.

Just like always.

She clenched her jaw and stepped inside. The first thing she saw was the clock, numerals blazing like the reddest of hellfire against the darkness.

4:06.

If she were holding a gun instead of a spray can of mace, she would have emptied the cartridge into that digital demon to exorcise the obscenity of its frozen time.

She could no longer fool herself that no one had been here, that she'd only forgotten to lock the door and left the window open and, gee, what an absentminded little thing she was.

No, some Creep had waltzed in, removed the clock from her trash, restored its strange programming, and left it as a message to Julia.

A message that he could get in any time, no matter how many locks she held keys for.

Why would a Creep advertise? If he wanted to jump her, he could wait in the dark wings for his moment and reach out like the long fingers of the past. Just as Mitchell had done.

The memory of her fiancé's attack flooded through her, made the room grow fuzzy, and she almost lost her balance. Then she shook her head clear. If the Creep were still here, she wasn't going to make it easy for him.

Julia eased into the room, elbowing the switch up and blinking against the sudden light.

Her room looked the same, except for the clock. The bed not quite neatly made, Mr. Ned and some CD's on her shelf, the Jefferson Spence paperback parted open on the bedside table. The window screen was gone, and the lace curtains shifted in the breeze like uneasy ghosts.

Julia crossed the room and closed the window, sliding the latch into place. Walter was right, the windows were of solid construction. She saw no scars in the frame that might indicate a forced entry. Either she'd overlooked a lock, or some Creep had access to a copy of her house key.

Without looking at the clock, Julia grabbed it, yanked the plug free of the wall, and tucked it under her elbow. She wondered if, even powerless, the clock's digits still blazed.

4:06. Why 4:06?

A thought fluttered at the edges of her memory, like a lost

bat that disappeared back into its cave. She had so deliberately kept herself from remembering that the past had become a place that she visited with effort, a place that required a travel agent. She would only go when Dr. Forrest told her so.

She went back through the house, locked the front door, and then checked all the other windows. She would unpack under the morning sun. For now, she was safe enough. As safe as she could ever be inside her own head.

Unless someone had a key to her head as well as her house.

Julia took a plastic shopping bag from the great mound of them under the sink. She slid the errant clock into the bag and tied it tightly closed. She wrapped a second bag around it for good measure and then tucked it under some coffee grounds and an ice cream box in the kitchen garbage. Maybe tomorrow she would find a big rock and smash the clock to bits.

Killing time. The image was almost funny, but the persistent buzz of adrenaline still tickled the surface of her skin. She felt as if she were being watched.

Was someone still in the house?

No, she had checked all the rooms. The attic access was in the bathroom. She'd covered a case in Memphis where a Creep had crawled through the maintenance access of his apartment, climbed over the rafters to the next unit, and drilled small peepholes in the bedroom ceiling. The woman had come home one day to find Sheetrock dust on her bedspread, saw the holes, and called the police.

The Creep was caught, but the woman never knew how many times he had watched her through his little series of spy holes. A hundred hot showers couldn't wash that kind of violation from your skin. Could the victim ever again undress without a tiny paranoid shiver? How much therapy had the woman needed before she'd quit scanning the ceiling of every room she entered?

Paranoia was partly a survival instinct. But at some point you had to let it go.

Julia thought of calling Dr. Forrest. Her wristwatch said eight o'clock, plenty early enough. But she suspected Dr. Forrest had a lover, the man Julia had overheard in the background of several phone conversations. Julia hated to be so needy, so dependent, so demanding of the therapist's time and attention. Most of all, she didn't want Dr. Forrest to tire of her.

If she could survive the night, she would be okay. If she could survive her *life*, she would be okay.

Julia went back through the house to her bedroom. She stopped herself from double-checking the window. An odd buzz sounded in her ears, the near-silent alarm of something amiss. The shelf where the engagement ring was hidden appeared undisturbed, Mr. Ned giving his friendly terrapin grin and books in an alphabetized row. But the top drawer of her dresser was slightly ajar.

She wasn't a neat freak by any stretch, but she did have a compulsion to close things. Doors. Windows. Lids. Cabinets.

She pulled open the drawer. Underwear and bras lay in ruffled tangles, a few of them black and red, most boring old beige or white. She dug into the pile, turned it over. The teddy was missing.

Mitchell had bought it for her in hopes that she would model it. And she would have, if Mitchell hadn't turned savage. How she had longed for the right moment, a moonlit holiday, maybe, or a romantic anniversary of their first time. But Mitchell never mentioned it again, and Julia could never be sure how he'd react to a seductive surprise. Turned out he was the one full of surprises.

She was glad to be rid of that reminder of their flawed

relationship, but there was the immediate problem of the teddy's disappearance. Did a Creep sneak into her house for the sole purpose of digging through her naughties? Was he, at this very moment, parading around in the negligee, shivering and swelling with a secret thrill?

Julia sensed the eyes on her again. Paranoia, she knew. And yet—

She turned to the window.

Two bright glints, reflecting the light of her room. Staring between the lace of the curtains.

The eyes faded back into darkness as Julia's breath caught. Then she heard a shout, the breaking of tree limbs, and a grunt of pain as bodies slammed against the siding and fell to the ground.

"Quit it, or I'll break your arm," someone shouted.

Julia stood undecided for a moment. Then she reached under the bed, got her Louisville Slugger, and ran to the window. In the rectangle of light cast into the back yard, she saw two men struggling on the ground. She gave the Louisville Slugger a little test swing. It was easier to handle than a wooden lamp.

God, I'm getting better with all this batting practice.

Julia hurried through the house, stopped in the living room to grab a flashlight and stuff the mace in her pocket. Feeling a little braver gripping the baseball bat, she went out the kitchen door to the side of the house. She edged around the corner into the back yard, shining the flashlight ahead of her.

"Get off me," one of the struggling figures yelled.

The two had rolled to the trees that grew near the house. Julia pointed the light at them, but her hand was trembling so much that she couldn't see their faces. "Who's there?" she said, but her voice was lost amid the sound of scattered leaves and grunts.

She raised the bat, hoping to be menacing, and tried again. "Who the hell is it?"

"Julia!" gasped the man who was currently on top.

"*Walter?*"

She held the light more steadily and saw that the man on bottom was pinned, belly down, his arm behind his back. Still his legs flailed, and he twisted like an eel on a spear. His face mashed against the dirt, bits of leaves stuck to his hair. Walter straddled his back, a bronco rider whose steed had collapsed.

Walter grimaced with effort as he tugged the man's wrist up to the shoulder blade. The man groaned sharply.

"I'll snap it," Walter told him. "I've wrestled a steer or two in my day, and if I can handle them, I can surely handle the likes of you."

Walter gave an extra push to emphasize his point. The man lay still, breathing heavily.

Julia approached slowly, stopping a few feet away. "What's going on?" she asked, not sure which of the two she should be prepared to slug with the bat.

"Call the police," Walter said, blinking into the flashlight's beam.

"You didn't answer me," she said, fingers clenched around the bat handle.

"He—" Walter panted. His face was strained, and she wondered if he really could keep the other man pinned. The man on bottom seemed younger and just as strong as Walter.

"I saw him climb out your window," Walter said. "Right, scumbag?" he said to the man beneath him.

The man turned his face toward the forest, away from the light.

Julia backed up slowly and ducked inside, still holding the bat. She dialed 9-1-1 from the living room, carrying the phone so she could watch through the window. Walter was still on top.

"Communications," came the clipped male voice.

"Yes, sir, I'd like to report a—"

"Yes, ma'am?"

What? A *Creep*? She thought of all the false reports she'd filed in Memphis, how the Metro cop had ridiculed her. She tried out the copspeak she'd learned as a crime reporter. "There's an altercation in progress."

"Altercation. You mean a fight?"

"Yeah."

"Any weapons involved?"

"Not that I can see. But you better hurry."

"Could you confirm that address, ma'am?"

"102 Buckeye Creek Road, in Elkwood."

The man on the ground flopped like a beached fish, but Walter held on.

"Yes, ma'am," said the communications officer. "I'll send a patrol car right away. Say, you live near Mabel Covington, don't you?"

Julia sighed into the phone. What was next, a recipe swap? "You may want to dispatch an ambulance, too."

"Why? Is somebody hurt?"

"Not yet, but may be." *Especially if you don't hang up and get on the damned radio.*

"You where you're safe?"

"Excuse me, but I'd better go help."

"I wouldn't advise that—"

Julia hung up before the dispatcher could finish his "ma'am."

Julia ran outside, her hand cramped from gripping the bat. Even Mark McGwire had to rest the lumber on his shoulder once in a while, steroid-stoked or not. But Julia couldn't rest yet. She wasn't going to let the bat go until the police arrived. And maybe not even then, because Snead might be on duty.

"You doing okay?" Julia asked Walt.

He shook his head "no," but said, "I've been whooping punks like this since I was six."

Then he jerked his head, urging her to help. His brown hair was damp with sweat and a nasty bruise welled up under one red and watery eye.

"If he moves again, brain him with the bat," Walter said.

"Bat?" the man grunted against the ground. "You're *crazy*."

"Hey, I ain't the one that was sniffing a woman's underwear," Walter said.

The teddy. This was the Creep. The one who had left the footprint, who had sneaked into her house, who had reprogrammed her clock. She fought a brief urge to tap his skull with the Louisville Slugger.

A siren wailed in the distance, coming up the valley and echoing off the slopes. The Creep gave another half-hearted struggle upon hearing the sound. Then he lay quietly again, his arm forced at a painful angle.

"Thank you," Julia said to Walter. "No telling what he would have done . . . "

"The thing that burns me the most is that people like this got no respect," he answered, giving another upward yank to the young man's arm.

"I was–*owww*–just here for the ring." The flashlight showed the reddened face of a college-aged man, and Julia recognized him from the apartment building down the road.

The guy's face clenched in pain, and Walter eased off the pressure a little. "What ring?"

"Some dude hired me to get it," he answered. "Called me out of the blue a couple of weeks ago, mailed me a money order."

Julia raised the bat. "And the underwear?"

"Christ, lady, it was a gag," he said. "The dude said to screw with her head."

Walter was ratcheting up the pressure again when the guy moaned and said, "No more till I get a lawyer."

Blue lights flashed across the trees as the patrol car roared up in front of the house. Julia ran to them, waving the flashlight, letting the bat drag on the ground. Two policemen bounced out of the car, one drawing his sidearm.

"Don't shoot," Julia said. "They're around back."

"Drop the weapon and step away," ordered the cop with the gun.

"It's only a souvenir bat," Julia said. "It's got an Ozzie Smith replica signature on it."

"Drop it."

She complied. Satisfied, the cop with the gun went past her while the other crept to the corner of the house. Julia didn't know what she was supposed to do. The cop hadn't ordered her to freeze or anything. She stood for a moment, watching the bar lights bounce off the nearby apartment building. Some of the college students had come out and were standing on the porch, talking and drinking beer.

Julia followed the policemen around back. The cop with the gun now had it pointed at Walter. The other cop knelt by the man on the ground, fumbling with a pair of handcuffs and shining a large-beamed flashlight.

"This guy was breaking into her house," Walter said. "I saw him peeping at her through the window."

"Get off him and slowly back away, sir," ordered the cop. "Keep your hands where I can see them."

Walter's eyes narrowed in anger, but he obeyed.

The second cop helped the other man to his feet. The man rubbed his elbow, glowering at Walter with a "You just wait" look.

"What's your side of it?" the cop asked the injured man.

"I didn't break in," he replied. "I was just cutting through the yard to walk through the woods when this freak jumped me."

"Oh, yeah?" said Walter. "What's that in your back pocket, then?"

The cop shined his flashlight at the man, turned him around, pulled the frilly black teddy from the man's pocket. The cop held it up, letting it dangle between his thumb and forefinger as if it were contaminated. The college guy looked sheepish.

"Is that yours, ma'am?" asked the cop with the gun. He had relaxed his stance and was now pointing his gun at the ground near Walter's feet.

Julia nodded. "Yeah. I just noticed it missing a few minutes ago. Someone had broken into my house."

"Anything else missing?"

"Not that I know of, but he said something about looking for a ring."

"Do you know this man?" the cop asked, waving the weapon casually toward Walter.

"Yes," Julia said. "He's a friend of mine."

The cops looked at each other, and then one led the Creep around the house, reciting the Miranda warning.

"Are you both willing to make statements?" the other cop said, finally returning his gun to its holster.

"Sure," said Julia. "You want to come in the house? I guess you'll want to check for fingerprints and all that."

"The crime scene tech is on duty at the hospital," the cop said, taking out a small notepad. "She's going to hate coming out this time of night. So, you going to press charges, Mrs. —?"

"Stone. Julia Stone. Of course I'm pressing charges."

The cop scribbled down her name and asked for Walter's name. When Walter gave it, the cop lowered the notepad and let his writing hand make a subtle crawl toward his holster. "Triplett?"

"That's right." Walter straightened a little and glanced at Julia. "*That* Walter Triplett."

The cop nodded and asked Julia, "So you're vouching for his side of the story?"

Julia considered the possibility that the intruder had actually been Walter, and the college guy may have caught him in the act. But Walter had a key and needn't bother sneaking in or out the window. And despite his reputation as a possible wife-killer, his kindness had eased her fears. "He's safe," she said.

The cop glowered at Walter, went to his car, and retrieved a clipboard. He spent the next fifteen minutes filling out an incident report. Then the car pulled away, lights still flashing. The college students jeered as the cops passed, holding their beer cans in the air.

"I thought they were going to check for fingerprints," Julia said.

"This is Elkwood," Walter said. He touched the bruise under his eye and winced.

"Come in and let me get you some ice for that."

Julia retrieved her Louisville Slugger on the way inside. If discretion was the better part of valor, she figured 34 inches of hardwood would bridge the remainder of the gap if necessary.

CHAPTER NINETEEN

Walter sat in the living room, looking at the baseball cards spread out on the table, as Julia wrapped some ice in a washcloth. She brought the cloth to him and then sat across the room in the chair at her work desk.

"Stan Musial," Walter said, noting the arrangement of the cards by position. "Didn't he play centerfield?"

"No, left," Julia said. She shifted restlessly on the couch. She had leaned the bat in the corner, but the mace still bulged in her pocket. "He couldn't throw well enough for center. He hurt his arm pitching in the minors. Three-time MVP. Led the Cardinals to two championships during World War II."

"I thought all the good players got drafted by the army. Wasn't Ted Williams a fighter pilot?"

Julia shrugged. "Maybe it was a conspiracy to make St. Louis look good. The old St. Louis Browns made their only World Series appearance in 1944. First time in 42 years. They won in 2006, too."

Walter pressed the impromptu ice pack to his cheek. "Ouch."

"Did that Creep slug you?"

"Nope. He accidentally elbowed me in the face when I tackled him."

Now came time for the question Julia had been delaying. She tried to sound casual, not like an interrogator. "When did you see him break in?"

In other words, what were you doing lurking in the woods behind my house? WATCHING my house?

"I do yard work for Mrs. Covington. She saw me fixing up

this house after Hartley moved out and she hired me. I was over yonder—" he waved with his arm, "—laying some mulch when I saw somebody go around back of your house. I didn't think much of it, figured he was heading down that trail in the woods. My Jeep was parked behind Mrs. Covington's, so I reckon he didn't know I was watching."

Julia slid her hand into her pocket, felt the contour of the mace canister. "He lives in one of those apartments. Mrs. Covington told me one of them had a history of peeping."

"Guess he took it a step further this time. When I didn't see him pass there where the trail goes by Mrs. Covington's back yard, I got suspicious. So I went through the woods and saw your window open. I figured somebody had been messing around there before, or else you wouldn't have asked Mr. Webster to check your windows."

"Maybe you should become a cop," Julia said. Just like T.L. Snead. Then Walter could be part of the great Satanic conspiracy and get his piece of the action.

"No, thanks," he said. "I don't like guns."

"You sure didn't flinch when that cop pointed one at you."

"Because I was frozen stiff. I thought old Barney Fife there would blow my head off if I so much as blinked."

Julia laughed a little, but her abdomen was too tense to put much force behind it. "I take it that the Elkwood police don't have a very good reputation."

"They thought 'Police Academy' was an instructional video."

Julia laughed more easily this time. She was so tired that she was almost giddy. Too much had happened in the last few days. The skull ring, a piece of the past unburied. The discovery of Snead's move to Elkwood. A sexual assault by the man she had thought loved her. A Creep stealing her underwear. If she dared to think at all, she feared she might just start laughing and never stop.

Walter must have noticed her weariness. "I seen him climb in the window right as it was getting dark. You drove up about two minutes later. I was afraid he might jump you or something, so I went to warn you, but then I saw him climb out with the . . . um . . . underwear thing."

He's BLUSHING.

Wait–if the Creep was only in the house for a few minutes . . . then how did he have time to find the clock, plug it in, unlock the front door, prowl through her dresser, and get out the window again?

Walter continued. "He went into the trees, and I saw your lights come on and heard the window close. I waited to see what he would do. Then, when he snuck back to your window and started peeping, he made me so mad that I wanted to bust him."

"Let's see, peeping, burglary, breaking and entering—"

"Oh, he didn't break nothing. Your window was already open. Which kind of made me wonder, since you were so worried about the locks."

"The window was open?"

"Yeah. What's wrong?"

"The ring. My fiancé gave me a huge rock and somebody wanted it. I better check."

He followed her into the bedroom and waited by the door as she pulled the burgundy velvet box from its hiding place behind Mr. Ned. She opened the box and the diamond glistened from its golden set.

"Man, that could keep a Creep fed and liquored up for a year or two," Walter noted.

She rubbed her head and yawned with exhaustion. "It's just dirt and metal, when you get down to it."

"Listen, I better go and let you get some sleep."

Go and leave her alone with the night and the locks and the mace and the Louisville Slugger and the skull ring and the haunted clock—

"Do you know much about electronics?" she asked.

Walter's head tilted inquisitively. "A little, yeah."

"I'd like to hire you for a job." She went to the kitchen, feeling his gaze on her back. She extracted the clock from the trash, took off the outer bag, and carried it to Walter. "Would you mind seeing if this has been tampered with?"

"This that broken clock?"

Julia nodded. She didn't want to tell him she'd found it plugged in when she'd arrived home, that the digits were still stuck on 4:06. Let him examine the clock without her imbuing it with any mystique.

Their fingers brushed briefly together as he took the clock, and Julia felt an odd tingle of electricity. Similar to what she had experienced when putting the skull ring on her finger.

No. The ring had no power. The clock contained no dark magic. Satan didn't exist, and therefore had no influence in the world besides in the minds of desperate, gullible people.

And Walter had no magic power, either. She was just tired, that's all.

He stood and their eyes met. One heartbeat, two, a third. They both looked away at the same time.

"Uh—I'll give this a look-over," Walter said. "But don't expect to pay me."

He moved toward the door, carrying the clock as if it were a football, in a hurry now, almost clumsy for the first time since she'd known him. She followed, but not too closely.

He paused in the doorway and pointed to the bat leaning in the corner. "Would you really have used that?"

She smiled. "You don't ever want to find out."

"Reckon not." He grinned back with strong, slightly-uneven teeth. Was he blushing again? None of the men she knew blushed. Rick O'Dell didn't blush. Mitchell had certainly never blushed in his life. "Well, see you later."

"Bye."

He went out into the darkness as moths clustered around the porch light. The college students had gone back inside, to continue their drinking in front of the television. Maybe having a friend arrested was just one more reason to party.

"Walter?"

He stopped beside the Jeep, his face shadowed. "Yes, ma'am?"

"My name's Julia."

He nodded.

"Thanks," she said. "For . . . you know."

"Might want to lock your door," he said, braver now with the distance between them. "There's bums and creeps everywhere, even in Elkwood. 'Night, Julia."

She waved, closed and locked the door, then stood leaning against it, replaying the sound of his saying her name. She found herself comparing it to the way Rick said it, the way Mitchell had said it back in more innocent days.

"Jooolia," Walter pronounced it, stretched out and lazy, a musical "ooo" in the middle. Jooolia, the way her dad had once teased. Mitchell's high-brow friends said "Jewlia," more precisely adding the "you" sound.

She took the wooden box from her purse and examined it. This relic didn't belong in Elkwood, in the new life she was trying to build. Maybe Mitchell, as screwed-up as he turned out to be, was right about one thing: perhaps the past should have been left buried.

If I were stronger, able to control my anxiety better, we could have been married years ago, and I'd be happy now. Mitchell wouldn't have resorted to—

No. The attempted rape wasn't her fault, no matter what kind of tricks her mind tried to play. And she wasn't to blame because Mitchell had tracked down and hired a Creep to prowl in her underwear drawer and try to steal the engagement ring. If he were in financial trouble, she would have gladly pawned the ring and given him the money. She would have been happy with a simple diamond chip, or no ring at all. Jewelry had never created a commitment or love through its precious substances alone.

Dr. Forrest would sort it all out in the morning. In the meantime, a night of hours must pass.

Maybe, if she acted as if this were the end of a perfectly normal day, she could survive. Papers waited on her desk, notes for articles. Other chores required her attention. Reality exerted its own brand of pressure. And reality offered an escape, however briefly, from dark thoughts.

Julia booted up her computer, surprised that the screen saver didn't exhibit some sinister message. Other appliances seemed to belong to the unseen forces of Evil, why not her computer? With any luck, her toaster might start spouting backwards Led Zeppelin lyrics.

She connected to the Internet, knowing she should get to work on her articles. But first she checked her e-mail, one of her strongest addictions besides coffee. A few posts from her Cardinals newsgroup speculated on a possible managerial change, Sue asked if Julia had arrived safely and said she'd soon have more info on Snead, and the director of the animal shelter had sent an e-mail of thanks. Nothing from Mitchell. Big surprise there.

Creepmail must have closed its accounts.

Julia closed the e-mail program without responding to the messages. She did a search for "Satan," then got the obvious, www.satan.com. Seemed like typing w-w-w-dot-*anything* brought access to some bizarre site. She linked and read through some sites built by self-styled Satan worshippers.

Not only were their edicts contradictory and juvenile, they were also poorly worded. Someone who was filled with the power of the Master of the World should at least know how to run their text through a spell check. How could these people not hold their hokey posturing up to a fire-lit mirror and laugh themselves into the grave, and thence to the hell they so eagerly sought? Except they didn't seem to believe in hell at all, and certainly in no everlasting punishment. They mostly held up their religion as an excuse for self-indulgence and vapid cruelty.

She finally reached the biggie, the official Church of Satan Web site. After reading through some of the Church of Satan's premises, based on the writings of the late Anton LaVey, Julia believed that Satanists were even crazier than she was. And, at the bottom line, the little rules and rituals were as demanding and tedious as those of the most disciplined and austere religions.

The Nine Satanic Statements. The Eleven Satanic Rules of Earth. The Nine Satanic Sins. So Satanism had its own sins. Its gate was just as strait and its way just as narrow as those of fundamentalist Christianity. Most amusing was the fact that LaVey, who actually had the audacity to die while positioning himself as Satan's High Priest, was as possessive and money-grubbing as the most odious of corrupt Christian evangelists. Here was his supposed "gift" to the world, his Satanic Bible, but it had the copyright symbol attached to every tiny segment, lest someone spread the Word without LaVey or his heirs drawing a percentage of the profit.

Other regalia was available for purchase through the site, such as black candles, silver calabra, ceremonial robes, daggers, and various herbal potions. And the Devil took credit cards.

Julia could easily separate these self-serving tenets from the cruel memories of her own past. This packaged-and-shrink-wrapped product bore no connection to the abuse she had suffered at the hands of Satan worshippers. As with all religions, it wasn't the words or the beliefs or the long-dead prophets that defined transgressions. It was *people*, those of flesh and blood and bone who mindlessly swallowed whatever was fed to them, blind to the true nature of the hand bestowing the blessings.

Julia shuddered as her own memories tried to spill from their carefully latched closet–goat's head and a silver blade and smoking crucibles and bad people.

Julia clamped her eyes shut and squeezed her temples between her palms. Her breath became shallow and her pulse accelerated to a flutter.

No, that's for Dr. Forrest and Dr. Forrest only. Not for here, not for now, not for YOU.

She took a deep breath, scared. The panic attacks were occurring more frequently. Despite her sense that she was being healed, despite her faith in Dr. Forrest's treatment, she felt on the edge of a great black chasm, and the next step would have her falling into the ink of oblivion.

She forced herself to inhale, thought of sunshine and clouds, heard Dr. Forrest's voice counting down from ten, let her fingers grow warm and plump and light. Let her body dream itself as a piece of the sky, apart yet part of it all. Let herself become air.

And, riding on the breath came a warmth and comfort and a soft, distant breeze that suggested a gentle voice.

God? Is that you?

But if it had been God, the very act of focusing had driven him back to his hidden hole in the heavens. She concentrated on Dr. Forrest's instructions and let herself relax further.

When she returned from her mental vacation, the computer screen still glared. Nothing but words. If she were to understand how Satanists worked, she needed to translate this nonsense. Maybe if she read LaVey's ideas with a cold and academic eye, without the preconceptions, Satan would lose his power to reach out from the past.

After a few minutes of going through the rules, she thought she understood something of Satanism's attraction. Indulge yourself in this world, right here and now, instead of waiting for an eternal reward. Seek gratification of the flesh and mind instead of the spiritual satisfaction of a life wasted helping others. Be kind only if it leads to personal gain, otherwise practice cruelty, and don't *dare* turn the other cheek.

Give in to nature instead of rising above your base animal instincts. Take what you want, because if you have the power to take it, it rightfully belongs to you.

Be selfish and petty and to hell with everybody else.

The "official" portrayal of Satan wasn't the damned, evil Prince of Lies presented by the conservative sects of the Christian church. This Satan was a smiling, benevolent uncle who always had a pocketful of candy to dispense. This Satan never punished. This Satan didn't require that his followers roast for an eternity to prove their devotion.

Well, which one is the real Satan? If God indeed wears many faces, the devil must have more masks than a Hollywood prop shop.

Even though LaVey urged his followers not to harm children or animals, only full-grown adults who happened to be standing in the way, the other camp believed that blood offered power and magic. And to them, what Julia considered the Crowley Camp, power was what Satan was all about.

Not that Aleister Crowley attributed his power to Satan. No, that would have deflected some glory from Crowley himself, who petulantly demanded to be called the Great Beast. So yet another false prophet inflicted the world with his self-aggrandizing beliefs, the magick so precious that an extra letter had to be added. Scariest of all was Crowley's espousal of blood as life energy, with sex as a source of power and magic. Naturally, the most potent "spiritual working" came from the fluids of the innocent: the children.

So Crowley basically built himself a religious system that excused the molestation of children, and in fact encouraged it. The idea of the fat, drugged-out satyr abusing a child made her want to vomit. Crowley's first law was "Do what thou wilt." Was there a hell hot enough to deliver the punishment someone such as that deserved?

"Joolia."

The call rode in on the whisper of breeze in the eaves or the rustle of a curtain. She looked around the empty room.

She pushed herself away from her desk and paced rapidly, trying not to hyperventilate. The darkness outside the house pressed against the doors and windows, searching for an invasion point. Her house was weak and shook with the shadowy wind.

She ran to the bathroom, turned on the tap at the sink, and splashed cold water on her face. When she looked into the mirror, she scarcely recognized herself. Her eyes were red-rimmed and watery, her hair stringy from sweat. Her skin was pallid, that of a walking corpse.

It was all her fault. If she hadn't kept sticking her nose in the past, if she didn't have to explore, if she didn't have to *know*, she wouldn't be freaking out over skull rings and Black Masses and false prophets and ritual abuse. If she were *normal*, she might have a happy future waiting.

She wouldn't be isolated in Elkwood, alone with the Creeps who were closing in with their devil masks. But she wouldn't have Dr. Forrest, either. Dr. Forrest was her light in the world of darkness, the one who led her through the tunnels of the past to the true Julia Stone that she knew she could become. The whole, healed Julia Stone, the one who would stand in light.

If only she were that person already, instead of this limp, weak Julia who was nibbled by shadows, gnashed between the teeth of invisible monsters.

As she leaned into the corner of the bathroom and slid down onto the cold tile, the walls of the world collapsed. The scars on her stomach throbbed, and the air smelled of mildew and rot. The temperature seemed to rise twenty degrees, and the room became as steamy as a swamp. Yet still her teeth chattered, her bones clacked against the tiles like a wind-blown skeleton on a string.

She was sliding into that inky ocean. This time the wave had swept its mighty arm over her, crushed her spirit, drenched her with doom. All that remained was to slip beneath the surface for the final time. This was the antechamber to hell, the waiting room to the rest of her life.

Had this been what she was born for, to end up shattered and mad, to go down without even a cry for help?

Dr. Forrest won't like this. She won't like this at ALL.

Because this isn't only YOUR failure, Julia. It's HERS.

Did she really want to disappoint the one person who had faith in her? Was this the proper repayment for someone to whom she owed so much?

She struggled for breath, her chest bound by hot bands of steel. She closed her mind off to the dark reaching fingers, the sinuous memories, the negative thoughts that were her jailkeeps. She thought of the light, of Dr. Forrest's calm voice.

"We can make it, Julia."

As if the therapist were right in the room with her. Julia

grabbed a pained lungful of stale air.

"We'll go through it together," came the voice of assurance. "Let me take you back, and then lead you forward."

Yes. Dr. Forrest could save her.

Julia exhaled, breathed again, trying to gain a rhythm. She ignored her pounding heart, afraid that its beat might be erratic. Sweat crawled over her flesh like slimy insects.

Dr. Forrest's words came to her again, like a voice in the wilderness.

"I'm here for you, Julia. I'll always be here. I'll save you."

And Julia shifted her focus onto the therapist's face, built her photograph to fill her mental field of vision. And Dr. Forrest smiled.

Julia smiled, too. Someone did love her. Someone did care enough to save her.

She lay against the tiles, aspirating easily until her dizziness passed. The shadows slid back to their odd lairs of hibernation, the panic drifted away like mist across a morning lake, the walls of fear turned to powder and crumbled.

Soon, seconds or minutes or hours later, she could stand. She wiped her face on the towel that hung on the back of the door, avoiding her reflection. She didn't want to see herself this way.

This wasn't how Dr. Forrest wanted Julia to see herself.

She went to the bedroom, holding onto the wall for support. The room still held that expectant air, fouled by The Creep's stealthy invasion. He had stood on this carpet, had breathed this air, had rummaged through her intimate things—

No. He was just a Creep. He would pay for his crimes and maybe taint Mitchell in the process. And he was out of her life, all of them were out of her life, Mitchell, her father, the bad people, everyone who had ever tried to hurt her.

All she needed was Dr. Forrest.

She made sure the curtains were tight, resisting an impulse to check the sash lock again. She thought of the bat and wondered if she should return it to its place under the bed. No, she was brave now, she gained strength through Dr. Forrest. Tomorrow she would tell the doctor all about this strange day, and by the end of the session, she might even be able to laugh about it.

For now, she needed to sleep, because the exhaustion had settled upon her flesh as soon as the panic had abandoned it.

She went to the closet to get a nightgown.

When she opened the door, she saw the yellowed paper pinned to a dress sleeve.

The drawing was done in red crayon, of a crude star shape in a lopsided circle, similar to the image carved on the wooden ring box.

Underneath the pentagram, written in a childish hand, was: HELLO JOOOLIA.

CHAPTER TWENTY

"Who do you think left the note?" Dr. Forrest asked.

Julia held her hands in her lap, fingers fidgeting, palms moist. The paneled walls of Dr. Forrest's office had always provided comfort, but today they seemed closer than usual, more oppressive. The smell from the coffee maker crowded the air. Julia's chair squeaked, the noise magnified by the long pause.

Julia couldn't meet the therapist's eyes. But Dr. Forrest was kind, was Julia's savior, was her tour guide through the house of her head. Dr. Forrest wouldn't let anything bad happen to her.

"Come now, Julia," the therapist said gently. "You can trust me, remember?"

"I don't know," Julia said, breath catching. Her eyes burned from lack of sleep, her knees trembled beneath her slacks.

"You don't know who left it?"

"No."

"The man was arrested for breaking into your house."

"Except Walter said the window was already open."

"This Walter . . . do you trust him?"

Julia looked outside. Dr. Forrest usually kept the shades drawn during their sessions, but today was so glorious that it invited cheerful thoughts. The sun splashing the red and golden trees, the sky a soft shade of blue, the clouds spread thin and wispy above the mountains. A day for hoping, a day full of optimism, the promise of coming winter's decay carefully hidden beneath the vibrant splendor.

"I don't know him very well," she finally said.

"Stay away from him. He's not conducive to your healing."

"But he was nice to me. Besides you, he's the only one that hasn't hurt me."

"It's only natural for you to feel vulnerable. After what happened with Mitchell—"

"You said we didn't have to talk about that anymore."

"Of course. We'll have to deal with it eventually, but today, let's work on the note."

"It's from one of the bad people," Julia said decisively. "They're back. They followed me here."

"Now, Julia, just because you found out that this Snead person moved to Elkwood is no indication of a conspiracy. The past is real, the abuse occurred, and you suffered tremendously. But we need to realize that the past is over, or we'll never heal."

Julia squeezed her eyes shut. "You're the one who says that I need to bring the past alive."

Dr. Forrest stood and walked to the window. "Why are you angry with me, Julia?"

"Angry?"

"Is it because I wasn't there when you needed me? That you've made these discoveries of self and suffered the panic attacks without my being able to help you?"

Julia gnawed at the end of her thumb, a new habit. "No, that's not it at all."

"Are you blaming me, Julia?"

Julia fought the urge to rise, to go to Dr. Forrest and kneel, to beg forgiveness. "It's not your fault. None of it. If I didn't have you—"

Dr. Forrest turned, a smile dying on her lips. The therapist was trying so hard to be pleasant even though Julia was acting like a spoiled child. Julia was being unfair, and she knew it.

Yet she couldn't help herself. Sometimes Julia thought Dr. Forrest carried more of her emotional baggage than she herself did.

If only I had your strength.

"You're the only thing that's kept me from going off the deep end," Julia finished.

Dr. Forrest returned to her chair and scooted it close to Julia's. She held her patient's hand. "Let's stop this talk of going crazy, Julia. You are not crazy. Your scars are not the product of your imagination. Mitchell's attack wasn't a dream. The man peeping through your window wasn't made up. The note is a fact, it exists, it's real."

Julia looked at her purse where the paper was carefully folded. She should have taken it to the police. But the thought of meeting Snead, or having him assigned to the case, frightened her more than a thousand creepy notes. This mythic Snead was gaining power in her mind. Soon he would be twelve feet tall, sprouting horns and breathing fire.

The wooden box containing the ring was also in her purse, next to the note. She didn't like carrying it around, and its proximity filled her with worry. Yet she didn't want to leave the box at the house which seemed so easy to invade. And its proximity provided a perverse comfort, an anchor to an insubstantial past.

"It's all real, Julia." Dr. Forrest continued. "And you know what else is real, don't you?"

Julia nodded. "The bad people. The ritual. The abuse."

"The memory lives in your body, doesn't it?"

Her scars throbbed. A sharp pain raced between her legs.

"They did it to you, didn't they?"

Julia shrank back in her chair, tossed her hair from side to side.

"Don't deny it, Julia. We've gone this far. You're ready to

take the last step."

"No," Julia moaned.

"We can heal these new injuries. But the key is to beat this old one first. We have to bring it out. It's the only thing holding you back, the only thing keeping you from becoming the new Julia Stone."

Silence. A truck passed on the road outside.

"You know who left the note, don't you?" Dr. Forrest said, voice lower.

The panic scrambled in from the corners of the room, on quick black legs. Why was Dr. Forrest doing this?

"You know, Julia. Share with me."

She *didn't* know. She twisted in her chair but had nowhere to run. Blind alleys in every direction, the nightmare edges of cliffs, the cold walls of deep cellars.

"The same one who held the knife." Dr. Forrest rubbed Julia's fingers.

"You—you said it was all in the past."

Dr. Forrest leaned close, her voice smooth, as seductive as that of Eden's serpent. "But the past informs the present, Julia. We are who they have made us."

Julia didn't understand, and her thoughts were racing too much to concentrate. The panic swirled, its black talons tickling paths across her skin. Why didn't Dr. Forrest help her?

"It's coming," Julia gasped. "Can we do a relaxation?"

"Soon, Julia. First, we need to approach this. We need to uncover the entire memory. Because part of it is still buried, and we can't go forward until we've completely exposed the past."

Dr. Forrest's hand clasped Julia's, squeezing reassuringly. The doctor continued, her breath on Julia's cheek. "Don't hold it back, Julia. Or should I say, 'Jooolia'?"

Julia tensed, her spine as brittle as chalk, her muscles

aching.

"Who held the knife, Julia?"

The panic had its hands around her throat, constricting her windpipe. Blood pooled in her head, she felt faint and dizzy, but there was nowhere to fall.

"Who did it, Julia?"

"He did," she whispered.

"He gave you away, didn't he? He betrayed you."

Julia gave a frantic nod.

"Say it, Julia."

She wanted to tear her hair out, to rip her eyes from their sockets, to slice her flesh with sharp blades. Anything but to deal with this. Anything besides facing the most terrible Creep of all.

"*Say it*, Julia," Dr. Forrest commanded, clamping Julia's hand so tightly that it hurt.

Julia sought escape in the rooms of her head, scrambled for the attic. Dr. Forrest was inside the house with her, slowly climbing up the stairs. No locks could keep the doctor out.

Just as no locks could keep out the truth.

"*SAY IT.*"

"Daddy," she tried to say, though she didn't think any air passed over her larynx.

"Say it, Julia. Bring him out. Don't protect him. You don't owe him any loyalty, not after what he did to you."

"Daddy," she whispered.

"He gave you away, didn't he, Julia? He's one of them. He loved them more than he loved you. He loved *Satan* more than he loved you."

She had reached the mental attic, was cradled by its dusty corners. If only there were a window from which she could jump. Behind her came Dr. Forrest's footsteps on the stairs, and the soft, insistent voice.

"Go back to that night, Julia."

No. Not that night. Not ever again.

"Go back."

And she was suddenly years away, without hypnosis, without undergoing the slow countdown. As if yesterday and today were really not separate things. The rooms of the past resided in the same house as the rooms of the present, always only a door away.

And Julia stood frozen in the doorway, four years old and scared.

The bad people in the hoods gathered around Daddy. They were yelling at him. They were going to hurt him.

Daddy looked over at her, standing in her pajamas, Chester Bear dangling by her side. Why was Daddy crying?

Then the bad people saw her.

"She belongs to him, not to you," said one of the bad people, the tall one. He held his fist near Daddy's face. "All things belong to him. The money and the flesh."

Daddy shook his head. He was wearing a dark robe, just like the others. Except his hood was down. She couldn't see the faces of the other bad people. She was so afraid she almost wet her pajamas, and she hadn't done that in a long time. She was Daddy's good girl who made him proud.

"You can't have her, Lucius," Daddy said to the bad man.

"It's not for me," he said, shaking his fist, his voice growing deeper, scarier. "The Master has ordered it."

"No," Daddy said. "I'm done with it. I want out."

"No one gets out," the bad man said. "You signed in blood. He owns you now, just as he owns this whore Judas Stone."

The other people in hoods moved closer to Daddy.

"*Daddy!*" Julia shrieked.

"It's okay, honey," Daddy said. Then he pulled his hood over his head. She couldn't see his face, and his eyes glowed like the glass eyes of a stuffed animal.

Daddy held out his hands, the sleeves of the robe drooping, full of shadows. "We won't hurt you. I'll take care of you."

She hesitated, afraid to leave her room. Darkness behind her like a long curtain.

"Come on, Jooolia," he cooed, just as he did at play, happy times of crayons and the blue pool in the yard and dolls making dinner and cars and trucks and wooden blocks on the living room floor. Just like normal.

She took a small step forward. Why was Daddy wearing the hood? Didn't he know how scary he looked?

"It's just a little game we play," Daddy said, coming toward her, his hands out. Like he wanted to hug her.

"What's he doing?" came Dr. Forrest's voice, as if from behind a wall. Dr. Forrest didn't belong here. Dr. Forrest belonged back *there*.

But Dr. Forrest was her friend. Dr. Forrest wanted to help her. Dr. Forrest wouldn't let the bad people get her.

"It's just a little game we play," Julia said.

"And he's holding your hand, taking you with the bad people," Dr. Forrest said. "What's happening?"

"Daddy's carrying me. It's nighttime because it's dark and I see stars and it's cold and I'm scared. I dropped Chester Bear somewhere. I smell the wet grass."

"You're in the barn, aren't you?" asked Dr. Forrest. Such a nice lady.

"There are more bad people here, and some smoke that smells funny. Stuff is burning in little pots. There's a big gray rock on the dirt. I can't see the stars anymore."

"Daddy puts you on the rock, doesn't he?"

Julia nodded, confused. She was supposed to be remembering, but she didn't want to.

Because this isn't happening. If you close your eyes, it goes away.

"Don't shut the door, Julia," came Dr. Forrest's voice again. "You're close."

Close. The bad man's breath is on her skin. Somebody takes her pajamas, and she's naked and cold. She tries to move, but she can't. The rock is hard under her back.

The man in the hood bends over her. He has a knife. It glows in the fire, candles all around, something stinks, why are there so many bad people? They all have hoods. Which one is Daddy?

They're singing now, a song that doesn't sound happy at all. She looks up to the other end of the rock, trying not to see the bad man. She sees the goat's head, the ragged threads of the neck dripping blood. She screams.

"That's it, Julia," said Dr. Forrest. "Let it out. Don't let the memory keep you chained anymore."

Something hurts inside her belly, she's crying but none of the bad people seem to notice, they just keep saying the scary words over and over.

Just the way she remembers it.

Just the way Dr. Forrest told her it happened.

And then the rest of it. She can't breathe, why is Daddy letting them do this to her? This isn't just a little game. Because games are fun, and this isn't fun.

Now the bad man has a knife, holding it over his head. The knife flashes like the skull ring.

"What does he say?" Dr. Forrest asked.

"You know," Julia murmured.

"Yes, I know, but *you* need to know. Say it out loud, and you'll kill its magic. It will have no power over you."

"I'm scared."

"I *know* you're scared, Julia. I know this is hard for you. But the only way to get better is to stare down your fears." Dr. Forrest sounded as if she were near tears herself, voice harsh and choked.

Julia recited the words, imitating the chant of the hooded man:

"Highness of Darkness, Satan, Master of the World, accept this offering from your loyal and humble slaves, that you may continue to make us free. So mote it be."

"And the rest of it," Dr. Forrest said, excited.

They said in unison, the bad people, Julia, Dr. Forrest, all combined in one chilling voice, "Lord Master Satan, we offer you this blood in your cursed name, that you may smile upon us and bless us. That you may—"

Julia stopped, caught in the doorway, not sure if she were in the past or the present. She opened her eyes, Dr. Forrest loomed over her, hands holding hers, face rapt, eyes closed.

Dr. Forrest completed the chant. "—that you may take as your bride, this whore Judas Stone."

CHAPTER TWENTY-ONE

Julia shivered, more frightened than she had ever been. She was on the precipice of a great gulf, it yawned out black and endless and inviting, a total madness.

"He cut you, didn't he, Julia?"

Dr. Forrest was her only link to reality, the therapist's grip the only thing preventing her from slipping into the abyss.

"He took your blood, and the eyes glowed." Dr. Forrest seemed nearly as faraway and lost as Julia. Even with the warm sunshine breaking through the office window, with the mountains spread bright and golden outside, with the reality of the chair and the floor and ceiling and walls, all the solid things of the world seemed as if they were melting away, swirling down some hidden drain into oblivion.

"The skull ring. You remember," Dr. Forrest said.

Julia couldn't suck any oxygen into her lungs.

"He did it."

Words like nails.

Julia stared into the therapist's rigid, twisted face. Suddenly Dr. Forrest's eyes snapped open, shining like candle fire, flickering.

"Say it, Julia. Don't let him have this last victory."

"He . . . "

"Say what he did."

"He let them—"

Dr. Forrest's lips curled in triumph. "Yes, he did. He had the power. All the power that Satan could offer. How could he resist?"

Julia jerked up from her chair, pulling free from Dr.

Forrest. "He gave me to that *Creep*."

Julia wrapped her arms around her chest, sobbing, her shoulders quivering. She collapsed back into the chair. She turned to look outside, to escape from the office, but the world was only a larger prison. Wherever she might flee, her mind would follow.

"I told you so," Dr. Forrest said, calmed by Julia's acceptance. "Now you know. Now we can deal with it."

"No," Julia sobbed. "It didn't happen."

"Julia, your denial has been holding you back."

"Not him."

"Julia, incest is common. So many of our sisters have suffered the same cruelty. And ritual abuse. Would you be surprised if I told you half of my female patients recover memories of Satanic masses?"

Half.

"I share your pain, Julia. I bleed with you."

"You don't understand," Julia said.

"Of course I do. I've been here with you. I've . . . been there before you."

Been there?

"I'm a survivor, Julia. Just as you will be."

"Survivor?"

Dr. Forrest stood, unfastened the bottom two buttons on her blouse. She showed her belly, the raised welts purple against her pale flesh. On Dr. Forrest, the work had been completed, the pentagram fully etched, the horror plainly written onto the page of her body.

"You?" Julia didn't know what to say. What use were words?

Dr. Forrest buttoned her blouse with quick, efficient movements. She smiled, but her eyes were distant, unfocused. Perhaps she was looking through the rooms of her own house, rummaging in secret cellars.

Julia glanced at the wall clock. Two hours had passed. She had given herself away, ripped open her skull and handed her brain to Dr. Forrest. And her spirit had slipped out through the wound, merged with the shadows and was lost.

"We can defeat it, Julia. Now we move forward."

"I'm sorry, Dr. Forrest. I'm sorry it happened to you."

"Don't be sorry. Sorrow is for the weak, the emotionally crippled, those who don't seize what lies before them. We should strive for balance, Julia."

Julia stared with wonder at the wise therapist's face. Dr. Forrest had exposed herself, had opened up her own dark rooms, and now was as calm as if she had commented on the pansies in the window planter.

If this woman, who has endured terror beyond imagining, could become strong enough to help others, it's time I stopped feeling sorry for myself.

But the stinging memory swarmed over her again, and the force of the nightmarish admission blew in like a hurricane. She closed her eyes tight, but all she could see was the hooded man on top of her, his skin hot and sweaty on hers, the skull ring on the fist that held the knife, the twin rubies glowing as brightly as the two eyes under the hood—

"Julia, look at me."

She opened her eyes, shivering, her tears cool on her cheeks.

"It's natural for you to be scared," Dr. Forrest said. "It gets easier. Accepting is the first part of healing. From here on, we go forward."

Julia nodded. Forward.

"Now you're ready to embrace the whole truth. But we'll have to go slowly."

Julia began putting away the memories, the emotional

trauma of the session, as if they were notebooks filed in mental cabinets. She needed to gather herself and go meet the demands of reality. She was behind on her work, and the paper's deadline was this evening. And the police were supposed to come by her house to dust for fingerprints.

She bent down to get her purse and stopped with her hand on the strap. "What about the drawing?"

"Let's not worry about the drawing right now." Dr. Forrest walked to stand beside Julia's chair. "I think you have enough to sort out right now without thinking about that. In fact, I believe it would be best if I kept it for you. At least for a week or two, until you're ready to face your recent problems."

Julia clutched the purse into her lap. She wasn't sure she should let the paper go. The police might need it to prove that the Peeping Tom had illegally entered her bedroom. It likely had his fingerprints on it.

But how would he know about the pentagram, about "Jooolia"?

Maybe Dr. Forrest was right. The drawing had caused her nothing but worry. If she were rid of it, maybe she could get on with her healing. Out of sight, out of mind.

She opened her purse and handed the folded paper to Dr. Forrest. The therapist smiled, her gray eyes almost mirthful. "You're going to be just fine, Julia. You're going to be perfect."

Julia closed the purse, the wooden box still buried under Kleenex, hairbrush, wallet, cell phone, and keys. She would keep the ring secret until the next session.

"Time heals all wounds, Julia," said the doctor.

Time, and maybe the band-aids and salve of hope. And faith, if she could find any.

CHAPTER TWENTY-TWO

Rick O'Dell came by Julia's desk after lunch, his confident smile a counterpoint to her dark mood.

"So, how was the vacation?" Rick asked. His shirt sleeves were rolled up, his tie carefully askew. He was eating a donut, nibbling it like a fastidious mouse.

"Refreshing." Julia glanced back at her computer screen.

"You look like you hardly slept a wink. Who was the lucky guy?"

Certainly not you, Mr. Stud-In-Your-Dreams. My private life is none of your business.

She controlled her annoyance. "Look, Rick, I'm way behind. I've got four articles to get done by deadline."

"Touchy. Don't you want to hear the latest on my Satanic sacrifice theory?"

Julia's fingers froze over the keyboard. She swiveled her chair, forgetting her resolve to be indifferent to him. "Actually, I was kind of wondering about that."

"You've still got it in you. Once you get a nose for the crime beat, you never lose it."

"Rick, I'm strictly features now. Don't worry about me trying to take your job."

Rick laughed, the confident boy wonder with two press awards on his desk. "I just got a copy of the medical examiner's preliminary report. Ritualistic markings, made with a blade. No fingerprint match, unfortunately. The victim is still unidentified. Autopsy showed traces in the system of morphine and—get this—belladonna."

"Belladonna?"

"Yeah. Also known as 'witch bane.' Long associated with black magic and Satan worship. It's taken as a hallucinogenic substance, even though it's actually a poison."

"I know what belladonna is. Hand of Glory, and all that. So what killed him, the wounds or the poison?"

"From what they can tell right now, he probably was just getting a decent buzz on when the knife fell the first time." Rick stuffed more of the donut in his mouth, crumbs dribbling down his chin. He wiped his hand on his pants. "If he was lucky, he was dead before they chopped off his head."

"You're saying 'they.' Any evidence that this wasn't the act of a lone psycho?"

"Who cares about evidence? This story is sweet."

"Is the daily onto it?"

"Don't you read the papers?"

"Not if I can help it."

"They're strictly soft-selling it. The cops are feeding them a line of crap, and as long as they can publish that quote-of-the-day, they're happy." Rick pulled a couple of wrinkled clippings from his shirt pocket and read from them.

"'Police say they are pursuing new leads in the case of a murder victim whose headless body was recovered last week. Investigators now believe the body was dumped into the Amadahee River miles upstream and that it's unlikely the murder occurred in this area.'" Rick looked at Julia over his glasses. "How's that for positive spin?"

"Not bad. The writer should work in P.R."

"The writer was the daily's editor. Rumor has it she's a bedmate of the sheriff and a couple of council members, and not just politically, either."

"Too much information, Rick. My day was hell enough without knowing that."

"Here's yesterday's. 'Chief Investigator Lieutenant T.L.

Snead says—"

"*Who?*"

"Snead. Supposed to be some hotshot detective from the big city. Only been here a few months, though, so the good-old-boy jury is still out on him."

"Snead." Julia stared at her keyboard, her belly tightening.

Rick moved closer, taking advantage of the broken eye contact to loom over her. "What's with this Snead? Do you know him?"

No. It's all a coincidence. Cops don't get transferred just in time for a ritual sacrifice to come bobbing up in the river. Snead didn't follow me from Memphis as an agent of Satan. The devil isn't stalking my immortal soul, because I'm not sure I even have one any longer.

Julia ignored the shadowy cloak of panic that hovered at the corners of her mind. "What does Snead say?"

"He believes identification will be difficult since the body was in the water so long. The skin was too far gone for fingerprints. And without the head, dental records are useless."

"Gee, that's convenient. It's almost like a forensic expert committed the murder."

"Or else a bunch of people who are insanely lucky." Rick leaned forward and arched his eyebrows, trying to look sinister. "Or maybe Satan's awesome power is protecting the coven from being discovered."

For a brief instant, a second face had superimposed itself over Rick's, a face with red eyes and a wide black nose and a goatish beard. A face distorted by evil.

Julia rolled her chair away. "Don't do that, Rick."

Rick grinned, but his grin was like that worn by the skull ring, sinister and sick. He tried to laugh but the wind died in his throat.

Julia stood and walked to the corner of her office.

Rick started to follow. "Hey, I didn't know you were so jumpy."

He put out his hand to touch her arm but she jerked away.

Satan doesn't exist. Dr. Forrest says monsters are only in the mind.

Oh, but monsters *could* wear flesh. Daddy. Lucius. Mitchell. The Peeping Tom. The people in the coven who had scarred her for life. And maybe, just maybe, there was a monster inside her, wrapped around her bones, owning her every movement and breath and thought.

"Hey, I'm sorry, Julia." His hands hovered as if he wanted to touch her or pass her a tissue, anything to ward off an uncomfortable show of emotion.

"Just leave," Julia said. "I've got work to do."

Rick backed away, pausing at the door. "Gee, hope you feel better. Guess you don't want to go out to dinner, huh?"

The worst part was she couldn't tell if he was serious or not. She waved him away, sat at her desk and pressed her palms against her eyes until the bright colors drove away the dark image of Rick's goat face. God, if she was going to start seeing things, she might as well check into the rubber room right now. Visions were the gift of only the blessed or the damned. Which was she?

Julia finished her articles and went home around seven o'clock. She drove fast, racing the sun because she hadn't left the house lights on. The thought of what might be waiting in the closet filled her with a gut-clenching dread. She arrived at Buckeye Creek Road just before dark. Mrs. Covington was sitting in her front-porch rocker as Julia drove by. The old woman waved her over.

Julia eyed the apartment building carefully. The Creep could be out on bail and already back at his window, binoculars in hand. The forest was quiet, the trees readying themselves for a long winter's sleep. The mountains were so solid and strong and peaceful that Julia almost convinced herself that everything was normal, that Elkwood was a safe place, and the past was not tiptoeing up behind her with arms outstretched.

If God existed, he surely would set up his Earthly kingdom in this granite stronghold. But would his gates be open or would he fortify himself against unwanted, unwholesome company?

Julia stopped in the yard just beyond the porch railing. Mrs. Covington sipped her tea and lit a cigarette. The red tip glowed in the dusk. "How you doing, Julia?"

"I'm fine, Mrs. Covington."

"Call me 'Mabel,' honey."

"Yes, ma'am."

"Cops made a big show of it last night, didn't they?" The woman sucked on the cigarette, its glow throwing strange shadows on her wrinkled face.

"Yeah. They arrested that guy for breaking into my house. He stole my—"

"Didn't I *tell* you to watch out for him?"

"He broke into my house and—"

"It ain't the first time." Mrs. Covington took a puff and let the smoke swirl around her face. The porch squeaked in rhythm with the rocker. "They done let him out. I saw him up yonder with his buddies, drinking beer like he didn't have a care in the world."

"The police were supposed to come today and dust for fingerprints."

"Never you mind about the law. You'd best just take care of yourself."

Julia patted her purse. "I've got a can of mace. And a

baseball bat under the bed."

The old woman cackled. "As good as a gun. Just make sure you use it on the right person."

The tobacco smoke wreathed Julia, sweet at first, but then cloying. "I thought mountain people were supposed to be trustworthy."

"That's just what they show on the TV set. People is people all over, I reckon. Some good, some bad, and sometimes you can't tell which is which."

"Well, I'm just glad Walter was here when the Creep broke in. No telling what might have happened if not for him."

Mrs. Covington quit rocking and leaned forward. "That's a mighty handy coincidence, don't you think?"

"Coincidence?" Julia preferred to think of it as good luck. She deserved a little, didn't she?

"He's been around right regular lately."

"He told me he was working for you yesterday."

Mrs. Covington stubbed out her cigarette. Her face was barely discernible in the shadows. Julia wondered why the woman didn't have on her porch light as usual.

"Sure, he was working for me. But he could have done that any time. And he come by your place twice while you was gone. Walked around the back of the house where I couldn't see him."

Julia's mind spun with this information, trying to match it up with what Walter had told her. "He seems okay to me."

As okay as anybody in this new future where my lover attacks me and my shrink has a pentagram scar and cops let perverted Creeps roam free and headless bodies float downstream.

"He's keeping an eye on you, but I'm keeping an eye on him." A cat padded across the porch like a moving shadow.

"Well, if you don't trust him, why do you let him work for you?"

"He's mountain. Knew some of his kin, and kind of felt sorry for him when he fell on hard times. He might not be innocent but so far I can't find a crack in his story. And I spend a lot of time looking. That's why I keep him close."

"He seems to be doing all right for himself." Julia fidgeted, changed her purse strap to the opposite shoulder. She caught herself wondering if her door would be unlocked. Or if Walter would be hidden in her closet, waiting for her, a man who had a key to her house.

Julia moved to the porch steps, feeling lost herself though she was only a few feet from the railing. A light came on in one of the apartment buildings, and Julia wondered if it was coming from the Creep's window. Would he dare to come back for a second helping of whatever pleasure he'd stolen in her room, or to finish the job of stealing the engagement ring?

And what if Walter had a secret agenda, and his kind face was only the mask of a sociopathic killer?

No. Julia refused to believe it, not of the man who had sat across from her in the living room last night. She couldn't see those same gentle but strong hands wrapped around a throat, squeezing, squeezing, fingers digging into soft flesh. That face with the cheeks that creased when he smiled couldn't twist into a punishing, murderous mask. And his Christian faith seemed sincere. Walter simply wasn't capable of harming anyone without a good reason.

But then, Mitchell had kept his own violent urges carefully hemmed in, hidden behind eyes that disguised whatever strange storms brewed inside his head.

"Cops been out again," Mrs. Covington said.

"Good. They said they would follow up on the breaking and entering."

"They wasn't doing much following. They went inside your house for a while."

"Inside? Where did they get a key?"

"Seems like nobody needs keys to get in the Hartley house." Mrs. Covington stopped rocking, and the cat hissed, leapt to the porch, and scurried away. "Company's coming."

Julia looked at the dim outline of the woman's face, with its wizened roadmap of wrinkles. The wind changed a little, rattling the leaves. Beneath it, hushed at first but rising, came the sound of a car engine on the road. Headlights swept around a bend and sliced across Mrs. Covington's house. It was Walter's Jeep.

"Speak of the devil," murmured Mrs. Covington.

Walter parked in front of Julia's house, got out and walked over to the porch. He carried something that Julia couldn't make out.

"Howdy, Mrs. Covington," he said, adding more quietly, "Hi, Julia. I came by to see how you were doing."

"How do, Walter," Mrs. Covington said. "Say, is your Aunt Peggy going to make her apple butter this year?"

"Soon as the apples finish falling."

"She always was the best cook in the Triplett family, in my book. Don't go telling your momma that, though."

Walter's grin flashed in the weak light from the apartments. "I'm not as dumb as I look." Then, to Julia, "I took a look at that appliance you gave me to fix." He held up the bag he was carrying.

"Great," Julia said, not wanting to talk about possessed clocks in front of Mrs. Covington, who probably already thought Julia was batty, the way she double-checked her locks, kept her windows shut in the heat of summer, and rarely ventured outside after dark.

"When you going to come finish up the mulching?" Mrs. Covington asked Walter.

"It's on my list." He moved closer to Julia. "Did you ever

hear back from the police?"

"The Creep's out," she said. "I guess he's got friends."

"Figures."

Mrs. Covington watched in darkness. Julia said, "I've got to go, Mrs. Covington. See you tomorrow."

"All right," she said. "Mind my words, hear?"

"Good night," Walter said to the old woman, whose hand flickered in a wave.

Julia walked toward her house, Walter beside her. When they were out of range of Mabel Covington's hearing, Walter said, "She's a strange old thing, ain't she?"

"Everybody's strange around here," Julia said.

"Everybody. What's that supposed to mean?"

It means if I weren't afraid that a Creep might be waiting in my house, I don't think you would be stepping foot across my threshold again. It means maybe I'm not crazy at all, maybe it's the rest of the world, and by my solitary saneness I'm the piece that doesn't fit the Life Puzzle.

"I'm just tired and babbling." She fumbled in the purse for her keys, tucked the canister of mace in her hand, and unlocked the door. Before entering, she glanced at Mabel Covington's porch. The woman had lit another cigarette, and its glow bobbed with her rocking. Julia stepped inside and turned on the lights, blinking against the brightness.

"Leave the door open, if you don't mind," she said to Walter.

"The bugs will get in and eat you alive."

"It's not the bugs I'm worried about." She slipped the mace into her pocket where she could quickly retrieve it if needed. She didn't sit in her chair, hoping Walter would take the hint.

"Your eye looks better," she said. The swelling had gone down, though the flesh around his eye was red.

Walter took the clock from the bag and set it on the coffee

table beside the baseball cards. "Like I said, I'm not any electronics expert, but I couldn't find anything wrong with it. The circuit boards look sound, and I've never heard of a microchip just going off the deep end."

"So your diagnosis would be to throw it away and forget about it?"

"Sometimes something's broke and you just got to go replace it."

She moved to the hallway and yawned, even though her pulse was racing. "I'm tired, Walter. Long day."

Walter nodded, not looking at her. Was he thinking of her bedroom waiting just a few yards down the hall? Or of his lost wife?

"Thanks for checking the clock," Julia said. She wondered if she could reach the bat under the bed if he decided to attack. She tried to look sleepy over the fear, and then became angry at herself for doubting the only person who had helped her.

"She got into it, didn't she?" Still Walter stared at the floor, or maybe past years.

"Got into what?"

"About my wife."

Julia put her hand in her pocket, touched the mace. "Well . . ."

Walter clenched his fists. His face tightened, the crease in his cheeks no longer cheerful. "She was probably in on it."

Julia didn't know if Walter was talking about his late wife or Mabel Covington. "Mrs. Covington?"

Walter went to the open door without looking at her. "Nothing. The past don't matter none."

He was going to walk out. He was going to act like nothing had happened. She couldn't let him do that. She didn't want to lose this little bit of whatever feeling stirred inside her chest every time he was around.

Julia hurried after him, wondering if Mabel Covington was over on her porch, watching and straining her ears for tomorrow's gossip. "Walter, the past does matter. Especially if it hurts."

Walter turned in the doorway, a sad smile across his face. "No. If it hurts, you forget it. You bury it deep as hell, like you do your favorite childhood pet when it dies. Then you get on your knees and pray, but mostly what you do is wonder why the Lord would do such an awful thing."

Julia found herself spouting Dr. Forrest's aphorisms. "No. You have to dig it up, bring it to the surface, acknowledge its power over you. And then you can heal."

Walter shook his head. "Sounds like the slogans on that New Age crap in that little crystal shop downtown."

"You're religious. What do you think God wants you to do about it?"

"Keep living. Finding something worth hanging on to, a reason to get out of bed in the morning." Walter finally met her eyes. His gaze was hot, the gray in his irises gone, a bright golden color radiating there. "And hanging on to faith despite it all. If this world fails you, at least you got the next."

Julia wondered why his anger hadn't scared her. Unlike Mitchell's, Walter's anger was directed toward something larger, something beyond his reach. If he was a Creep, his belief made him even more threatening, because it touched a larger mystery she couldn't understand.

Walter looked out the door to the dark forest. "We were asleep in our tent, up in the woods north of town. I woke up in the middle of the night and she was gone. It was pitch black, the moon was down, there was hardly a star in the sky. I wandered all over the woods looking for her, yelling her name until I was hoarse. It's a wonder I didn't fall off one of those cliffs."

Tears glistened on Walter's cheeks. He turned away and continued. "When morning came, I drove all over the mountain, calling for help. We looked for a solid week. Never did find any sign of her. It was like she up and walked off the face of the Earth."

Julia wanted to touch him, to hold his hand, but she hardly knew how to deal with her own emotions, much less comfort someone else. "What do you think happened?"

After a long pause, in which Julia could hear the cold chirping of crickets outside, Walter said, "I figured she was close by. She left her shoes in the tent. They found some of her footprints the next day. Other footprints were found up there, too, so the trail got confused. The hounds hit on her trail for awhile, but then it disappeared into a creek. Even if she was sleepwalking or something, that cold water should have woken her up."

"I'm sorry, Walter."

"It ain't your fault."

"I know, but—"

"Forget it," he interrupted. "That was a long time ago. When something bad happens, you can either freeze up like your busted clock yonder, or you can get over it and move on. She's with the Lord now, so maybe she's better off anyway."

Get over it. Was Walter like her, only half alive, part of him having been fatally wounded years ago? Even his Christianity wasn't enough to fix his damage.

Julia folded her arms across her chest. "You're not telling me the whole story," she said.

"There ain't no story," he said. "Hell, most of the people in town think I did away with her. Do you know how it feels to have eyes latched on your back when you walk down the street? Like somebody's always watching from the shadows?"

Oh, yes. Julia knew what that was like. She was the poster

child of panic and paranoia.

"Sorry to keep you up," he said. "You don't need my problems. You're the one that had a Creep break into her house."

"Thanks for watching out for me. Helps me sleep better."

"Got that deadly bat handy?" he asked.

"I'm ready for anything."

"I'm praying for you." He waved goodnight and left. Julia looked at the clock and the baseball cards and hurried after him.

From the door, Julia called, "If I can ever do anything for you—"

He was gone, lost in the dark, and she heard the Jeep's ignition fire.

"Just let me know," she whispered.

She thought of his parting words, and considered a possible double meaning for them. Maybe praying for her didn't mean he was asking God to help her. Maybe he was asking God to make Julia his possession. If she were braver, or more scared, she would ask God herself, but she was afraid she might get an answer.

She closed and locked the door.

CHAPTER TWENTY-THREE

The phone call woke Julia sometime before dawn. She rolled over, kicking at the blankets, trapped for a moment in some strange dream in which she'd been buried alive. The bed was damp with sweat. She squinted for the clock before remembering that it was in the trash can.

She fumbled for her cell phone on the dresser and nearly knocked it to the floor before finally getting it to her ear. Only important calls came during sleep, usually with bad news. But lately, there had been no other kind of news. "Hello?" she said, trying not to sound groggy.

"Julia."

"Dr. Forrest?"

"You're not obeying my orders."

"Uh?" Julia fought into a sitting position.

"I told you to stay away from that man. He's not conducive to your healing."

"Which man?"

"You know. Did you dream?"

Julia tried to remember, though she knew only bad things waited in the gray shadows of semi-consciousness. "Yeah. I think Daddy put me in a room, except the room was really a box, and I couldn't breath, and I beat on the sides trying to get out—"

She realized her arms were sore, and wondered if she'd been lashing out in her sleep.

"You know what that means, don't you, Julia?"

"No," Julia said, afraid to find out.

"Your father oppressed you for years before the actual

ritual abuse occurred."

"But I was only a small child. How could I remember all of that?"

"The memory is in the meat, Julia. Some women have reported experiences of attempted abortions, memories made while they were still in the uterus."

"Before they were even born?" Julia was wide awake now, her heartbeat racing, any relaxation she might have gained from sleep long gone.

"We're just beginning to understand memory and how the mind stores information. It's possible that memory works at a cellular level, so that even the moment of conception is recorded somewhere. Of course, it's the retrieval system that's flawed. That's why you need help."

Julia thought of Walter's words, about how sometimes the past is best left alone. "Maybe it's not such a good thing to remember all that."

Dr. Forrest sighed. Julia wondered if the woman ever slept.

"Julia, we need to heal you. We need more survivors. There's strength in numbers. It's all about the truth. And it's all about sharing."

"I . . . why didn't you tell me before that you had been abused, too?"

"Because I'm the doctor, Julia. And the only reason I told you was so you'd know that you're not alone."

Julia tried to wipe the darkness from her eyes. "What time is it?"

"A little after four."

"Why are you calling?"

"You need me, don't you?"

"Of course."

"Tell me what else happened in Memphis."

"I've told you everything."

Except for the part about the wooden blocks spread across my table and the silver skull ring and maybe one or two other things which either I have forgotten or am lying to myself about.

"Julia. Don't keep secrets from your therapist."

"I'm not keeping secrets."

"You talked to a detective. You went back to your childhood home. You saw the barn where you were the victim of Satanic ritual abuse. Why didn't you call the police and tell them about remembering the barn?"

Who had told her those things? "Because I was afraid."

"Afraid of what? Never be afraid of the truth."

"Because I don't think the police would have believed me. I don't think they would have believed me about Mitchell's assault, either."

"Am I the only one you can trust?"

No. Maybe she could trust Walter. Or could she? Her pulse throbbed in her temples, and she rubbed at her forehead. "Yes, Dr. Forrest."

"Then you'll do what I say?"

"I want to get better."

"Come to my office today. There's someone I want you to meet."

"Today?" Julia thought about her staff meeting at the paper. She still had a lot of work to catch up.

"Ten in the morning."

"I don't think I can make it."

"You'll come. You want to be healed, don't you?"

"Yes."

"You want to become the person you're supposed to be."

"Yes."

"You want to be free."

"Of course I do."

"He owns you, Julia." The earpiece clicked as the doctor hung up.

Julia put down the phone and sat on the edge of the bed. *He owns you.* The darkness around her grew substance, pressed against her like a thick black jelly.

The smallest of noises came from her window, like a bird's feathers scraping glass. Julia turned in the direction of the curtains. Two red specks glowed there.

Julia nearly dove into the blankets, to bury her head and let the panic consume her and maybe take her breath for the deepest and final time. The eyes couldn't have been red. It must be the Peeping Tom, back for a second helping.

Her face flushed with anger. She wanted to make sure he would never peep again. She reached under the bed, grabbed the Louisville Slugger, and ran to the window.

She heard the voice, plainly, clearly, "He owns you, Jooolia."

She dropped the bat. The twin red specks disappeared.

Eventually dawn came, the gray light filling the room. Julia numbly took a shower, dressing in the bathroom. She kept the bat close. When she was dressed, she called the Elkwood police desk. She gave her name and asked if the investigating officer in her Peeping Tom case could meet her at Dr. Forrest's office at ten. When the communications officer asked for more information, Julia hung up.

The morning was dark, oppressive clouds spread in a solid drab sheet overhead, the air still. Even the colored leaves seemed washed out, yellows and reds edging toward brown. A soft fog hid the surrounding mountains, and the smell of coming rain fought with the sweeter odors of autumn decay and grass. No one stirred at the apartments across the street, and Mabel Covington's rocker was empty.

Julia arrived at the *Times* office to find Rick waiting by her desk. "Gee, you look terrible," he said, stirring his coffee with a pencil.

"Good morning, Mr. Compassion." Julia expected him to again ask who was the lucky guy who'd kept her up all night, but he only pressed his lips together and nodded.

"Anything new on your Satanic murder theory?" she asked.

"Nope. Got an interview with Snead this morning. The editor's going to love me for this one."

If she loves you half as much as you love yourself, that would be a romance for the ages. "Good luck. Well, I've got work to do. As usual."

"We've got days until deadline." He moved closer to her, looming. "What's your hurry?"

Julia nervously eyed the corners of her small office. Her heart was beating fast, the panic creeping in on a black tide.

"Hey, is something the matter?" Rick set his coffee on her desk, stepped back, and held his palms up, his expression as innocent as a teddy bear's.

Julia put her elbow on her desk and propped up her head with one hand. "Just tired, is all."

"Well, I was going to ask you if you wanted to go out tonight with some of my friends, but I guess not. He owns you."

Julia spun in her chair, tried to rise but her knees were weak. She gasped a couple of times, fought some air into her lungs, and whispered, "What did you say?"

"Jeez, what's wrong with you, Julia?" he said.

"You said 'He owns you.'"

His eyebrows lifted. "I didn't say anything of the kind."

Julia's pulse machine-gunned through her veins, her throat constricted.

"You ought to go home and get some rest," Rick said,

taking a step back. "You don't look so hot."

Julia pulled a water bottle from her purse and took a couple of swallows. Her hands trembled so much that the water sloshed inside the plastic container. She was ashamed to have Rick see her this way. "I think I'm catching a little bit of the flu."

Rick edged closer to the door. "I'd go see a doctor if I were you."

"I am," she said. "Ten o'clock."

"Well, don't die or anything before then," Rick said, glancing at two graphic artists passing in the hall as if they might provide emergency medical assistance, or at least provide cover for his escape.

"I'll be fine," she said. "I just want to get a little work done before then."

"Yeah," Rick said, avoiding her eyes. "Well, I've got to get ready for my interview."

"Bye," she said, but he was already gone. Julia looked into her open purse. The box waited under her wallet, key chain, and tissues. Her fingers itched to touch it, though the memory of its strange electricity still haunted her.

She reached in, dug toward the bottom of the purse until she felt the wooden box. Her fingers explored the etched emblem. She thumbed the lid free and rooted in the cloth. She touched the cold metal and pulled the ring free of the purse.

Julia held the ring between the thumb and forefinger of her right hand. Again it seemed to guide itself toward her left hand as if possessing a gravity of its own. Then the ring was on her finger, its heat expanding through her in orange radiant waves. Words popped into her head, spoken in the guttural voice of a madman: "With this ring, I thee wed."

She wrestled the ring free and flung it into her purse. Her ears rang as the blood rushed from her head. She bent over, fighting a surge of nausea. The walls closed in, as sinister as the sides of a living coffin.

Breathe, Julia.

Count.

Just the way Dr. Forrest taught you.

She started, concentrating on each number, picturing the numerals as crystal clear shapes, and their edges softened as she mentally melted them. Ten was the tough one, because it fought and squirmed, wanted to slip away before she could pin it down. Nine came and went a little more slowly. By the count of eight, she thought she could breathe again. Seven, six, and she would survive.

Five, and she could open her eyes, focusing only on the deep cleansing breath and the exhalation that carried away the fear. Four, three, now more slowly, two, and she almost yawned. Then *one*, the end, relaxation, an effective enough self-hypnosis that she could clearly think about the things Dr. Forrest had advised.

Bring it out. Let the pain surface. Face the nightmares. Don't surrender.

But maybe surrender was better. She could crawl into the cellar of her head, put her hands over her eyes, and wait.

Wait for what?

For Daddy to come out of the shadows, in his hooded robe and wearing his skull ring, the knife cold and cruel in his hand?

She shuddered herself back to the present and found herself gazing at the blank screen of her computer. She flipped on the power and the screen burst into brightness. The computer ran through its loading commands and the screen saver came up, a field of deep red.

In the middle, in letters as white as corpses:

He owns you, Jooolia.

She jabbed the computer's power switch with her index finger, half expecting a tremendous bolt of electricity to leap from the machine. She grabbed her purse and hurried into the hall, nearly knocking down an advertising rep. The rep called after her, but she staggered from the building into the gray morning. The parking lot was like water, something to be waded through.

If only I can make it to Dr. Forrest's.

She struggled into the Subaru and drove to the therapist's office without running off the road, though several drivers honked at her. An Elkwood police patrol car was parked by the office door, gleaming even though the sun was veiled. The secretary ushered Julia through, telling her that the doctor was expecting her. Julia glanced at her watch and saw that it was only a few minutes after nine.

She knocked on Dr. Forrest's door.

"Come in, Julia," came the therapist's muffled voice.

Julia entered to see Dr. Forrest standing beside the window with a tall, thin man who smiled at her. In a tweed jacket and wearing no sidearm, he could have passed for an English professor. His face was creased from age, but his dark hair had only the slightest touch of gray. The cop's eyes were cold and dark.

Dr. Forrest said, "Julia, this is Chief T.L. Snead."

Snead.

Julia swayed as if the floor had been yanked from underneath her. She recognized him now, an aged version of the cop in the old newspaper photographs.

This was Snead, the man she had built into a monster in her own mind. Here she was, face to face with the man who she believed might have covered up Satanic murders, who had failed to solve her father's disappearance, who had tracked her from Memphis to this small Blue Ridge town.

Snead extended his hand in greeting, and she saw that the tip of his pinkie was missing, the stump healed to red scar tissue. She backed away.

"So you're Julia," Snead said, with no hint of emotion. "I always wondered what kind of woman you would grow into."

"What are you doing here?"

"I decided to take over this case myself," Snead said. "Invasion of privacy is such a terrible offense, as I'm sure you know firsthand. I want to make sure the right person is convicted."

Julia's anger momentarily overwhelmed her fear and confusion. "What do you mean, the right person? They arrested that guy last night. You have statements from both Walter Triplett and me."

"The suspect tells a different story. He says Mr. Triplett was the one who was inside your house."

"And you *believe* him?" Julia looked to Dr. Forrest for help, but the therapist crossed her arms and said nothing. "That Creep said he was hired to steal my engagement ring and harass me."

"Allegedly. But Mr. Triplett has some—shall we say, *suspicions*—surrounding him. We need to investigate the matter more thoroughly."

"Then why didn't anyone from your department dust for fingerprints?"

Snead gave a smile. His lips looked like a reptile's that had just swallowed a satisfying bug might. "How do you know we didn't? Your house is a busy place."

"Somebody was at my window again last night. Right after I talked to you on the phone, Dr. Forrest."

The doctor frowned. "Julia, you probably imagined it. You know that paranoia is one of the side effects of non-specific panic disorder."

"No. It happened. He said, 'He owns you.'"

Snead and Dr. Forrest glanced at each other. Then Snead said, "Do you have any evidence?"

"Maybe you could go check for footprints or something. I don't know. It's not like I had a video camera running."

"Why are you so afraid, Julia?" Snead said.

She stared at the beige swirls in the carpet. She remembered something James Whitmore had told her in Memphis, how cops never forgot the cases they hadn't solved. "How come you followed me from Memphis?"

"I didn't follow you," Snead said. "I was here already."

Before her? Then he must have kept track of her whereabouts. Did Elkwood have some connection to her father's disappearance? Even though Dr. Forrest had convinced Julia that her father was a terrible and abusive man, she would love to have that riddle of the past resolved. But Snead's interest in her was a more enigmatic riddle.

"I'm a friend of Dr. Forrest," Snead continued. "We grew up together. And I've had several conversations with both her and your therapist in Memphis, Dr. Danner. I thought getting some insight about you might help me solve your father's disappearance. Plus, I was curious about how the tragedy affected you."

"I thought doctor-patient information was confidential." She looked accusingly at Dr. Forrest. The older woman touched her abdomen as if to remind Julia of the pentagram that had been carved into her flesh.

"A doctor can share a diagnosis, Julia," said Dr. Forrest. "What we can't do is give transcriptions or relate specific incidents or confessions that emerge from therapy."

That didn't sound like anything Julia had ever heard, though most of her legal knowledge came from reruns of *Law & Order*.

"Why don't you make yourself comfortable?" said the doctor. She crossed behind Julia and closed the office door. Snead waited by the window at parade rest. Julia took her usual chair, her purse in her lap.

Dr. Forrest returned and sat in her own session chair. "Now, Julia, what brings you here this morning?"

Julia gripped the arms of the chair. "You *told* me to come in."

The therapist's face saddened, and the wrinkles around her mouth deepened. "Julia, Julia. That's not the way to healing. You can lie to me all you want, and that doesn't matter. What matters is that you're lying to yourself."

"You called me in the middle of the night," Julia said. "Remember?"

"You imagined it, just as you imagined the person at your window."

Julia squeezed her purse, the leather moistened by her sweaty palms. Even sitting, she was as dizzy as if riding on a mad magic carpet.

"Okay, let's assume you're not making it up," Dr. Forrest said. "What did you think this person at the window said?"

"'He owns you,'" Julia managed to whisper.

"'He owns you.' And what do you think this means, Julia?" The doctor tented her fingers, her legs crossed. Snead looked on as if Julia were a white rat ready for another run at a familiar maze. Why didn't Dr. Forrest make him leave?

"I don't know what it means."

"I'll tell you, then. That was your subconscious mind telling you that you're still letting the sins of your father control your life. You're still a slave to the past. But the fact that you're ready to hear the message is a good sign, whether it came in a dream or not."

"I don't want to hear any message," Julia said. "And I don't want to talk about this in front of *him*." Julia avoided Snead's eyes.

"You trust me, don't you?" said Dr. Forrest.

"Well, yes."

"Then you know I'm doing what's best for you."

Julia pressed back in her chair. "I . . . I'm not sure about anything anymore."

Dr. Forrest leaned forward and touched Julia on the knee. She rubbed it lightly. "The memory's in the meat, Julia. Cellular memory. Just let it escape. Breathe."

No. Dr. Forrest wouldn't try to hypnotize her here, not in front of Snead. Julia didn't want to go back to that dark, bad place anymore. She was tired of the pain, anger, and the sick feeling in her belly, that emptiness that only grew with each visit to the past.

She wasn't getting better. She wasn't moving forward. If anything, she was getting closer to becoming the helpless four-year-old again. She closed her eyes and tried to ignore Dr. Forrest's soft, lulling voice. She sought a connection with something larger, a Higher Power she'd always denied. But the woman was too much a part of Julia, had opened the doors to the house of her head, stood always in the halls, calling.

"You know who did it, don't you? You know who the bad man really is. What did he do, Julia? Tell us what he did."

Julia shook her head and moaned, trying to shove away the memories that threatened to surface. Her eyes were pressed so tightly closed that small tears seeped from the corners.

"Julia, you can trust us. We understand, more than anybody in the world. We know what it's like, how hard it is to accept the truth. How hard it is to accept the master."

Master?

Dr. Forrest continued, in that soft, mesmerizing cadence. "We don't want you to fight it any longer, Julia. *He* doesn't want you to fight. He's been very patient with you because he cares for you so very much."

"*Who* cares?" Julia wasn't sure if she'd said the words aloud or not.

"Why does he bother, when he has so much power that he can take easily what is his?"

Julia sensed that Snead had moved from the window, but she couldn't force her eyes open to see. She tried to burrow into the chair to escape the horrors of the past, to keep from sliding into that black, yawning gulf.

Daddy can take what is his. He has always owned you, in life, death, or absence. Daddy can hurt you no matter where you try to hide.

"I'll tell you why, Julia," continued Dr. Forrest. "Because he *loves* you."

Love?

That was the first time Dr. Forrest had ever uttered that word. In all the months of treatment, in these accelerated sessions of the last week, the doctor had talked of sharing, healing, hope, and all the other abstract things that meant nothing. In the religion of the brain, even God was off limits. Now she had to bring out this last hollow word, the one that deserved a special place on the altar of useless words.

Snead's voice came to her as if he was on the foot of the stairs and she were hiding in the attic. "He owns you, Jooolia."

Her eyes snapped open, her abdomen clenched in a knot, her hands curled into fists as she sat forward. She blinked, her vision blurred. Snead still stood by the window.

Dr. Forrest wore her usual look of kind concern. "What's the matter, Julia?"

"What's he doing here?" Julia said, this time staring into

Snead's small, dark eyes.

"You asked for him to be here, remember? When I talked to you on the phone last night."

Wait. Didn't Dr. Forrest just say I imagined the phone conversation?

Maybe she shouldn't have tried to resist Dr. Forrest. Because she was confused, her thoughts screwed up. How could she trust her memory when she had long ago lost the ability to tell what had been real? How could she even trust what she thought *now*, much less 23 years ago?

But since a policeman was here, she decided that there was one thing she hadn't imagined, a solid piece of evidence that might prove once and for all that The Creep had been in her house, and that Walter was innocent of breaking and entering. It was something she'd held in her own hands. Even though she didn't trust Snead, at least Dr. Forrest was present as a witness.

"There's something I found the other night," Julia blurted to Snead. "It was in my closet."

Snead's eyebrows arched, and that bug-eating smile slid across his face again. "What's that, Miss Stone?"

"The drawing."

"Drawing?"

She talked rapidly, glad to be relieved of at least one secret. "A picture of a pentagram. With 'Hello Julia' underneath, only 'Julia' was spelled 'Jooolia' with three *O*'s in the middle, just like Daddy used to spell it when he was teasing me."

"Where is this picture now?"

"I gave it to Dr. Forrest."

Dr. Forrest looked sadly at Julia, and then at Snead. The therapist shook her head.

"What?" Julia asked.

Dr. Forrest held her hands apart. "There's no picture, Julia."

She stood. "What do you mean, there's no picture? I gave it to you yesterday, right in this office."

"Please sit down," the therapist said.

"What did you do with it?"

"Sit down," the therapist commanded. Julia stared at her.

"She's worse off than I thought," Dr. Forrest said to Snead.

"It's not *me* that's crazy, it's all of *you.*" Even as she said the words, she realized that was exactly the kind of thing a crazy person would say.

"Julia!" shouted Dr. Forrest. Snead moved after her, but she was already gone, through the office door and out of the building, into the reeling gray world outside, into her car and then forward into the mad, strange future.

CHAPTER TWENTY-FOUR

The climb up the winding road to her house was treacherous, the Subaru's tires squealing with each curve. The asphalt was covered with damp leaves, and a film of mist clung to the surface of the road and the windshield. Julia's panting fogged the window, so she wiped a clear circle with the bottom of her fist. She peered into the thickening gloom ahead, occasionally glancing into the rearview mirror, expecting Snead to come rocketing up behind her with bar lights flashing.

Why are you running? They know where you live. HE knows where you live.

She didn't have any kind of plan. All she wanted to do was get home, slam and lock the door, huddle in the house. But that wasn't an escape. Because, wherever she went, she was always inside her own head. She couldn't outrun the rising tide of shadows.

When Julia drove up, Mabel Covington was on the porch of her big house, leaning on her wooden walking stick, cats prancing around her ankles. The old woman waved frantically with a trembling hand. Julia slowed the car and pulled along the edge of the woman's yard. The apartments were quiet, their tenants off at school or work. Unless the Peeping Tom had his binoculars at the curtain's edge.

Julia rolled down the passenger window as Mrs. Covington hobbled over to the car.

"What is it?" Julia asked, looking down the drive to see if Snead was after her.

"He's here," Mrs. Covington said, her face nearly as white

as her thin hair.

"Who's here?"

"He come back." The woman leaned against the door, wheezing as she put her head inside the car.

"The Peeping Tom?"

"Hartley. The one that used to live in your house."

The old woman had gone as mad as the rest of the world. "I'm sorry," Julia said. "I'm in a hurry."

"You don't understand. He was *here*. He was messing around your house. I called the cops, figuring he come back to get something he left."

"Why would he come back here?"

The woman's eyes narrowed, as cold and clouded as marbles. "Didn't nobody ever tell you, child?"

"Tell me what?"

"Oh, Lordy." The old woman backed a few steps away. "You don't know, do you?"

"Tell me what happened," Julia said, suddenly remembering the murder of the little girl that Rick had mentioned. That name, Hartley, struck a dismal note of recognition.

"You must have found out something. I was hoping and praying they'd leave you alone."

"Maybe we'd better go inside."

The old woman shook her head, the weathered flesh of her neck quivering under her chin. "They told me to stay out of it. I done said too much."

Mrs. Covington turned and struggled across the yard and levered her way onto her porch, planting the walking stick before her with each step. The wooden knocking was swallowed by the silence of the shrouded forest. Then the woman disappeared into her house. Julia rolled up the window and parked in front of her own house.

Hartley was here. What did that mean? Was he really the one that had killed that girl two years before? A crime like that must have sent seismic shock waves through this little community, and Rick O'Dell probably would have woven it into his pet conspiracy theory. Why hadn't Walter told her about it? Walter, the man she thought she could trust?

Julia tiptoed around the side of the house, wishing she had the Louisville Slugger with her. One hand was tucked in her purse, ready to draw the mace, but the spray would have little effect if someone really intended to harm her.

No one was behind the house. She thought of checking around her bedroom window for footprints, to confirm that someone had actually stood there last night and called to her. But more leaves had fallen, covering the ground in a damp carpet of dying color.

The trees somehow seem closer today, surrounding the house.

She almost laughed at the absurdity of the thought. But she was afraid that if she started laughing, she might never stop.

Nothing stirred in the woods, and through the thick autumn mist came the soft gurgling of the creek. She glanced toward the shrouded hill beyond. For a moment, Julia pictured a child sprawled in a clearing, people in hoods gathering around. Then she blinked away the image and hurried to the front of the house.

No Snead yet. He must have decided not to pursue her, for whatever reason. Even the Chief of Police needed some kind of justification to come after her. Maybe Julia *was* a threat, both to herself and others, and should be locked away for her own good.

Maybe she had imagined the pentagram drawing, the man at her window, the message on her computer at work. But she hadn't imagined the skull ring. The skull ring was real, solid, a link between the past and present. As she searched for her house keys, she dug into the bottom of her purse to reassure herself with the substance of the engraved box.

A weird fetish object to make yourself feel better with—

The box was gone.

She held the purse close and raked through the contents. Wallet, keys, mace, tampons, hair brush, note papers. No ring.

But the purse hadn't been out of her sight.

Julia checked again, but the box and the ring inside it were gone. She unlocked the door, her hand trembling so much that she could barely fit the key in the lock. Despite the muted daylight, the house was dark and forbidding.

Once the door was locked safely behind her, she put her purse on the couch and went to get the Louisville Slugger. She was bending down to reach under the bed when he grabbed her from behind, one hand clamped over her mouth to keep her from screaming. She struggled and kicked, nightmare visions of Mitchell's assault forcing their way to the surface. But Mitchell was in Memphis.

And this Creep was stronger than Mitchell. She tried to drive an elbow against his ribs, but he pulled her back into the dark open closet.

"Shh," he hissed, his voice like the moist flickering of a snake's tongue near her ear.

She bit his hand, and he grunted in pain. "Damn it, Julia."

Walter!

So he was a Creep after all.

He had her in the closet now, and clothes fell from their hangers as they struggled. Walter pulled his hand away from her mouth and whispered, "Hush, they're probably listening."

Listening?

Julia pushed herself from his grasp, falling against a thick row of coats and sweaters. "What in the hell do you think you're doing?"

Walter put his index finger to his lips. A purple half-moon marked the flesh where she had bit him. He looked as scared as she felt, his eyes showing white all around the irises.

"Shut up for a second," he said. "I'm not trying to hurt you."

She almost believed him. But in this new world of secrets and lies, no one deserved her trust. If she was going to go crazy, she was determined to do it the old-fashioned way, without any help from anyone. She was going to walk straight up the stairs, stand in the middle of that dark attic of her mind, and scream at the warped walls until they collapsed in upon her.

She didn't need a nudge from Walter. She didn't need a carpenter to fix her house. All she wanted was strong locks and tightly nailed shutters, all light barred from her rooms. All she wanted was to disappear, into the shadowed corners of her attic or the musty depths of her cellar. Alone in the ruins.

Walter pressed against her in the cramped closet. He shook her and whispered, more urgently this time. "Listen to me. Don't break down right now. I need you."

Need? He needed *her*? Again she almost laughed, but even that took too much effort. As always, surrendering was the most painless option.

"They're outside," he continued. "Deke Hartley, Snead, and the others."

"Snead?" She wondered how the cop could have gotten to the house so fast. And how had Walter gotten inside? Was he the one with the key, the one who had left the pentagram drawing, who stole the skull ring, who tricked her with the digital clock?

That made sense. Foolish Julia, she had asked him to check

the clock. She had turned to him for comfort, had made the insane mistake of putting faith in this man who now seemed the most desperate of Creeps. This stranger hovering over her, sweat on his pale face, eyes flicking, lips pressed white.

You don't have to let the Creep into your house. HE'S ALWAYS INSIDE.

Before she could scream, Walter crouched in the corner of the closet. He pulled at a plywood panel set in the wall. The wood came loose, revealing water pipes and insulation. Walter ripped the insulation away in clumps.

The musty smell of the crawl space rose up and filled the closet. The gap between the shower stall and the wall was about two feet wide, with the subfloor cut out. "What are you doing?" Julia asked.

"Access," Walter said. "For working on the plumbing. Or sneaking out."

Walter wriggled down into the narrow opening between the floor joists. His feet touched the dirt beneath the house and he turned, looking almost comical, like a Jack-in-the-Box that was too large for its container. "Come on. Or do you want to stay here and wait for them?"

Julia thought she heard a scrabbling sound at the front door, but she couldn't be sure. "Did you take the ring?"

"What ring?" His eyes met hers, blazing brown not with anger, but with a strange determination.

"And the clock. What does '4:06' mean?"

"Don't talk crazy," he said. "Let's get out of here." He ducked into the opening, contorting his tall frame. His shoulders disappeared, and then his head, and lastly his arms. He called her name from the crawl space, his voice muffled.

Julia got on her hands and knees, pulling her purse behind her. She looked longingly across the room at the Louisville Slugger beneath her bed. Even if she had the bat, she wouldn't be able to wield it in the cramped crawl space. Snead and the rumored Deke Hartley might be outside, and might be after her for whatever reason, or they might not. Despite Walter's strangeness, she would rather go with him than face Snead and Hartley.

She peered down into the darkness of the crawl space. This was worse than the cellar of her dreams, bones or no bones. This was surrender without oblivion, this was a willing, conscious decision. This was a leap into an unknown future.

But then, the future had never been known, and even the past was uncertain.

Julia dangled her legs into the crawl space, the fabric of her slacks scraping on the rough plywood edge. She lowered herself into the dank air, feeling Walter's hands on her. His touch was cool and moist, but was gone as soon as her feet were planted on the ground three feet beneath the floor. She bent the rest of her body into the crawl space just as a loud knocking came from the front door.

Walter reached up and tugged the panel back into place, throwing the crawl space into almost complete darkness. The only light leaked from several vent grills set into the walls of the block foundation. Julia's heart thudded in her chest. Voices came from outside the house, a man's which sounded like Snead's giving orders, followed by a woman's.

Julia couldn't see Walter, but she could sense his body several feet away. "What the hell is this?" she whispered.

"I should have told you," he said, barely loud enough for Julia to hear.

Julia grabbed out blindly and caught his shirt. She tugged herself closer to him, scooting along in the moist dirt. "Why the hell is everybody keeping secrets? What do they want?"

"Everything. But they ain't going to get it." He started

toward one of the air circulation vents, his elbows and knees scraping softly on the ground. "Follow me," he whispered.

The weak daylight from one of the vent grills was momentarily blocked as someone passed by. How many were out there? Were they members of Snead's department? Were they *all* Creeps?

As she scrabbled along after Walter, she felt disembodied, outside herself, wondering whether she should scream for help. She bumped her head on a water pipe and the pain drove the nonsense away. The pipe vibrated along the bottom of the floor from the blow, and Walter stopped and shushed in warning. Julia rubbed her head, grateful for the pain. Now she had something to focus on, something that was real. She wrapped her purse strap around her wrist and wriggled onward, her eyes adjusting to the dimness.

Her hands raked across hard things which she thought were rocks. One of the objects was tilled from its resting place by her fingers. It gleamed pale in the muted light, showing its curved length.

A BONE. Sweet merciful God, a bone!

It looked like a small rib, dry and smooth. Julia knocked it away and it clattered against a concrete support pier. She rolled away from the burial ground and pressed her hand against her mouth to muffle a scream. Walter heard the choking sound and turned, crawling to her side.

She grabbed his hand, thrust it toward the soft dirt where the bones were scattered. They both touched the tiny skull at the same moment.

Walter's eyes widened. "Hartley," he whispered. "That goddamned scum."

His body trembled, either from fear or anger. Julia thought of Rick O'Dell's theory, about a widespread network that offered human sacrifices to a supposed dark master. Those bones were so tiny. The devil liked them young. Or perhaps only the devil's worshippers did.

Julia stretched so that her mouth was near Walter's ear. "It's a child," she said, her voice breaking.

"I know," Walter said, tears glistening on his cheeks.

The pounding at the front door grew louder, and someone shouted into the house. If the Creeps entered the house, they would soon find out she was gone. And presumably they wouldn't think some angelic hand had lifted her up to the clouds. Not while Satan was spinning his dark spells below.

"What are we going to do?" she asked, squeezing Walter's arm.

A crashing sound reverberated along the floor. Someone was kicking in the door.

"My Jeep," Walter said. "It's on the other side of the woods."

"Do they know you're here?"

"I don't think so."

"What do we do now?"

"Crawl." He wiped at his eyes and moved underneath the floor, Julia close behind, her elbows and knees sore. A splintering sound erupted above them.

Walter reached the service access, a small wooden door set into the foundation at the rear of the house. Feet pounded across the floor, and shouts rang out overhead. At least three people, maybe more, were in the house.

"Now!" Walter said, knocking the access door open. "Run for it," he said, pushing Julia through the opening.

Julia tumbled into the back yard, grateful for the trees, hoping all the Creeps were inside and that no one had been left to guard the rear of the house. If they were going to get her, they'd have to take her down running.

God, give me flight.

As she dodged between the branches, leaves falling around her, she felt almost giddy with a new freedom, September on her face, the smell of creek mud in her nose, nothing to lose but a past that she had been trying to lose for years. Leaving behind bones, Creeps, almost everything except fear.

Yet even the fear was welcome now, because it gave her energy. Life had simplified, reduced now to its basic purpose. Live in order to have more life. Flee so you can make it to the next breath, to the next fleeing, part of the biological cycle that was as old as bacteria. This was God's solo spectator sport, the survival of the fittest or the luckiest. If God cared to grant her strength, she would gratefully accept. All else in the world had failed her, even her father.

She glanced behind her, saw Walter enter the forest, running toward her. He motioned to the creek that slid silvery and cold down the slope, the water splashing between dark mossy rocks. She almost took off along the creek bank, ignoring Walter and choosing her own random path. But she thought of the tears he had wept under the house. Creeps couldn't cry.

She leaned against a big oak to wait for him, catching her breath. "Did they see us?" she asked as he dashed up.

"Shh," he panted, stopping and putting his hands on his sides. Soft forest noises filled the silence, the settling of leaves, the high chatter of a bird.

"I don't hear anybody." Walter looked into her eyes. Dirty streaks ran down his face where he had cried.

"Are you going to tell me what this is about?"

"Later. My Jeep's over that ridge. They're probably already searching for you."

"How many?"

He took her hand. "Don't know. Enough. More than

enough, knowing them."

"Who is 'them'?" Julia asked, but Walter was already tugging her along, leading her to the creek. He helped her across, stepping on slick stones. Julia scrambled up the muddy bank, holding onto a flaking grapevine. Walter nearly lost his balance and fell, but Julia grabbed his shirt and pulled him onto the bank.

They ran onward, Walter leading the way, Julia holding up her arms to keep the branches from slapping her face. Briars tugged at her clothes, and she stubbed her toe on a root. Once she thought she saw movement out of the corner of her eye and nearly shouted, but she turned her head and saw nothing but more trees, the corridors between them full of still shadows.

They slowed as they hiked uphill, reaching a clearing on the top of the ridge. Jagged hunks of granite protruded from the edge of the slope. A flat slab of gray rock sat in the middle of the clearing, worn smooth by the elements. Between the trees, Julia could see the mountains rolling away, blue and smoky in the distance. Layers of clouds wended over the ripples of land. Under other circumstances, the setting would have been peaceful and humbling. But the trees surrounding the open ground were a little too gnarled, with knotholes like obscene eyes.

"Here's where they found the girl," Walter said, fighting to catch his breath.

Julia looked around. Flat stone. Cold against her own back. Bad people around her. The knife's blade touching her belly.

Her muscles quivered from the exertion of the climb, but she didn't dare sit on the rock. The place *felt* evil. Like the barn near her childhood home in Memphis, the air here tasted like poison, and a sick energy worked its way through the soles of her feet.

Julia wondered how many other altars of human sacrifice existed. Was the entire earth stained with blood and bones, the substance of the innocent given to the dirt for the satisfaction of a demanding master? The devil might not exist, but his followers most certainly did. His followers were legion. More widespread than anyone dared guess.

Walter knelt with his back to her, scanning the woods below for any sign of Snead's people. "Hartley disappeared right after they found the body."

"Didn't the police do anything?"

"Hartley had ways of keeping folks quiet. One way or another. I reckon that's Snead's job now."

Julia shook her head. She couldn't believe that Snead and Hartley were connected, that Snead took the job when Julia moved here. The only people who knew she was thinking of moving to Elkwood were Mitchell and Dr. Danner. But the conspiratorial network apparently existed long before she left Memphis.

She stared at the flat stone. Julia tried not to picture the girl, small and shivering and nude on the stone, mad people dancing around her under the cold and soulless moon, chanting their sadistic prayers. She shut her eyes to fight back tears.

She felt Walter's hand lightly touch her shoulder. "Let's get out of here," he said.

"It's all too crazy to be real."

He wiped at her face with the sleeve of his flannel shirt. "I've been telling myself that for a long time. Ever since my wife walked off the face of the Earth."

She opened her eyes and looked into his. The loss was there again, inside him, that big hurt that would stay hidden if she didn't know it was there. "Do you believe in the devil?"

"I believe in *Hartley*," he said, looking away, up at the veiled sky. "The Lord never makes it easy."

He took her hand. "The Jeep's only a few hundred feet from here. There's an old logging road that runs down the valley."

They left that sorrowful clearing, Julia wondering just how many sacrifices had been offered at this unhallowed site over the centuries. She walked gingerly, as if over the graves of infants.

CHAPTER TWENTY-FIVE

The Jeep was parked in a high bank of weeds, amid goldenrod and white Queen Anne's lace in fall bloom. Walter stepped onto the leaf-covered logging road that wound between the trees across the slope, looked in each direction, and climbed behind the wheel. Julia got in beside him, tired both from tension and exertion.

"What now?" Julia asked as Walter started the Jeep.

"I know a place where they might not find us."

She touched his hand that was cupping the gear shift. "Why are you helping me?"

He looked at her. "Let's just say I got a debt to pay."

Walter pulled out onto the dirt road, the Jeep bouncing on the ruts. A few saplings had taken root in the roadbed, and the Jeep's bumper pushed them over. Their tracks were barely visible in the damp leaves.

The Jeep lurched over a rut and a book slid from beneath the seat and bumped Julia's ankle. It was a Holy Bible. Walter saw her looking at.

"I got somebody riding shotgun," he said. "You ought to try it sometime."

"I'm not ready to believe in anything," she said.

"Except the devil?"

She picked up the Bible and opened it. "I'm hardheaded, okay? Just don't try to save me."

"I can't save you. You can only save yourself."

The Bible fell open to a page with a folded-back corner. "Luke" was printed in bold in the header. A section of the text was highlighted in yellow and Julia read it aloud. "'To thee will I give all this power, and the glory of them; for to me they are delivered, and to whom I will, I give them.'"

"Luke chapter four, verse six. The devil said that to Jesus. I use it to remember to stay on my toes."

Or maybe to remember who's the real boss. 4:06, huh?

She closed the book and tucked it back under the seat. "We're going to have to tell the police."

"Julia, those *were* the police."

"They can't all be in on it. The sheriff's office, the State Highway Patrol, the S.B.I. The devil doesn't own everybody."

"Maybe not, but how do you tell?" Walter kept glancing in the rear-view mirror. "We better guess right on the first try, or else we're in even deeper trouble."

Julia fished in her purse for her cell phone. "Can't we make an anonymous tip?"

"They screwed with your clock and VCR in ways I can't figure out. You reckon they won't be able to trace a phone call? For all I know they've planted a GPS tracker on my Jeep."

Julia glanced at the cell phone and saw that it had no bars. "Dead."

"Not many towers way out here."

The logging road widened as the slope became less steep. The forest was a blur of gold, red, and brown as the Jeep gained speed. Julia fastened her seatbelt and held on to the roll bar overhead to keep from being thrown around by the juddering. Walter slowed briefly, engaged the four-wheel drive lever, and accelerated down the muddy road.

The trees thinned out, and they came to a stretch of pasture bounded by a barbed-wire fence. A few cows gazed at them, not pausing in their cud-chewing. The Jeep crossed a shallow creek that intersected the road.

"They were after me in Memphis," Julia said over the roar of the engine.

"On your last trip?" Walter kept his eyes on the road.

"No. Before I moved here. I didn't know it until recently."

"What do they want?"

"I'm not sure. Either to shut me up or finish the job."

"Job?"

"My father was one of them. One of the Creeps. When I was four years old . . . "

She didn't want to tell the story again. She wanted to leave it undisturbed in the basement of her head, to let it gather dust and cobwebs until it was safely insulated, forever lost in shadows. Telling Dr. Forrest was difficult enough, but telling someone she'd only known a few days was impossible. She didn't want Walter to think she was crazy.

But Walter wasn't exactly unscarred, either. He'd suffered his own loss and harbored his own sorrows. But he still was holding something back, and she realized faith couldn't be based on logic. She'd either have to trust him or jump from the Jeep and take her chances, and she was out of second chances.

"What happened when you were four?" Walter asked.

She studied his face. His jaw was set in determination, as if he were a man with a mission. He'd already made sacrifices for her. If only she could be brave enough, for once in her life, to let somebody reach her. And maybe help him in return.

Walter stepped on the brakes and the Jeep slid to a stop. "What's wrong?"

Julia put her hands over her face. "You wouldn't understand."

Walter grabbed her wrist and pulled one of her hands away from her face. "Listen here, damn it. I don't know what I got myself into. I just might be heading for a bullet, for all I know. I walked through hell to drag you away from the devil and now we're driving into who knows what. Don't tell me I won't understand."

Julia tried to look away from him, to the rolling hills, pastures dotted with barns, and stretches of woods that surrounded them. But she couldn't escape the magnetism of his anger. She gathered air to speak.

"They took the ring," she managed to say.

"Ring? You make it sound like some kind of elf quest or something."

"They gave me to Satan," Julia said, finally shattering, her tears erupting. But the panic quickly faded, became something new, transmuted into a calm, cleansing anger like lead changed into gold by a philosopher's stone. "My father gave me to the Creeps so they could cut me up as a blood sacrifice and have a party with my body. At least, I *think* that's what happened."

It was Walter's turn to look away.

"My father disappeared that same night," Julia continued, before Walter joined those who judged her a hopeless head case. "The police never solved the case. My injuries went on the record as trauma from trying to climb out my broken bedroom window. I spent the next ten years in foster care, going from home to home, trying to forget anything had ever happened. I got lucky for a teenaged foster kid, was adopted by a kind, well-to-do couple. They died in a car crash when I was nineteen, but left me enough money to finish college and not have to struggle to make ends meet."

Julia was surprised at herself because the story was falling out so easily. It had taken two years to tell Lance Danner that much about her past. Dr. Forrest had elicited such detail in a few months. Walter had drawn it out of her in two minutes, even after she'd promised herself not to tell him.

"Maybe you'd better drive on," Julia said.

Walter nodded, seeming grateful at having something to divert his attention. He put the Jeep in gear and continued down the dirt road. The vehicle smelled of grease and gum, foam spilling from splits in the vinyl seats, the windshield grimy with bug guts.

"I'd met Mitchell Austin during my freshman year, during a summer house party at my adoptive parents' country club," she said, realizing that refined world was totally different from Walter's rural, working life. "I know, boring old coots who play croquet and drink, it sounds more like a prison sentence than a vacation. But Mitchell was—"

She searched for the right word, fumbled over "pleasant," "trustworthy," and then found the most accurate one. "Reliable. He comforted me when my new parents were killed. He kept in touch while I finished college at Memphis State, and then asked me to marry him. That was about the time I started having my . . . little problems."

"Problems," Walter said. Not questioning, but not judging, either.

"Sleeplessness. Irritability. Forgetfulness. Fatigue alternating with periods of manic activity. Then it got worse. I broke out in a cold sweat when I was in cramped quarters or surrounded in a crowd. I'd have episodes of anxiety, when my heart rate doubled and my ears rang and I was afraid I'd never be able to take another breath."

Julia actually laughed. After all the give-and-take, the careful baiting, the strategic questioning of psychotherapy, she'd forgotten what it was like to just *talk* to somebody. Somebody real. She had so little left to lose that she had embraced this different kind of surrender.

"Panic disorder," he said, keeping his eyes fixed on the road. "Sort of like freaking out?"

"How do you know about that?"

"My wife started having that. Before she—"

His wife. Who had walked off the face of the Earth one

night, just as Julia's father had done.

Julia was going to ask about his wife, despite the sadness in his eyes, when Walter whipped the Jeep to the right. A police car was coming up the road toward them, silent but with its bar lights flashing.

"Damn," Walter said. "They've cut us off."

He steered the Jeep into an open hayfield. The Jeep bounced over the rugged terrain, Julia holding on, tools rattling in the back. She looked through the rear window and saw that the police car had stopped at the edge of the road.

"Thank God they don't have four-wheel drive," said Walter.

"Do you think the whole department's in on it?"

He shrugged, heading for a copse of trees on the far side of the meadow. "Doesn't matter. Snead can put out an APB and get his people out in force."

They drove into the trees, and the police car was out of sight. The Jeep climbed a steep grade and, for one stomach-grabbing moment, Julia thought it was going to flip over. Then they crested the hill and reached the stream they had crossed minutes earlier, only now it was wider, the current slower.

"They've probably blocked the highway," Walter said. "But they don't know the back country like I do. Hang on, and say a prayer or two if you know any."

He steered the Jeep into the water and headed upstream. The wheels fought over the damp rocks, but the water was only a few inches deep. "I learned this from Clint Eastwood," Walter said with mock seriousness. "Except he used a horse."

"You'll have to work on your wounded squint."

Walter flashed her a bad-guy glare that actually made her giggle, a crack in the stress that had a manic quality to it.

"Gee, I really must be crazy," Julia said. "Here we are,

being chased by who-knows-how-many Creeps and cops, and you're making goofy faces."

"It's normal to be crazy," Walter said. "If you're not crazy, something's wrong with you."

They drove about two hundred yards up the streambed until they came to a bridge. Walter veered onto the low bank. The highway was clear, and Walter gunned the engine, accelerating toward the east.

"Where are we going now?" Julia asked.

"Well, I think we can take our chances once we get out of Snead's jurisdiction. He might trump up a resisting arrest charge or something, but I'd bet he won't push it too far."

"You don't know how badly he wants me."

"I'm starting to get an idea."

"Snead was a detective in Memphis. He worked my father's disappearance. He was also in charge of several mutilation cases that were never solved. There was evidence of ritual activity."

"You mean Satan murders?"

"You said it, I didn't. A guy I work with at the *Courier-Times* thinks it's happening here, too."

"That body they found in the river last week?"

"Yeah. And what about that girl you said Hartley killed?"

Walter's hands were white from clenching the steering wheel. "There's something I didn't tell you. Something I've never told anybody."

Secrets. The asphalt hummed by underneath the Jeep. A few farmhouses stood off the road, with weathered barns and rusty tractor equipment.

"My wife was pregnant when she disappeared."

"I'm sorry," Julia said, realizing others had guessed the secret. "That must have been awful."

Walter rubbed at his eyes with one of his scarred hands. "I

guess I should be over it by now. It's been seven years."

Julia gently touched his arm. "You can't escape the past. It lives inside you. You just have to let it out and make it harmless."

Jeez, now you're starting to sound like Dr. Forrest yourself.

Walter nodded as if he'd barely heard her. "The bones under your house . . . do you think those were human bones?"

"If Hartley was into ritual sacrifices, he might have done it more than once. I don't know how many times these Creeps think they have to please their idiotic Dark Master."

A pickup truck was in the oncoming lane, driven by a man in a green baseball cap. He waved as he passed. A goat was in the truck bed, chewing on the rope that tethered it to the tailgate. Julia stared at its curved horns, at the ragged beard and black eyes, until the truck went around the bend and out of sight.

"We're out of town limits now," Walter said. "I guess they've probably got my house under surveillance, too. But I bet they don't know that my cousin owns a piece of the mountains over this way."

"Do you think we're safe?"

"I don't know. I'm not even sure what we're running from."

Julia thought that Mitchell would have lied just then. Mitchell would have jutted his chin out and said, "Don't worry about a thing. I'll take care of you."

Yeah, he tried to take care of me, all right. With his fists.

They went three more miles down the winding road and came to a small gas station. Walter parked behind the building so the Jeep couldn't be seen from the road. "I'll put in a call to the sheriff's office," he said. "We should be able to tell pretty fast whether Snead's got to them yet."

"The pay phone's out front," Julia said. "More people know

you here. I'm just a nobody. Let me make the call."

Walter opened his mouth as if about to protest, and then nodded. "If you see anything strange, get back here quick."

"That's what I had in mind," she said, shouldering her purse. She climbed out of the Jeep, her leg muscles sore from tension. She walked stiffly to the pay phone, studying the flaking antique signs nailed to the front of the store. A man in overalls came out, nodded at her, and went back inside. Only one car was parked by the pumps, a big Chevy from the days when gas was cheap.

Julia flipped through the phone book, glad that the pages hadn't been ripped out. She found the listing, pushed coins into the slot, and dialed the number. A woman who sounded like she'd been awakened from a nap answered the phone. "Sheriff's."

"Hello," Julia said. "I'd like . . . I need to report some bones."

"Bones? Did you say 'bones'?"

"Yes, ma'am."

"What kind of bones?" The woman yawned.

"I think they're human."

"This ain't one of them high school kids, is it? 'Cause you're going to go through this big long to-do and then I'm going to go, 'So where is these bones?' and then I bet you're gonna go, 'In the *graveyard*' and then you're gonna laugh like it was the funniest thing that ever was thought up."

"This isn't a joke," Julia said.

"Sure, it ain't. Okay, I'll fall for it. Where is these bones?"

"Under my house."

The woman laughed. "Under your *house*?"

Julia chewed her thumb. The man in coveralls came to the window of the store and stared at her. "I'm Julia Stone and I live at—"

"Stone? You're the *whore Judas Stone?"*

"What?" Invisible fingers clutched at her throat.

"He owns you, whore, so give him what's his."

Julia let the phone drop. She leaned against the phone box, her brain swimming and her chest tight with sudden panic. This was a big one, the inky tidal wave, the ocean roller coaster, the earthquake chasm beneath her feet.

He owns you.

The words raced through her head, in the dispatcher's voice, in the low rumble she'd heard outside her window last night, in the menacing voice on the night of her Black Mass.

Take this whore Judas Stone.

She felt light, displaced, again outside herself, gasping for air.

Run to the Jeep. Get out of here.

Except–

No matter where you go, you take it all with you. It's part of you. And he OWNS you.

She tried to relax, to begin the slow countdown from ten. But she couldn't find ten, she couldn't make balloons of her fingers, she couldn't concentrate enough to let her mind stray. Only one person could help her now. She scrambled through her purse for more coins, thumbed down the receiver switch, and fed the phone as she punched up a well-remembered number.

Dr. Forrest answered before the first ring ended. "Where are you, Julia?"

"It has me."

"Relax, Julia. Breathe."

"I can't." Her heart was going to either explode or collapse upon itself.

"You trust me, don't you?"

Julia leaned against the wall of the store. A car whisked by on the highway, but she didn't bother to see if it was the police. "Why was Snead in your office?"

"You asked him to be there, remember?" Dr. Forrest's tone switched from concerned to chiding. "You called me last night."

"No, *you* called *me*." Even as she said the words, Julia was no longer sure she believed them.

"Julia, you need help. You need *my* help."

"You lied about the pentagram drawing."

"Julia, do you want to be healed?" Dangled like a treat before a scolded puppy.

Julia hammered her fist against the wall of the store. "Healed of what?"

"Healed of resisting. Let it out, let it possess you. He owns you, but you've been such a very bad girl. So very difficult."

Julia's inhalation froze in her lungs. Numb tears filled her eyes.

"Julia, we've all tried to help you. Lance, Lucius, your father, everyone. That's all we've ever wanted, for you to embrace him. For you to become the whore Judas Stone."

Julia couldn't pull the phone from her ear. In that horrible black moment, she realized that Dr. Forrest owned her just as Lance Danner had. All wanting her to remember that night. All making the monster real.

"Julia?"

"Yes." The word hissed from her lips in a slow leak of air and soul.

"Where are you now?"

"I don't know."

"We want to help you. He loves you, Julia."

"Julia?"

That last voice hadn't come from the phone. "Walter?"

He ran to her, grabbed her by the shoulders and turned

her to face him. "Shhh. Just relax. It's okay. They can't get you here."

He took the phone from her hand and placed it on its hook. A door slammed shut. The man in the coveralls peered at them, twisting his mouth sideways. "You folks okay?"

"Breathe," Walter whispered. He called to the man, "She's fine. Just had a dizzy spell."

The man nodded as if he didn't believe them and went back inside.

"Listen, Julia." Walter's face was so close she could feel his breath, could see the hundreds of flecks of brown and green and gold in his eyes. "You're standing on the clouds, the sun is out, you're laughing and playing. There's a soft, golden light shimmering in the sky. You don't have to be troubled. Open your heart and–"

"That man—he's probably calling the cops. He's in on it. He's one of them."

"Shhh. Look way off, where the mountains meet the sky. Up there where the clouds are. Be a mountain. Even the devil can't break a mountain."

Julia looked at the thick folded clouds that hung over the ridge, and the strong and timeless slopes that fell away into a river valley. *They can't break a mountain.* Silly, maybe, but it worked. Maybe Walter sensed she wasn't ready for a leap of faith, and maybe his sales pitch for Jesus was waiting in the wings, but for now he was an anchor, as solid as his metaphorical mountain.

When she could finally breathe again, Walter led her around the corner of the store and helped her into the Jeep before climbing into the driver's seat.

"He owns me," Julia said.

"Satan doesn't own you." Walter jammed the Jeep into gear and sped onto the highway, heading for the soft blue mountains ahead. "Not while I'm still alive."

As they roared away too slowly to lose the past, Julia wondered if, no matter the route they took, Satan was already the master of all her possible futures.

CHAPTER TWENTY-SIX

The Jeep came to a stop in front of a weathered cabin. The cabin's two small windows were separated by a gray door. A stone chimney leaned precariously from one end of the structure. The cedar shake roof was covered with moss, and the walls were made of thick, hand-hewn logs.

The climb into the mountains had been a blur. All Julia remembered was the vehicle bouncing and roaring as Walter climbed into the hills, a mad kaleidoscope of autumn leaves overhead, and Walter's occasionally reaching out to touch her arm. She had imagined hearing sirens and once thought she had seen Snead running between the trees alongside the old logging road.

Julia looked out of the Jeep at the forest that surrounded the cabin. The dirt track dwindled to a footpath on the ridge behind the cabin. The surrounding mountains were lost in the mist, adding to Julia's disorientation. The air had grown heavier with an imminent storm.

"What do you think?" Walter asked.

"Where are we?"

"Ten miles past nowhere, at our hunting cabin. Been the family getaway for three generations. I don't reckon our creepy friends will be able to find us here, at least not before we figure out our next move."

"They'd better not follow us," Julia said. "It looks like we've run out of road."

"That just means we're that much harder to find," Walter said. He got out of the Jeep and came around to the passenger side. Julia was already out of the door before he reached her.

She leaned against the Jeep until she was reasonably sure she'd regained her balance. The fresh pine-and-loam aroma of the woods cleared her head.

"I'm sorry to drag you into this mess," Julia said.

"I was in this mess long before you came to town."

"I don't have anything but my purse," she said. "I don't know if I can be much help snaring rabbits or whatever you mountain men do for food."

Walter laughed softly, as if the surrounding forest relaxed him. "If we get that bad off, there's a couple of fishing poles inside. Got a few days' worth of canned goods, too, and a backpack of stuff in the Jeep. Compared to running from the devil, starving to death is the least of our problems."

Walter unlocked the door and it swung inward with a groan of hinges. He stepped into the dark cabin while Julia studied the towering hardwoods. Walter emerged after half a minute. "It's safe," he said, glancing at the oppressive sky. "Come on in."

Julia went past him into the cabin. The interior was chilly and steeped in old woodsmoke, and her eyes took a moment adjusting to the darkness. She made out a small table in the center of the room, a counter with a basin in the corner, and a small loft along one wall that she assumed contained the bed. Walter came in with an armload of firewood and soon had a blaze roaring in the fireplace.

Julia knelt on the floor before the fire, grateful for the warmth. The flicker of flames threw jagged shadows up the walls, but the close quarters were comforting instead of threatening. The sky outside the windows was now charcoal streaked with silver, and the first drops of rain fell on the shake roof.

"We'd better get the stuff out of the Jeep," Walter said.

He'd said "we." He didn't expect her to sit there like a

helpless child. They were in this mess together. Together, such a strange word. After all those years with Mitchell, she'd never felt "together" with him.

Thunder rumbled across the mountains as they waited in the door. "If one of us gets struck by lightning, the other gets all the food," Walter said.

The static electricity in the air revived Julia. "Let me see what you've got before I get my hopes up."

They dashed to the Jeep, and Julia climbed in the front while Walter wrestled with the zipper at the rear of the canvas top. She passed him a rolled-up sleeping bag and slung his backpack over her shoulders. The rain fell harder as they ran back to the cabin, and they were both soaked by the time they stood panting before the fire.

Walter pulled some cans from the backpack. "Sardines or Vienna sausages?"

"You don't have any caviar in there, do you?"

"Nope." He flashed his uneven smile. "Don't have any breath mints, either. I didn't expect to have anybody to please on my next trip up here."

"I'm not hard to please." Julia peeled off her sweater, hung it from the log mantel, and checked the cell phone. Still no signal.

Walter pulled a small bundle of clothes from the backpack. "Here," he said, tossing the clothes to Julia. "You don't want to be catching a cold. Makes it harder to run from devil worshippers."

Julia stared at him.

"Don't worry. I won't peek," he said. "I'm no gentleman, but I'm a man."

Julia went to the corner beneath the loft and kept her back turned as she took off her shoes and changed clothes. She looked down at the scars on her belly and shivered at more than just the chill. Walter's blue jeans and red flannel shirt were too large for her, but the dry fabric felt good against her skin and she gleaned a strange comfort from wearing his clothes. She went back to the hearth with her wet clothes in her arms.

"Okay, you can look now," she said.

Walter kept his attention focused on opening the cans. The smell of the food mixed with the smoke. "I didn't lie," he said. "That creep really was climbing out of your window."

"I know. I think my fiancé–I mean, my ex-fiancé–"

Walter finally looked at her, and his gaze was hungry. "You don't have to be alone. You can let somebody ride shotgun once in a while."

She blushed, but hoped it was hidden by the firelight. "I think Mitchell hired him to harass me and play tricks to make me think I was going nuts. He thought I'd have to cave in and then he could control me. He seemed obsessed with my money, but I don't have any."

"You're starting to sound as paranoid as me."

"It ain't paranoia if they really are out to get you."

Julia spread her wet clothes out on the stone hearth, and then suffered a sudden attack of shyness as she draped her bra and panties on the mantel. She scolded herself and finished the job. No need to keep secrets anymore. Secrets had never done her any good.

Walter handed her the sardines. Julia had rarely eaten sardines and had always been repulsed by the smell. Now, though, her hunger was stronger than her distaste. She pulled one of the small oily fish out of the can with her fingers and ate it like a seal would, her head tilted back.

"Your turn not to look," Walter said, pulling another change of clothes from the backpack. "Can I trust *you?*"

Julia licked the fishy taste from her lips. Not too bad,

though a bit overpowering. "My therapist said not to trust anybody."

"Therapist? What can a therapist tell you that you don't already know? All they do is pass their own problems onto you, instead of the other way around."

Julia looked at him. "That's a relief. You really *are* crazier than I am."

"And from that phone call you told me about, your Dr. Forrest is crazier than both of us put together. Now, keep your back turned."

"I'm no gentleman, either," she said.

Walter went to the corner and changed clothes while Julia ate another sardine and wondered whether or not she was considering peeking. She couldn't decide, and she was on her fourth sardine when she realized that nearly a minute had passed without her thinking of Mitchell, Snead, or Dr. Forrest.

Or of her father.

Walter joined her before the fire and ate the sausages. They then had an apple each, passing a canteen of water back and forth while they finished the makeshift dinner. Julia put a large oak log on the fire and watched sparks fly up the chimney. The rain had held steady, and darkness settled heavily on the mountaintop.

Julia stared into the deep red embers and wondered if that was what hell looked like. "Tell me about your wife."

The rattle of rain on the roof filled the pause. Walter said, "Her name was Rita Faye. We were married right out of high school. We knew we'd most likely be poor all our lives, but we had a little bit of land and figured other people had it a lot worse. She loved to keep up flowers. I always thought dirt ought to be used for vegetables, but I sure do miss the smell of those flowers now."

Walter leaned against the fireplace and continued in a

barely audible voice. "I can picture her now, bent over her marigolds and daffodils, her hair tied back in a ponytail, the sun catching on it and making it shine. She was five months' pregnant when she disappeared."

"I'm sorry," Julia said. "I shouldn't have brought it up."

"No. It's in the past. And the past can't hurt you none unless you let it."

"It's hard to believe she just got up in the middle of the night and walked off. My father disappeared like that, too."

"In the middle of the night?"

Julia took a smoky breath. "I think he was a Satan worshipper." Somehow, the accusation sounded even more unbelievable when said out loud, beyond the safe madness of Dr. Forrest's office.

"Satan. Not many believe in him these days."

Julia crossed her arms. Walter's face was soft and kind in the firelight, with a touch of sadness in the shadows of his eyes. She could trust him. She was consumed by a sudden desperation to completely trust somebody, after the betrayals of Mitchell and Dr. Forrest.

Maybe her borderline personality disorder drove her to leech sympathy out of everyone she met, a soul vampire who needed constant affirmation. Or maybe she had always been alone, unconnected, adrift in a world where even the past wasn't reliable. She had no tether, no foundation, and Walter seemed as solid as the Appalachian granite.

Her face was hot from the fire. "He was one of them. A member of their coven. He let them take me across the field behind our house. They carried me into the barn. They were all in robes, and there was smoke in the air, and somebody had cut off a goat's head and impaled it on a stake. The bad people starting chanting, and they held me down while the man with the ring cut my stomach—"

Another long silence. "And you were just a child," Walter said softly. "Like the girl Hartley killed."

She nodded. She couldn't look at him. She hated her father, hated the Creeps, not just for the pain, but for the memories they had shackled her with. For the evil, poisonous seeds they had planted in her mind. She hated them for teaching her to hate. "The one who held the knife . . . I think it was my father. That was the night he disappeared."

"Why do you think it was your father?"

"Dr. Forrest told me."

"The shrink that pretty much said you were the bride of Satan?"

Julia gave a bitter laugh. "I know it sounds crazy. But the man with the knife wore a skull ring, with two rubies set in the eyes. I found the ring in my father's house when I went back to Memphis."

"That's the ring you were talking about."

"Someone took it from my purse."

"Does anybody know you had it?"

The bands of red and orange heat alternated in the glowing embers, hypnotic and ethereal. The rhythm of the rain had made her drowsy. She couldn't think clearly. "No. But I gave Dr. Forrest a pentagram drawing that somebody had left in my closet. Whoever it was had written 'Hello Jooolia' on it, misspelling Julia with three O's in the middle. Exactly the way my father did when he was teasing me."

"So she knew someone had been in your house. Did you tell her about the ring?" Walter had moved closer, though he might have just shifted to be nearer the fire.

"I don't think so." She glanced at him. The light was golden on his face.

"Don't you remember what you told her?"

Julia shook her head. "It's not that simple. You don't know

what it's like to have the past all screwed up, so that you can't tell who to hate or who to trust or just who you're even supposed to be."

Walter put his hand on her shoulder and stroked her wet hair. "One thing's been bothering me. You say you were part of a Satanic ritual when you were four. Well, if Snead was in on it, and knows that you're starting to remember, why didn't he just *kill* you? Why go to the trouble of all these tricks? The clock and the pentagram drawing and the ring and all that."

Julia put her hands over her ears. Panic crept up in the form of shadows in the cabin's corners, all dark and sharp like the fingers of the past. She didn't want to fold up again, not in front of Walter. She bit her lip hard enough to hurt.

"Hey, are you okay?" Walter asked.

Walter had lost somebody he loved, and he hadn't been driven into the dark cellars of his own head. He got on with his life, hid his scars, and kept on breathing. He clung to his faith, however simplistic she thought it. Whatever was going on between him and God, it seemed to be working. And what did she have?

She stood and paced the narrow room. Tears welled in her eyes, making her ashamed. She wasn't the only one who had suffered in this world. "I don't want be crazy."

Walter moved quickly to her side. He cupped her chin in his hand and forced her to look at him. "Snead's real. Hartley's real. It's not your imagination. I don't know what they want from you, but I'm betting it's no good. And this Dr. Forrest— how long have you been going to her?"

"Since I moved here."

"And what good has she done?"

"Well, at first we were making progress. She brought me out of my denial. She made me see . . . what really happened way back then." Julia closed her eyes to escape the intensity of

Walter's gaze.

"She told you your father gave you away as a sacrifice to Satan. Sounds to me like she did you one hell of a favor."

Julia turned away from his sarcasm and sat with her back to the fire. "You can't run from the past."

"Who says? What's so great about the past, anyway? Do we have to keep rubbing our faces in the stuff we ought to forget?"

Julia said nothing. She watched the shadows dancing in the firelight along the ceiling. The rain had eased to a slow but steady downfall. If only the rain would wash the whole world away.

Walter went to one of the small windows and peered out. "I'm sorry," he said, subdued. "We shouldn't be arguing. We're supposed to be on the same side."

Maybe Walter was right. Did knowing the truth make the wounds heal, or only keep them fresh? Yet even after Dr. Forrest's bizarre behavior, Julia wondered how she'd face her problems without her therapist's help.

"Look," Walter said, sitting down beside her. He fumbled in the backpack and took out the baseball cards that had been lying on her coffee table. "I brought these. I wasn't thinking too clearly, or I'd have grabbed something useful. I got kind of scared when I saw Hartley snooping around."

Julia took the cards and flipped through them. The ludicrousness of their situation struck her like a cold slap. Holed up in a tiny cabin in the woods, not knowing whom to trust, unable even to call the cops because the cops were Creeps. Nothing to do but wait for the boogeyman to come claim her. Unless she went insane first.

She moved aside so Walter could put more wood on the fire. Exhaustion hit her all at once, and she yawned.

"Go on up in the loft," Walter said. "Might as well get some sleep."

Julia wondered if he would try and join her in the tiny loft. She didn't want to deal with any more emotional entanglement than they had already been thrown into. Still, it would be nice to have someone close by, just in case the bad dreams and panic came in the night. And maybe, just maybe, she could summon up some small comfort and warmth to offer Walter. "What about you?"

"I'm going to stay up a while," he said. He went to an old cedar chest in the corner and took out some quilts. He shook them and tossed them up on the loft. "I'm pretty sure they wouldn't be able to follow us in the dark and the rain, but I'm not too sleepy, anyway. I'll just keep the fire going for a while. Got my sleeping bag here if I need it."

Julia moved wearily to the ladder and climbed as if someone else were controlling her tired muscles. The quilts were spread over what felt like a thin foam pad at the top of the loft. The bedding smelled faintly of smoke and leaves. Julia rolled onto the quilts and bundled herself up.

She inched to the edge of the loft and looked down at Walter. He was turning their wet clothes over so they could finish drying. His hands were oddly gentle with her clothes. When he finished, he returned to his vigil at the hearth and opened his Bible.

"Walter?" she murmured.

"Yeah?"

"Thanks. For everything."

He looked up at the loft. "It ain't nothing. Sweet dreams."

She recalled the image of the meadow that Walter had helped her summon when she panicked at the gas station phone. She watched the shimmering clouds floating around in her imagination, and her breathing fell into a slow, even rhythm. Once, she saw the barn of her childhood rise in the midst of the meadow, but she was able to drive that horror from her visions.

I am a mountain. They can't break me.

And behind the mountain was a face, swirling in mists and clouds. She tried to focus, to believe, and though its features were veiled, she sensed a gentle smile.

Sleep soon drifted over her like a thick fog.

A noise awoke her in the night, the creak of wood. She opened her eyes to utter darkness. Her feet were cold. Something was touching her, tugging the quilts from her body.

Some*one* was touching her.

She tried to sit up, but her arms were pinned. Then the thing was on top of her, crushing her breath from her lungs. She couldn't even cry out. Two glowing red specks appeared in the darkness inches from her face, and the smell of rotten eggs and matches flooded her nostrils. The specks grew brighter, and in their glow she could see the face that wore those impossible eyes.

The skull ring.

The skull had taken flesh and now was coming to get her for good. She wrestled an arm free and clawed at the eyes. Her fingernails sank into meat and she ripped. The face came away in her hands, like a rubber mask, but still the eyes blazed.

Beneath that face was her father's, unshaven, cruel, leering, the way Dr. Forrest had made her remember him. His tongue snaked in and out between rotted teeth. A goatish scrap of beard sprouted from his chin, and his hot breath slavered across her cheeks. She raked her hand again and grabbed the cloth of his hood.

She yanked the cloth away and this time it was Mitchell who was on top of her, his hands groping and pinching, his expression simultaneously desirous and wicked. He laughed at her struggles, smug in his power. She closed her eyes against the intensity of his red stare and slashed at his face.

More skin and muscle came away, and a voice at her ear said, "He owns you, whore," and it was Snead's voice, a voice she knew from 23 years ago.

Snead. The man in the hood. The monster with the knife.

Julia opened her eyes to look at him, but now it was Walter who was above her, his cheeks burning with hate, saliva leaking from between his sharp teeth, the hands gripping her now even more powerful and cruel, bruising, twisting, taking what he wanted. The face shimmered, the features bulged and became the decapitated goat's head of her childhood.

"You're mine, Judas bitch. And I take what is mine."

She screamed as the sinister animal face pressed close and flickered its tongue across her lips. Its foul breath poured into her, burning her from the inside, arousing agony in her scars, awakening every bad memory and switching on the circuits so that pain spasmed through her body. She moaned in disgust as the creature's feverish flesh pressed against her.

"Julia?"

Walter's voice, from somewhere behind the goat-thing.

But Walter was *in* this thing, wasn't he? Part of it. All of them the devil.

Fingers clutched her ankle, shaking her. She kicked and clawed blindly.

"Hey!" he called again.

She opened her eyes. No darkness, no twin red specks, no goat-creature. The room was suffused with orange light, the fire down to embers.

Walter stood on the ladder, looking at her. "You okay? You were yelling out in your sleep."

She tried to blink away the nightmare. But her nostrils held the memory of the hellish stench and her flesh was warm from the imagined assault. "Are you one of them, Walter?"

"Shhh. You were having a bad dream, that's all."

"Tell me you're not one of them." She pulled the blankets to her chin.

"No, I'm one of *us*." He patted her leg. "You're safe here. They won't get you."

"I'm scared." She felt almost as helpless and lost as she had felt as a four-year-old.

The ladder creaked, and then his body lay alongside hers. "It's going to be just fine," he whispered.

His arms went around her. She accepted the embrace, snug in the blankets, and drifted back to sleep. This time, no Creeps stalked her dreams.

CHAPTER TWENTY-SEVEN

The morning light trickled through the small windows, indicated the storm had passed. Julia left Walter sleeping in the loft and kindled another fire. She rummaged in Walter's backpack, found some tissue, and went outside to relieve herself. The sky was clear, and Julia's breath made a mist in front of her face.

The view was spectacular. The cabin stood in the clearing between two stands of hardwood, and a sheer rock cliff rose behind the trees. The ridge was the tallest point for miles. The blue mountaintops rolled out in the distance like the waves of a gentle sea. The clean, brisk breeze brought Julia fully awake, and she welcomed the forest smells.

Walter was right. The Creeps couldn't get her here. This was the final outpost, a majestic castle, a place where trouble and danger had no business. The woods weren't threatening. Instead, they formed walls that kept enemies away. Being out under the big sky was like being paroled from the cramped prison of her head.

She went among the trees into the hush of forest. A gray squirrel skittered along the treetops, gathering its winter stores. As she squatted behind an oak, she thought of the night before. Walter had come to her rescue yet again, her very own knight in shining armor. Just like in the bedtime stories her daddy had told her—

"And what else did Daddy do, there in your bed?" came Dr. Forrest's voice, as if from nowhere.

She stood, pulled up the baggy jeans she had borrowed from Walter, and hurried back toward the cabin, afraid more voices would slip from the shadows beneath the oak and hickory. The sun was like the bloodied yolk of an egg over the eastern horizon. A few wisps of pale clouds were all that remained of the storm. Julia looked down the old logging road to make sure no one was approaching, and then went back inside the cabin.

Walter was up, his clothes rumpled, his chin and cheeks bristled by faint stubble. "Morning," he called cheerfully, though his voice cracked from sleep.

"Hi. Storm's over."

"I don't know if that's a good thing." Walter rattled around in a corner cabinet and pulled out a dented tin coffee pot. "Makes it easier for them to find us. If they're even bothering to look."

"What do you mean?"

"I'll tell you when I get back."

Julia stacked some logs on the fire and went outside to gather another armload from the woodpile. Walter came back from the woods with the coffee pot. He hoisted it, and some water sloshed out. "There's a spring around back. The purest water you've ever tasted."

"And we're going to mess it up by turning it into coffee?"

Walter smiled, the sun on his face and his tousled hair making him look young. "Sounds like an improvement to me."

A soft rhythmic sound filled the air, rapidly becoming louder, beating at the air between the mountains. Walter dropped the coffee pot and raced to the Jeep. The engine started and he backed the Jeep under a canopy of spruce. Julia finally recognized the sound, and went inside the cabin as the whir grew louder.

From the window she watched the helicopter cross to the west. The Creeps couldn't have that much influence, could they? What did they want from her so badly that they were dragging out all their resources? And if she tried to dismiss her paranoia, right there was Walter, ducking under the trees and staring up at the sky.

When the whir of the blades subsided, they looked at each other.

"Do you think it was them?" Julia asked.

He pointed at the chimney. "They would have seen the smoke. If it was them, they'd already be back."

He gathered the coffee pot and returned to the spring. Julia went inside, gathered her dry clothes from the hearth, and changed quickly before Walter returned. He didn't remark on her change of clothes, nor on having slept with her. Julia realized it was the first time she'd ever slept with a man without having sex. But then again, Mitchell was the only other man to ever share her bed.

Quit comparing him to Mitchell. They're not even on the same playing field.

He poured some coffee grounds into a metal sieve and placed the sieve in the pot. Then he hung the pot over the fire from a metal hook. "What's so funny?"

"Just figuring out which way I'm going crazy this time."

"I told you, you're not crazy. You're miles from civilization, with all the time in the world, with a nice guy who makes a mean cup of coffee. What's the downside?"

"Uh, you forgot the part where Satan worshippers want to claim my immortal soul."

"Oh, yeah. I figured this was too good to be true."

Walter brought some chipped ceramic mugs from the cupboard as the smell of coffee slowly filled the cabin. Julia sat by the fire and watched Walter.

"What are we going to do now?" she asked.

"Wait, I reckon."

"For them to find us?"

"We ought to just let things die down a little."

"I wonder what's happening back at my house."

"Depends on what they were after. Maybe all they want is you."

"I still can't understand why."

"Maybe they don't like to lose. Maybe they feel like they have to finish the job or their Big Bad Boogeyman will get upset." Walter sat beside her and placed the mugs on the hearth. He drew a couple of granola bars from the backpack and passed one to Julia.

"This doesn't fit the image of the rough-and-ready mountain man's breakfast," Julia said.

"Well, I hate to say it, but I ain't much of a mountain man. I don't even like hunting. My dad used to take me up here and make me stumble through the woods after him with a gun, but I never could stand to shoot anything."

"How long do we stay here?" Julia asked.

Walter shrugged. "A day or two. I don't know."

She leaned forward and touched his knee. "Do you think Hartley had anything to do with your wife's disappearance?"

He stared into the fire with a wounded expression. "Sometimes I'm scared that she was one of them. Then I think I'm crazy to even think that. But then you hear people talking about Satan worshippers and what they do to fetuses and babies and kids . . . and she changed after she became pregnant. She became faraway, panicky, suspicious of everybody."

Julia scooted next to him and wrapped her arms around him, feeling the hard muscles underneath his shirt. She squeezed as tightly as she could and his head leaned against her shoulder.

"Shh," she whispered. "Just let it go. Don't let them win. Don't let *him* win."

"Him?"

"Satan." Walter tensed under her embrace, but she continued. "A lot of Christians don't think he's real, that he's some superstitious relic. Call it evil, bad karma, whatever. The name doesn't matter. What matters is that we don't let darkness eat us alive, from the inside out."

She looked past him, lost in the warmth of his body. Here she was, playing analyst when her own head was cluttered. It was a miracle she hadn't gone over the edge months ago. She pictured Dr. Forrest's strangely earnest face, the woman unbuttoning her shirt to show the pentagram etched in her belly.

"You're not alone, Julia," Dr. Forrest had said.

She shuddered with the memory. How many women were out there thinking they were the brides of Satan? Were most of them willing, like Dr. Forrest, or were they like Julia, lost and scared and screaming as the panic and doubt ate them away from the inside out? Were Satanic sacrifices born or were they made?

"You're not alone, Judas," Walter said.

Julia jerked away from him, stood and fled to the door. *"What did you say?"*

Walter blinked, confused. "I didn't say anything."

"Yes, you did. You said 'You're not alone, Judas.'"

"What the hell?" His confusion turned to anger.

She backed away another step, hand reaching for the door latch. "It was *you.* You took the ring, didn't you? You're the one who planted the pentagram drawing with 'Hello Jooolia' on it. And you messed with the clock. You had a *key.* An inside job."

Walter stood and held out his hands. "I don't know what you're talking about. Don't flip out on me now, Julia. *Please.*"

His wounded expression almost convinced her. Almost.

Julia flung open the door and ran into the cold morning, through the trees and away from the cabin. She ran blindly, branches clawing at her face. She glanced back and saw Walter erupt from the cabin door, chasing her.

"Jooolia," he called, but she didn't slow. Her heart hammered in her ears. Thoughts spilled out in jagged counterpoint to the rhythm of her legs.

Walter. HE was the Creep. One of THEM, Satan's sick little servants. He probably killed his wife himself and ripped out his unborn son as a token to his master.

And stupid, gullible Julia Stone had fallen right in with him, had opened herself up and trusted him on the flimsiest of reasoning. She was nothing but the perfect victim, always had been and always would be. She might as well just drop to the ground and wait for Satan to come and do whatever he did with his brides, serve whatever his dark needs were.

Her lungs burned with the coldness of the air. She headed down a slope between trees, slipped on some leaves and fell. She scrambled to her feet. She reached an outcropping of rocks and slithered between two slabs of granite. While resting, she strained her ears to listen for Walter, but all she could hear was her own frantic, ragged breath.

Giant oaks and maples surrounded her, their gnarled branches reaching across the sky. The mountains were obscured, all signs of civilization lost in leaves and bark and laurel. This was the world of nature, the one that Satan ruled. He ruled the world of human nature, as well. He owned Julia. He owned them all.

Surrender. Lie down. Let him have you.

"He owns you, Julia," came Dr. Forrest's voice.

Then, Snead: "Time for you to become the whore Judas Stone."

Walter: "You're not alone, Judas."

She clamped her hands over her ears but couldn't squeeze the voices from her brain. She staggered from the rocks, the sun crazy through the treetops, the mist of her breath making sinister shapes before her face. Satan owned it *all*.

She closed her eyes, took a few more shambling steps, and fell again. The panic rose like fingers from black graves, twisting, clawing, impatient. When the fingers–*his* fingers–touched her, she couldn't even summon the strength to slap at them. They clutched her, tugged possessively.

"Julia," it said.

Something stirred in the dark corners of her mad house. That voice. Not Walter, not Snead, not Dr. Forrest. Not Satan.

Mitchell?

"Are you okay?"

Her eyes snapped open, and it *was* Mitchell. His tie was askew, hair mussed, but he was Mitchell Austin, Attorney-at-Law, former fiancé and would-be rapist. The devil made the flesh.

"Mitchell," was all she could gasp.

"I saw him chasing you," he said. "Come on, get up. He'll see us."

He pulled her to her feet. Julia wobbled and leaned against a tree. "How . . . how did you find me?"

"Deed records." Mitchell came to her, and she couldn't will her legs into motion. He took her arm and led her toward a thick stand of laurels. "The cops told me somebody named Triplett had kidnapped you. They didn't have any leads, but we both know cops aren't too bright. The cabin was on the family property tax listing."

Julia let Mitchell pull her into the rhododendron tangles. They were hidden by the thick, waxy leaves. "Now we just have to wait for the cops to show up," he said.

"Did you tell them where we were?"

"I wanted to see you first. Maybe some dumb part of me wanted to be a hero, hoping that you'd forgive me for what I . . . " His voice fell, losing all its courtroom authority. "For what I almost did."

"*Did you tell them?*"

He nodded. "I called from my cell in town. I left my car down on the road and hiked up."

"No," she whispered.

"Look, I came to Elkwood to make things right. I'm sorry. I was stupid, I lost my temper, I guess I was afraid I was going to lose you."

"So you tried to *rape* me?"

Mitchell's eyes shifted from side to side as if he were searching through some memorized law journals for a case to cite. He looked out of place in his power suit, huddled in the middle of the forest, miles from a golf club or stock broker. The wool of his jacket was frayed where branches had picked at the fabric. "I don't blame you for hating me. But it's your fault."

"Screw you, Mitchell." She stood in the thicket, anger reviving her strength. "Screw you and the goat you rode in on. You can't save me."

She started from the laurel, but Mitchell grabbed at her. "No," he said. "I need you."

She jerked her arm free.

"You're *mine*," he said.

"Like hell."

"*You're not going to walk away from me, whore.*" He threw himself at her, knocking her to the ground. They struggled on the frosty leaves.

"She walks wherever she damn well pleases," Walter said. He emerged from behind a stand of white pines. "She makes up her own mind. And you or nobody else is going to stop her."

Julia's eyes met Walter's, and she wasn't sure whether it was fire or madness in them. Mitchell let her go and stood up, brushing the leaves from his clothes.

"So you're the Creep," Mitchell said. He was a couple of inches taller than Walter, but Walter approached him steadily, fists clenched.

"Hey, I'm not the one beating up a woman."

"And I'm not a lunatic wife-killer."

"Don't believe everything you hear. She came with me because she wanted to. Ain't that right, Julia?"

Julia looked from one to the other, searching for the devil in each.

"You might as well give up," Mitchell said. "The police will be here soon."

Walter glanced at Julia. She couldn't meet his intense gaze. He took a step toward Mitchell.

"Stay back," Mitchell said, fumbling inside his jacket. He brought out a pistol, and the sun gleamed off its menacing barrel.

Walter's mouth fell open as he stared at the pistol. He froze but didn't raise his hands. Julia didn't know much about guns, only what she'd seen in cop movies. This pistol looked like an automatic because it didn't have a revolver chamber. But she knew that a gun fired bullets, and Mitchell was crazy or possessed, and that made a bad combination.

"Come here, Julia," Mitchell said. "If you'd have let me buy you a gun like I wanted, this loser might not have kidnapped you in the first place."

Julia glanced at Walter, and then took a step toward Mitchell.

"It wasn't me, Julia," Walter said. "You've got to believe me."

"What's he talking about?" Mitchell asked, holding the gun steady as if he were accustomed to using it.

Julia shook her head. She couldn't fight anymore. She would go back with Mitchell, he would take care of her until the police came, Walter would be arrested, and everybody would live happily ever after.

"He didn't kidnap me," she said.

Mitchell's gun hand quavered. "Julia, you're confused," Mitchell said. "Your . . . *problems* are probably aggravated by the trauma. You can't trust what you think right now."

"I don't know what I think," she said.

"I do care about you."

"No," she said. "You just don't want to lose me. No matter what, Mitchell Austin can't stand to lose."

Mitchell's jaw muscles clenched and he squeezed the grip of the pistol so tightly his hand shook. Walter kept his eyes fixed on Mitchell's face.

"Don't be stupid, Julia," Mitchell said, as if she were a disobedient dog or a wayward child. "Look at all I can do for you. You know I can. Money talks, and when we get back to Memphis and away from Snead and his sickos, we're going to be babbling like idiots. You don't know the half of it. If you're in trouble, we can buy your way out of it."

"I'm scared," the four-year-old inside her said. But she couldn't rescue that lost little girl. She was a woman now, new and improved and ready to battle for her soul.

Mitchell's eyes darkened. He raised the gun to chest level, still pointing it at Walter. "You want to stay out here with this redneck?"

This is it, decision time. The safe and insane world of the past, Mitchell's world, where she could stay in her dark shell forever? Or an unknown and perhaps equally mad freedom with Walter and his bloody past? The devil you know or the devil you don't?

Walter stood his ground, eyes fixed on the gun.

Mitchell spoke to Walter now. "So, you're trying to steal her from me, huh? And the money. I ought to put a few holes in your ugly face. Hell, they wouldn't convict. I know a good lawyer."

He laughed, a cruel, maniacal sound that was out of place in the still forest. The panic swarmed up the base of Julia's spine, wriggling like a bucket of black worms. Walter was going to die, and she might be next. No telling what Mitchell was capable of. His face twisted into a sinister mask, eyes bright with a secret madness.

"I'm not one of them," Walter said to Julia.

"I don't believe you," Julia said to Walter. She kept the lie locked on her face, hoping her eyes didn't betray her. She must have succeeded, judging from Walter's look of hurt shock.

She moved close to Mitchell, rested her hand on his arm. "You can take care of me," she said. "You can save me."

Mitchell's lips curled into a sneer of triumph. She felt him relax, and then chopped down on his wrist with all her strength, fueled by the memory of his assault in Memphis. Three loud reports ripped through the forest, and she heard Walter's shout over the roar in her ears as gunpowder smoke burnt her nostrils. Her rage burst forth like the waters behind a storm-swollen dam, and she chopped again. The pistol spun from Mitchell's hand and landed on the carpet of leaves.

"Bitch," Mitchell grunted, backhanding her across the face. He stooped for the gun, but Julia dug her fingers into his sleeve. Walter dove to the ground, clawed among the leaves, and came up with the pistol. Mitchell flung Julia away and stared at Walter.

"You going to shoot, redneck?" Mitchell smiled, all white teeth and wickedness. "I don't think you have the balls for it."

Julia rubbed her stinging cheek. "You sent me to Elkwood, didn't you?"

Mitchell frowned at her, the slightest hesitation flashing across his eyes. "You're crazy."

"Not as crazy as you wanted me to be," she said. "You and Dr. Danner set me up with Dr. Forrest. You wanted me to move here. You wanted her to make me so helpless that I'd fall into your arms and stay there forever."

Mitchell looked at Walter. "Can't you see how loopy she is?"

"But there was one thing you didn't count on," she continued, glad that she wasn't the one holding the pistol. She might have shot him. "Dr. Danner had his own agenda. He was doing his part to be a good little member of the Brotherhood."

"Brotherhood?" Mitchell looked confused. But all lawyers were actors on some level.

"Satan worshippers," Julia said, pleased to see Mitchell's face go pale.

He looked at Walter and shook his head. "She's crazy. Now she's babbling about Satan. She really fell for her doctor's shrink job."

Walter held the pistol and said nothing.

"You know Snead, don't you?" Julia said. "You knew him in Memphis. I wouldn't be surprised if you helped him get a job here so that he could keep an eye on me."

Mitchell took a step toward the pistol, but Walter said, "I wouldn't if I were you. Semiautomatic .45 with three shots gone still leaves four in the clip."

"Did you know Snead was in Satan's little circle, Mitch?" Julia smiled as Mitchell squirmed from the sarcastic nickname. "Maybe you're just playing Satanist. The truth is that I can't see you bowing down to anybody or anything. You'd never worship anything besides yourself."

"I'm in it for the money, just like them," Mitchell said. "Why else would anybody want to marry you?"

"Money? I don't have any."

"What do we do with him?" Walter asked Julia.

"I just want him out of my sight," she answered wearily. "Out of my life."

Walter motioned with the gun down the forest slope. "You heard her. Get out of here. And I wouldn't plan on coming back, or this here redneck might pull a 'Deliverance' on you." He gave a leering wink that would have made Julia laugh under other circumstances.

Mitchell's eyes widened, unable to tell if Walter were joking or not. He backed away a few steps, turned, and started down the slope. His leather shoes kicked at the leaves, his shoulders slumped. When he was nearly out of sight, near a gathering of scrub hemlocks, he looked back.

"You know that guy that lives next to you?" he called through cupped hands. "I paid him to play with your mind."

Mitchell took a few more steps, turned, and shouted again. "He mailed me a pair of your panties. Think about that the next time you're laid out on some shrink's couch. Or taking it on the devil's altar."

He ducked behind the hemlocks and the sound of his running footfalls soon faded.

"Your panties?" Walter said.

"He's a Creep," she said, crossing her arms and hugging herself. "To think that I ever let him touch me."

"Sorry," he said.

"Don't be. I'm just glad to be rid of him."

"What did he mean by 'I'm in it for the money'? I thought he was rich."

Julia frowned. "Who knows, with Mitchell?"

"You reckon he's in on this Snead deal?"

She shook her head. "He just wanted me as his little toy. Snead wants me for Satan, and I don't believe Satan likes to share."

"They probably heard the shots. They'll be coming soon." Walter flipped on the gun's safety and looked back up the hill in the direction of the cabin.

Julia just wanted to sag down to the forest floor, to join the rotted loam beneath the leaves, to decay in peace. She was tired of being owned. She had been owned by therapists, owned by Mitchell, owned by the memories of something that may or may not have happened when she was four years old.

And now Satan wanted her, or at least his misguided minions did. But she'd be damned if she was going to surrender now, not when she was on the verge of freedom. And she was no longer alone. She wasn't locked inside the house of her head anymore. She could *trust*.

She glanced at the sky but the clouds were still silent. But maybe that was the definition of faith, believing even when there was no evidence.

"Let it come, God," she said. "I'm not afraid anymore."

As they climbed the slope, Julia wished she could tap Walter's strength of faith. With Walter's help, she could fight Snead, Hartley, and Dr. Forrest. But she didn't have any weapons against a creature built from the flesh of bad faith, or the darkness that crept from the depths of her soul and was expanding to fill all she knew and believed.

CHAPTER TWENTY-EIGHT

"The Jeep won't do us any good," Walter said when they returned to the cabin. "They could block off the road easy."

"Maybe we should stay here," Julia said. "You've got the gun."

Walter shook his head. "I told you I'm no Clint Eastwood. I'd be just as likely to shoot myself as to shoot one of them. And they got us outnumbered."

The sun was high overhead, with all the night's rain burned away. Julia studied the woods around them. The Creeps could already be here, surrounding their hideaway. She shuddered at the thought of holing up in the cabin, waiting for the Creeps to call up their stupid dark master or whatever it was they did. She pictured a mad scene of torchlight and shadows, low sinister chants, the air filled with bitter smoke from strange herbs. She shuddered the image from her mind.

"Which direction do we go?" she asked.

Walter nodded toward the north. "If we head over the backside of the mountain, we can follow the creek down to the Amadahee. If we keep at it, we ought to be out of the county in a couple of days."

"A couple of *days*?"

"I don't think we ought to risk trying to get any help around here. There's no way of telling who's on their side. On the *devil's* side."

Julia shook her head, staring at the ground. "I don't want to believe in Satanic conspiracies."

"Me neither, but they still keep on coming. You go in and

pack up the stuff and I'll go down to the spring to gather some water. If we figure on two days of hiking, we'll have to travel light."

The smoke had thinned from the chimney, the fire nearly dead. The forest was reflected in the cold black windows of the cabin. The peace of this place had been shattered. Now the cabin looked forlorn, soulless, only wood and stone.

She went inside, the room steeped in the glow of the dying fire. She gathered the clothes and the remaining food, stuffed them into the backpack, and threw the pack over her shoulder. Walter's can opener was on the hearth. She unzipped one of the pockets of the backpack and slid the can opener in, but decided the sharp edges might make a tear. She should wrap it in something. She reached into the pocket and her fingers touched a warm, round shape.

It felt familiar, and a shiver raced up her arm. Her heart skipped a beat as she pulled out the object, feeling its strange pulse even before she saw the twin rubies.

The skull ring.

The silver face leered up at her, the rubies gleaming in the firelight.

Something stirred in the loft. A voice came, muffled by the quilts.

"*Hello, Jooolia.*"

She recognized the voice from her childhood. An icicle speared her chest.

The quilts rose in the darkness. Julia looked away from the shadowy loft before the nightmare could come fully into view. She flung the ring into the fire and ran for the door.

As she fled the cabin, dark laughter chased her, crawling from both the fireplace and the loft. Walter was out of sight. She was going to call him, but was afraid *they* would hear. The thing in the cabin called her name again.

Creep, her mind screamed at her as she ran. *Creep, creep, creep. Devil made flesh.*

She ran toward the high rocks along the peak. The granite protruded from the Earth like the bow of a sinking ship, its gray mass cracked by eons of wind and weather. The trees blurred by, branches slapped at her face. Her breath burned in her lungs and she was dizzy, in danger of collapsing at any moment. Fear served as fuel, though, and kept her legs moving.

She reached the rocks and peered back through the bare trees. No one was chasing her. Had she imagined the voice, the figure in the cabin? Oh, God, she wasn't going to start having delusions out *here,* was she?

She hugged the backpack to her chest, fighting for breath. Below her, the rocky slope dropped off a hundred feet or more, broken only by moss and a few stubs of pine that sprouted from cracks. She leaned against the sun-warmed stone and closed her eyes.

Two steps forward into the air and she would be rid of them. Now and forever. Satan couldn't chase her beyond the grave. The pain, the past, the tricks and lies, nothing would be able to touch her.

But that would be a different surrender, and she was sick of surrender. She was a mountain. They couldn't break her.

And she didn't know what lay waiting on the other side. A ceaseless darkness promised peace, but that suicidal leap might end in the roasting pit of the one who had owned her all along.

She edged along the granite shelf, pushing the panic away from her mind. The wind was stronger here, shaking the stunted balsam trees below. A few clouds had spun their gray threads together, with another storm pushing in from the west. It was as if Satan were controlling the weather just to play with Julia's moods.

And why shouldn't he? Even God and Jesus acknowledged Satan was the master of this world, according to Luke's little chapter in Walter's Bible.

Voices came from somewhere in the forest. She ducked into a crevice and eased back into the shadows. She held perfectly still for what might have been minutes or an hour, hardly daring to breath, thinking that at any moment the shadows would swell and turn into the fingers of panic, to clutch her heart until it stopped.

Her legs were asleep from crouching, so she stood and leaned against the walls of the narrow cave. Julia pressed her back against the granite as footsteps came up the rocky trail.

Walter.

She stepped out of the crevice, but the footsteps had faded. The wind between the black trees was the only sound.

Except for the harsh breathing behind her.

She spun, dropping the backpack. Snead stood there, wearing a crooked smile.

"Are you ready, Judas?" he said.

He had crept up on her without a sound. Or else popped out of thin air. How could she fight the master of the world?

"Did you find her?" shouted a man's voice from somewhere below. Julia recognized it from her house, from the cabin, from the night her father disappeared. Hartley.

"She's here." Snead tugged her arm. "Come along, Julia. He's waited far too long. You've made him very angry, you know."

As if to support Snead's words, thunder rumbled over the far hills. The sky had gone from sunny to dismal in scarcely half an hour. The wind gained force, and branches creaked on the slopes below. More clouds massed overhead, black and gray rags torn in anger.

Julia allowed herself to be led along the cliff. She was numb, as if her blood had stilled itself in her veins. A lamb to slaughter.

They squeezed between two large boulders and emerged into a flat clearing. Hartley was waiting, dressed in a brown wool robe, the hood thrown back to reveal the dome of his bald head. His eyes were set deep in the bones of his face, condemned to always look out at the world from shadows.

"Anybody follow you, Lucius?" Hartley said.

"Nobody," Snead answered. "Triplett ought to be in custody by now."

"Should have put him out of the way a long time ago."

"Don't worry. I'm sure we can arrange a little 'accident.' A chase through the woods, he falls from a cliff trying to elude arrest, nobody will think twice about it. Not with his past."

Hartley pulled a gun from his robe. "Unless the Triplett whore's bones turn up. And the bones of the baby she gave us. Then somebody else might start snooping around, like Judas Stone here."

The Triplett whore? Walter's wife. Oh, God, no. What kind of woman could give up her infant as a sacrifice?

Julia's anger revived her, and she fought against Snead's grip. Three more hooded figures emerged from the trees. It was as if Satan had summoned them out of earth, wind, fire, and water. They surrounded her, rough hands groping and clutching her limbs.

"Tie her," Hartley ordered.

Julia struggled but was overpowered and forced to the ground. Her hands were yanked behind her and her feet bound with rope. A faint scent of perfume crossed her nostrils, and a slender hand touched her cheek. The whispers went into her ears and through the lost rooms of her soul.

"You're one of us," Dr. Forrest said. "You've always been

one of us."

"You bitch," Julia spat. "I've never been one of you."

"You were born one of us," Dr. Forrest said. "You belong."

"The master is ready," Hartley said, looking around, the gun pointed at the turbulent sky. The wind had risen, now was chattering and screaming through the trees. "He's given us the signs."

"What do we do after we finish her?" Snead asked Hartley.

"Let Satan decide."

"There are too many loose ends, Hartley. Satan's supposed to blind the weak. But bodies have turned up, and sooner or later somebody's going to link us to Memphis."

"Are you doubting, my Brother Judas?"

The hooded figures stood around Julia, watching the confrontation. Julia noticed two of them wore patent leather shoes. Cop shoes.

Snead said, "He has truly blessed us. I'm just thinking about it from a law-enforcement perspective."

Hartley's voice rivaled the low thunder that crept over the hills. "There's only one law, and only one enforcer."

Julia looked up at Snead, saw the man's aquiline face redden in anger. "That's easy for you to say. You make the messes, and I have to clean them up."

Hartley raised his left hand as if addressing the sky. "Even the book of fools acknowledges the master of this world." Hartley smiled at Julia. "Four-oh-six, Judas."

A gunshot echoed over the hills, coming from the rocks near the peak of the ridge. Julia's heart clenched.

Walter. They must have found him.

She pictured him slumped in the leaves, blood pouring from his chest. Shot while trying to escape, they'd say. But Julia would know the real truth: that he had given his life trying to protect her. And she had doubted him and his God.

Hartley had ducked at the sound and now motioned Snead to investigate. Snead and two of the hooded figures disappeared among the boulders. Hartley whispered, "Watch the whore," and then slipped into the trees. Julia lay on the ground, tied and helpless, alone with Dr. Forrest.

The doctor knelt beside Julia, gently stroking Julia's hair. Julia cringed from the contact, sickened by the possibility of Walter's death. She sobbed.

"Hush, Sister Judas," Dr. Forrest said to her. "You're nearly healed."

What was this crazy woman saying? How many others had she polluted in her role as a therapist? How many other vulnerable victims were led to this wicked end by Dr. Forrest's manipulation?

Dr. Forrest smiled down at her, like a Madonna upon a child. "If only your father could see you now."

"What about my father?" Julia managed to ask through her confusion.

"He was weak, a fool. He lost his courage just when he was about to enter the Inner Circle. Imagine the power Satan would have bestowed upon him if only he'd have had the strength to seize it."

"No," Julia said. "You told me—you made me remember that he molested me."

Dr. Forrest laughed, a sound as sinister as the whipping of the rattlesnake's tail. "Douglas Stone couldn't molest a lamb, much less a living human being. Your mother was the strong one, the one willing to sacrifice everything. Then, when it came time to deliver you unto the master, Douglas stole you."

Dr. Forrest's face grew dark and her eyebrows made arrow tips. "But *nobody* runs away from the Brotherhood. And the Master doesn't suffer fools."

"What did you do to him?" Julia fought against her bonds, but now, just like 23 years ago, she couldn't break free. She was angry at these monsters, a rage that almost drove the colors of her mind from black to red. But she was even angrier at herself, to think she could have let someone else build false memories in her head, to have allowed someone to own her so completely.

"He's in a better place now," Dr. Forrest said, a vacant smile on her face. "The master surely saved one of the hottest pits of hell for that pathetic worm. I was one of those who came for you that night. Douglas had called the cops, and we could hear the sirens. If Snead hadn't been there to protect us—"

Dr. Forrest closed her eyes as if to control her rage. After a moment, she opened them and continued. "Your father broke the window and tried to shove you through. Your belly was cut on the glass. There was so much blood, so much magic. And Douglas wasted it."

The scars on Julia's abdomen. They weren't the beginnings of a pentagram after all. They were wounds, not the brand of a possessor.

She knew Dr. Forrest couldn't resist talking, so she decided to learn as much as she could. "Why me?"

"Your mother believed enough to offer her own flesh and blood and breath. But Douglas betrayed us. A Judas among Judases. You must come to Satan to pay for your father's betrayal."

Julia's eyes filled with tears. "Wasn't killing him payment enough?"

Dr. Forrest had returned to the soothing tones she'd used in their therapy sessions, adopting her familiar role. "You're still so confused, Julia. Don't fight the truth. Just giving your life isn't enough. You have to give him everything. You have to *believe.*"

Believe. In a belief system crafted to teach morality, but also offering an alternative to those who didn't want to wait a lifetime before receiving eternal rewards. Satan wasn't a snake, a silver ring, or anything that wore flesh. It was only a symbol for the naked human lust for power. For selfish gratification and twisted indulgence, no matter the ultimate cost.

And she had paid all her life in their sick coin. Now Walter had cashed out, too.

"We wanted you to come unto Satan in willing innocence. After all these years, the only way to do that was to make you see his power and accept it. Satan demands a total surrender from his whores." Dr. Forrest gave a leering grin. "That's how I serve him."

Someone shouted in the forest, and another shot rang out. Julia's heart leapt with hope. *Walter must still be alive!*

And if he were willing to keep fighting, so was she. She didn't have a gun, but she had a different weapon. Dr. Forrest craved one thing greater than an imaginary master's blessing.

For years, people have tried to make me someone I'm not. So maybe it's time to 'become' that person. Let's see what Judas Stone can do.

"I . . . I was willing," Julia said. "You're right. I was confused. But you and Dr. Danner have helped me so much."

Dr. Forrest beamed with approval. "Lance thought it was best that we get you away from Mitchell. Lucius thought so, too. I'm glad they sent you to me. I feel that I understand you. We're the same."

"Yes," Julia said. "I couldn't have made it without you. I would still be so lost."

"The truth will set you free."

"I want to be free."

The doctor's eyes shone with a manic gleam. "Embrace him, then. Surrender yourself."

More shouting came from the high rocks. The wind was roaring now, clouds colliding like the ragged sails of warships, the sky nearly solid black in the late afternoon. One of the hooded Satanists emerged from the trees and came into the clearing. It was Hartley.

"Bring the whore," he said, anger in his voice.

"What's wrong?" Dr. Forrest asked.

"Triplett has a gun. We have to hurry. Bring her to the altar."

Hartley disappeared into the forest again. Julia fought an urge to scream, "If Satan's so almighty powerful, why can't he stop bullets?" But in every religion, even the ones predicated on evil instead of good, faith was blind, frail, and ultimately human.

"I want to give myself," Julia said. "I'm healed now."

Dr. Forrest frowned. "But you were angry—"

"Only at myself," Julia said, imitating the blissful drone that Dr. Forrest had instilled in her during dozens of sessions. "But now I see. The Master has gone to so much trouble. I am honored."

"You are his favorite," Dr. Forrest said. "And I've helped bring you to him."

"Please. Untie my feet, so that I can go with a willing heart."

Dr. Forrest hesitated.

"You heard Brother Hartley," Julia continued. "We don't have much time, and I don't think you can carry me, even if the Master lends his strength."

Julia almost choked on this false testimony she was babbling. She tried to remember the words of the televangelist from the misdirected—or planted—videotape. If she could adopt some of that same self-righteous flavor and use it to the "Master's" glory, Dr. Forrest might swallow it.

"I want to be one of you," Julia said. "I want to go to him in glory. I've seen his power. Untie me, so that I might embrace him. So I can go to him of my own free will."

Free will, which the Satanists worshipped almost as much as they did their hollow deity and their own selfishness.

"You'll have to be marked." Dr. Forrest rubbed her own pentagram scar through the robe. "Serve him through the pain and blood."

Julia tried a sincere, rapt look. It felt thin on her face, an obvious fake. But Dr. Forrest was blind. She saw only what she wanted to see. Her eyes were bright in the eagerness to heal Julia, to bring a new Sister into the fold, to claim a victory so that her dark master might smile upon her.

"I'm ready to wear his ring," Julia said, hoping that was the right thing to say. "I'm ready to become the whore Judas Stone."

Dr. Forrest's strong fingers pulled at the rope that bound her feet. The double-hitch knot came free and Julia wriggled the rope from her feet. Dr. Forrest pulled her into a standing position. "The altar's ready," the doctor said. "We've been working so long for this day."

Julia glanced up toward the granite peak. A robed figure clung to the face of a boulder, peering down the opposite slope. They were going to ambush Walter. Julia started toward the rocks, but Dr. Forrest grabbed the rope that trapped Julia's hands behind her back.

"This way, Judas Stone," she said, tugging Julia in the direction in which Hartley had gone. Julia thought about pulling free and running, but she wouldn't be able to help Walter while her hands were tied. She'd have to be patient and wait for her chance.

They went through a stand of balsam and hickory and came upon a second, smaller clearing. In the middle was a flat boulder, surrounded by brown grass. A worn path circled the boulder. The altar had been used before, maybe to sacrifice Walter's wife and child.

Hartley crouched beneath a tree, sharpening his knife. He tucked the knife in his robe and approached them. His eyes were like pockets of fire beneath his heavy brow. "Judas Stone," he said, smiling. "Are you ready to join us?"

She nodded. She didn't want to appear too eager, at least not in front of Hartley. Dr. Forrest was deranged, but Hartley's face was crafted by a mixture of shrewdness and cruelty. Julia supposed that so-called High Priests didn't ascend to their positions by accident. The Master chose wisely.

"Put her on the altar," Hartley said.

Snead rushed into the clearing, his hood back, his robe askew on his shoulders. "We haven't got him yet. We're trying not to shoot him. A bullet's harder to explain than an accidental fall."

Hartley gave a reptilian smile. "Brother Snead, that's why the Master made you Chief of Police."

Snead again looked angry, and Julia saw that she might be able to use the in-fighting to her advantage.

"It's too much," Snead said. "I can control my end, but if outsiders start snooping, the cracks start to show. Some reporter called me yesterday asking if we suspected Satanic activity in the death of the floater. The SBI might start asking questions, too."

"Just take care of your business, and let the Master take care of the rest."

"Damn it, Hartley, she'll give you the money," Snead said, looking at Julia. "All you have to do is tell her you'll cut her eyes out if you don't. Do we have to go through more of this damned mumbo-jumbo?"

Hartley's eyes grew even brighter. "Silence, Judas," he roared.

"What money?" Dr. Forrest asked.

"The money Douglas Stone stole from the Brotherhood," Snead said coldly. "Three million goddamned dollars. With interest, it could be twice that now."

Julia stared at the ground, pretending to be dazed and driven to the babbling edge by Dr. Forrest's mental manipulation. *Three million.*

"Brother Hartley?" Dr. Forrest asked. "What's he talking about?"

Snead continued. "Do you think we keep all these little covens going just for the hell of it? All our brothers and whores work for the Master, all right, but it comes down to money. Hookers, crack, guns. Or haven't you heard that Satan rules the world?"

Julia sneaked a glance at Dr. Forrest's face. The woman looked as if she'd been clubbed in the head, her mouth fallen open, her eyes wide. "B-but the Master—"

"The Master smiles, Judas Forrest," Hartley said. "We spread wickedness. Love of money is the root of all evil."

"And take a cut of the profits," Snead said. "Well, *my* cut's going to be a little bigger. After all, I'm the one who stole drugs from the evidence locker. I'm the one who made sure those missing persons stayed missing and didn't turn up as bones somewhere. And I want half."

"That wasn't the deal," Hartley said slowly.

"New deal." Snead pulled a gun from his robe, and for a moment Julia thought he was going to shoot Hartley. Instead, he stepped over to Julia and pressed the gun to her head.

"Don't!" commanded Hartley. "She's the only one who can take the money out of the trust fund."

The barrel of the pistol was cold against Julia's temple. She held her breath, counting down slowly. If she was going to die, she didn't want to die in the blinding darkness of panic. She wanted to die thinking about what might have been, a future that led away from pasts that had never have occurred. She wanted to die healed and whole.

She visualized the mountains, where the ridges met the clouds. Walter was there on that imaginary horizon, waiting. And maybe something behind him, the shadow of his soul, the light of his heart.

Walter's God had ceded this world to sickness, lust, and greed, but even the frail hope of salvation was better than the certainty of nothingness.

CHAPTER TWENTY-NINE

The cold gun drew Julia back to the windy clearing. Three million dollars. The price of Julia's soul.

Mitchell must have known about the trust fund. With his connections, he probably knew about it before they'd even started dating. That made his possessiveness more understandable. Money and stolen underwear. The two ways into Mitchell's worthless heart.

Too bad she'd be dead before she ever had a chance to laugh in his face.

"Come on," Snead said to her, holding the gun steady. It was the same type as the one Walter had taken from Mitchell, a black automatic.

Dr. Forrest stood near Hartley, her hands clasped together under her chin. Hartley glowered, his thin white hair tangled by the fierce wind. The surrounding forest had grown dark, with the spaces between trees filled with black shadow. The thunder was nearer now, and the ground seemed to shake under Julia's feet.

"She stays," Hartley said. "She belongs to the Master."

"Cut the crap," Snead said. "It's just us now. No need to put on your Satan show."

"She belongs to him," Hartley said.

"This plan was screwed up from the start. You think she's going to join the coven now and willingly give you the money? I don't know why we had to waste all those years letting the shrinks mess with her head. The best way to mess with somebody's head is to put a bullet it in."

"You forget your station," Hartley said. "I'm the High

Priest here."

"Circles within circles," Snead said. "And who do *you* have to cut in on the deal? How many other people get a piece of the devil's money?"

"Brother Snead, don't interfere with the Master," Dr. Forrest pleaded. "Judas Stone was chosen. She was born to be one of us."

"Damn, 'Sister,'" Snead mocked. "You sound like you've fallen for your own brainwashing. You can stay here and try to explain all these bodies to the cops. The *straight* cops. Me, I'm taking this whore back to Memphis, where we're going to stroll into Stone's favorite S & L and make a little withdrawal."

He pressed the gun barrel more tightly into Julia's temple. "Ain't that right, Sister?"

If they expected Julia to be insane after years of abusive psychotherapy, she wouldn't disappoint them. After all, Dr. Danner and Dr. Forrest had been hammering away at her, building false memories, turning her past inside out, making her believe in monsters. The first rule of victimhood was to have an obsessive desire to please others. If Snead wanted her insane, she'd be glad to deliver.

"If the Master so wishes," she said, giving a smile that she hoped was appropriately empty.

Snead pushed her toward the rocks. She nearly lost her balance, her hands still tied behind her back. "Go on," he said to her. "It'll be night soon. I don't want to be out here in the woods with all these idiots running around with guns. A guy could get hurt."

They started up the narrow trail. Laurel thickets bordered both sides, the waxy leaves dark. The undergrowth was too dense to try for an escape. Snead pushed her forward, and she had no choice but to stumble toward the peak.

The last of autumn's leaves flapped in the trees, and the air tasted of static. Julia looked for a chance to flee. She almost didn't fear getting shot. At least that would be quick and merciful. But she hated to lose to these Creeps, now that she knew how pathetic and weak they were.

"Snead!" Hartley shouted, his voice nearly lost in the howling wind.

As Snead turned, two hooded figures burst from the laurel. One swung a long heavy branch, hitting Snead across the back. The other tackled Snead around the waist and grabbed at his arm. Julia was shoved to her knees in the struggle. The pistol fired twice, and one of the men groaned in pain.

Julia lurched to her feet. Hartley and Dr. Forrest hurried up the trail. The two men in robes held Snead down. Snead's face was bright with anger, blood seeping from one of his legs.

"Damn you fools," Snead hissed. "Don't you see what he's doing? He wants it all for himself. He always has."

"No, Judas Snead," Hartley said, breathing heavily. "Our *Master* wants it all. Because everything is already his." Hartley pulled a knife from his robe. "Including your sorry soul."

Julia edged toward the laurels, momentarily forgotten by the Brotherhood. Snead kicked beneath the grip of his captors, but couldn't free himself. Julia noticed one of the hooded figures had a hole in the back of his robe. A dark wetness surrounded the hole.

Shot through the heart. And still WALKING? What were these people made of?

Hartley lifted the knife and shouted to the sky, "Accept this sacrifice, Satan, O Master of the world, though this soul be of little worth."

Hartley bent over Snead, who uttered a string of curses. Julia looked away as the knife descended. Snead's scream turned to a gurgle and was stolen away by the wind. Julia looked at Dr. Forrest. The woman's eyes were hot with a mad inner bliss.

Hartley stood and cleaned the knife on his robe. "Sorry to taint the blade with his blood," he said, smiling at Julia. "But the Master will forgive you. Are you ready to finish the mark and join us?"

The pentagram. Hartley wanted to carve the final three lines to complete the scar. Then would come the surrounding circle in her flesh, the knife like cold fire beneath her skin. And at last she would be his, mind, body, and soul.

And trust fund.

If Satan owned the world, why did he need three million dollars? Sins were common. Evil was cheap. And spiritual emptiness was absolutely free.

But she couldn't run, not with her hands bound and her path cut off. If she dove into the laurels, she'd become tangled in the branches. The peaks ahead were too treacherous to navigate with her hands behind her back. And the hooded Brothers had proven their cruel efficiency.

The best option was to stall for time. Walter wouldn't give up, not while he still had a breath.

"Join us, Julia," said Dr. Forrest. "Become the whore Judas Stone."

Dr. Forrest held out her arms. Everything would be fine, all wounds would heal, the Master would forgive Julia's waywardness. Satan was the most compassionate of all the deities ever devised by humans. Satan allowed his followers free will.

But free will also belonged to those who *didn't* follow.

Walter wouldn't want me to surrender. He'd want me to keep fighting. I am a mountain. They can't break me.

Julia imitated Dr. Forrest's rapt smile. "I don't want to be alone anymore, Sister."

She stepped forward, between the two Brothers, and bowed her head slightly toward Hartley. "I'm ready to submit."

"He will be pleased," Hartley said. He looked up at the strange swirling sky, the bare trees like a thousand black fingers in the wind. "We must hurry, though. Austin might have reported the whore to the state police."

Dr. Forrest peeled her robe over her shoulders and threw it on the ground. She stood naked in the fading afternoon, trembling from either the chill or excitement. "Make her Satan's," she said, her voice high.

"What do we do with Snead?" said the hooded figure to Julia's left.

Hartley stroked the edge of the knife with his thumb, his tongue poking slightly between his lips. "Remove his head and throw him over the cliff. Let the waters take him, like they did Judas Triplett."

The Brother to Julia's right released her arm and moved in front of her. He smelled of wood smoke. The blood on the robe's torn fabric was thick and congealed. She recognized the ring on his left hand, though the silver was blackened with ash.

The skull ring.

From the fireplace in the cabin.

"Brother Snead can wait," said Dr. Forrest. "But Satan is eager. He's waited so long for this whore. He told me how badly he wants to take her, to burn her, to taste her blood." The woman rubbed her hands over her scarred belly in a grotesque parody of allure.

"So mote it be," said Hartley. "Remove your robes and partake of his pleasures. Come to Satan in purity, with nothing to hide." He leered at Julia. "And you're next, whore."

Hartley began pulling up his own robe, revealing his thin

and mottled legs. The skull ring on the man's hand glowed, as if the twin rubies were lit by inner hellfire. Hartley must have been in the cabin, found the ring, and brought it to be blessed by the kiss of Julia's blood.

No, *her* skull ring was worn by the hooded figure in front of her, the one who wasn't removing his robe.

The Brother who smelled of wood smoke.

She recognized Walter's boots beneath the hem of the robe.

As the Creep to the right of Julia released her arm to remove his own robe, Walter sprang toward Hartley. The High Priest's arms were tangled in the cloth, and he grunted in pain when Walter shoved a shoulder into the man's stomach. Hartley gave an awkward swing with the knife, his robe falling back around him, and gasped, "Help me, Judas."

The hooded Creep jumped Walter and they both fell to the ground. Hartley struggled to his feet and held the knife over the two struggling figures. "Guide my hand, O Satan," said the crazed man, spittle whipped from his mouth by the wind.

The knife plunged toward the hooded figures, and one of them groaned in pain. Julia stumbled forward, praying that Walter had not been hurt. Dr. Forrest grabbed Julia, her fingers like talons.

Hartley stood back and pulled his gun from the folds of his robe. One of the hooded figures rolled to his knees while the other lay still. The kneeling figure peeled back his hood.

Walter.

He slumped before Hartley, looking up at the bloody knife like a penitent before a shrine. Hartley's gun pointed at his face. Julia glanced at the forest floor surrounding Snead's body. The Creeps had forgotten about Snead's gun. She saw it, a muted glint against the dark leaves.

But even if she could get to it, she couldn't aim it with her hands tied behind her back.

She had only one weapon. Her mind. The crowded, multi-roomed house that had harbored so many doubts and shadows, that had closeted so much pain, that had scrambled its memories like so many alphabet blocks. She had allowed others to open and close her doors, but all her housekeepers had been mad. Now it was time to clean house herself.

"Don't," she shouted, seeing Hartley about to strike. The High Priest froze with the knife over his head. A drop of blood fell onto his bald head and trailed down his face.

"The Master doesn't want any more worthless sacrifices," Julia said. "It's me that he wants." Her words seemed amplified by the wind, rushing from the trees on all sides of them. The sky grew darker, night swallowing night.

Julia stepped toward Hartley, bowed, and knelt beside Walter. She avoided Walter's eyes, unable to bear the betrayed look she would see there. Dr. Forrest went to Hartley's side, grinning down at Julia, her eyes as bright as morning stars.

"She wants to join," Dr. Forrest said, shivering. "I told you she was ready."

Hartley frowned, confused. "But we won't be able to get the money."

"The Master can always get money," Dr. Forrest said. "But how many times does he get such sweet revenge? Imagine the power, imagine his blessings upon us, if we give him the daughter of the one who betrayed him?"

Under other circumstances, Julia might have laughed at the idea of someone's betraying the prince of betrayal. But, no, she wasn't a skeptic, she was a true believer, willingly offering her flesh to the master of the world. She mirrored the crazed, beatific smile that Dr. Forrest wore and was horrified to find how easily it slipped onto her face.

"Give me to him," Julia begged Hartley. "I want Satan to have me, body and soul. Of my own free will."

"No, Julia," Walter said.

"Shut up," Hartley said to Walter. "If it wasn't for your meddling, this whore would already belong. But I suppose Satan owes you a small debt of thanks. After all, your whore wife and child were worthy sacrifices."

Walter gasped and trembled with rage. Julia knew she couldn't wait much longer. She said to Dr. Forrest, "Untie me, so that I might come to him, pure and willing. We are all part of the Circle."

The nude woman stooped behind Julia and began tugging on the knots. "Oh, Sister. I'm so glad you want to belong. We'll be together forever, in him."

Hartley held the knife menacingly above Walter. "Watch the whore," Hartley said.

"She trusts me," Dr. Forrest said, as if talking to the forest and rocks and river. "And Satan will smile on my work. Because I've helped make Julia who she is. I've helped her become Judas Stone. Haven't I, Master?"

The knots loosened and the rope slipped down Julia's wrists. Dr. Forrest began pulling Julia's sweater over her head, preparing her for the completion of the pentagram. Julia kept the acolyte's smile, though her eyes were fixed on Hartley. His skull ring glowed in the rising darkness, the rubies making two red specks even though there was no light to reflect.

Julia looked at the ring on Walter's finger. *Her* ring. No reflection came from it. Her breath caught. She'd thought this was all a game, that "Satan's" tricks were explained by the manipulation of Creeps. The power of Dr. Forrest's suggestions combined with false memories.

But what if she'd really been born unto Satan? What if her father had given her away, but changed his mind and rescued her? What if the long-ago ritual had been interrupted, and Satan had delighted in Julia's long, torturous path back to the

Inner Circle?

No matter. The words were out like a rote magic spell before she could reconsider. "I want Satan to have me, body and soul. Of my own free will."

When Julia had said those words, hadn't a sick warmth filled her chest? Hadn't she felt giddy with strength, as if the master of the world would share the world's sick spiritual wealth? Didn't Satan promise absolute freedom, freedom to kill or scar or lie or lust? All sins without a price, because the ultimate price had already been paid?

She gazed at Hartley, half-expecting to see a goat's head sprouting from the top of his robe, expecting the master to don flesh so that he might taste his world's mortal sins. But all she saw was a depraved, aging man, his face reddened by the cold wind.

The skull ring was just a piece of metal set with ornamental stones. A symbol for the fools who lacked hope, who saw no value in the living and so had to fabricate a monstrous illusion. And daggers, robes, pentagrams, rituals were nothing but stage props for a nonexistent deity, contrived mockeries to give meaning to meaningless lives. The ultimate worship of self and ego.

She looked at Walter, and in his eyes saw life. The fires of the soul were never lit by fallen angels. They were lit by compassion. Power was created by a sacrifice that was selfless, not a sacrifice that was made to gain approval. Walter had made sacrifices for her, and he had sparked hope in her own heart. And love was the brightest of powers, the hottest of fires, the force that brought even gods to their knees.

Or maybe she was simply insane.

Either way, Julia stood, energy flowing through her limbs. She felt Dr. Forrest pulling on her blouse, trying to expose her abdomen so that Hartley could bring the knife to bear. The forest seemed like a wild beast, pulsing and throbbing beneath the skin of night. The wind rose and fell in a melody that might have been as old as the earth.

Julia shrugged away from Dr. Forrest's clutching fingers, turned, and walked up the path toward the high rocks. "O Satan, my Master, come take me," she shouted at the sky.

Hartley called after her, or it may have been Walter. She heard Dr. Forrest's footsteps in the dead leaves, chasing.

"Jooolia?" Hartley yelled, his voice barely audible above the gale.

They had killed her father. *Hartley* had killed her father. And though her father may have been spiritually weak, seduced by the attraction that corrupt moral freedom offered, he had rescued Julia when the Brotherhood sought to carve her up. No one was beyond redemption.

"Satan calls me," Julia said, continuing up the path, feeling her way between the laurels. She hoped her shambling gait was appropriately zombie-like.

She came to the spot where Snead had fallen. His gun was invisible in the darkness. She stumbled, swooned, and dropped to her knees, running her hands over the ground while pretending to regain balance.

"You need *us* in order to get to the Master," Dr. Forrest said from a few feet behind Julia. "You can't do it alone. Come before the High Priest. Let us help you belong."

Julia's fingers brushed over the gun and closed on the grip. Snead had been tackled in the act of firing, so the safety was off. She didn't know much about guns, but she knew how to point. And, if necessary, pull the trigger.

Dr. Forrest caught up to her and embraced her, the woman's bare skin feverishly hot. Julia allowed herself to be led back down the trail. She could scarcely make out Walter and Hartley, who were two gray silhouettes against the shadow of the world, Walter still on his knees.

Dr. Forrest nudged Julia toward Hartley. The High Priest turned the knife so that it caught some of the scant light.

"Why use the knife?" Julia said. "Does the Master not love bullets?"

Dr. Forrest touched Julia's shoulder. "Sister?"

"Or is a bullet too quick? Does Satan like to hear the little children scream while you cut them up? Or is it *you* who gets his jollies out of other people's pain and suffering?"

"You *whore*," Hartley said.

"Finish it," Dr. Forrest said, though Julia couldn't tell whether the woman was addressing Hartley or Satan.

Hartley swung his pistol toward Julia. "You can't fool the Master. He's the *original* liar. And he's got a place for you in hell."

Walter chose that moment to attack, lunging into Hartley's knees. Hartley swung the pistol toward Walter's head, the metal cracking against the hard bone of Walter's skull. Walter slumped, moaning, while Hartley fought to regain balance.

Julia pulled Snead's pistol from behind her back. "Tell Satan I said 'hello.'"

Hartley's mouth fell open in surprise. A surge of electricity flowed through Julia and she could have sworn the wind whispered, "Do it." She pulled the trigger three times.

Dr. Forrest screamed, and for an impossible moment, Hartley still stood, gazing at the wounds in his chest. He looked at Julia, and then at the pistol in his own hand. He smiled. She was so paralyzed with fear that she couldn't pull the trigger again, as if Hartley had stolen her energy in order to keep himself upright. As if he were drawing up the life of the trees, dirt, and rocks.

The blood of the world.

For the briefest of moments, the goat's face appeared over

Hartley's and the capricious lips—*surely an illusion?*—parted in a smirk of victorious surrender.

The wind rose, the music of the woods screaming to a crescendo, the devil's orchestra drawing its bows—

Stop it, Julia.

No music, only Dr. Forrest's wail and Hartley swaying.

Then, with a gurgle in his throat, he collapsed.

As Hartley hit the ground, the clouds tugged themselves apart and a sliver of sunset bathed the mountain. Somewhere over or beneath the mountain, thunder rumbled, as if the Master were laughing. Or perhaps God had broken his lifelong silence and finally spoke to her. Any message was lost in translation.

Julia stooped and gathered Hartley's automatic and helped Walter to his feet.

"You okay?" she asked.

He rubbed his head, steadying himself against her as he stared down at Hartley. "Doing better than him, anyway."

Dr. Forrest knelt by her tainted leader and wept, her arms over her flaccid breasts. "You were *one* of us," she blubbered to Julia.

"No," Julia said. "I was never *anybody's.*" She put her arm around Walter, helping support him.

Dr. Forrest looked up. The wind died and the soft fading light caught the tears on the woman's cheeks. "He owns you."

"I choose who I belong to," Julia said. She kicked Dr. Forrest's robe toward the pathetic, trembling woman. "You'd better put that on before you freeze."

Dr. Forrest snatched at the robe, jumped to her feet, and ran toward the trees. Her sad, broken laughter filled the clearing. "Satan calls me," mocked Dr. Forrest, in a strange falsetto. "I hear him in the trees. He's everywhere."

Walter tried to stagger after her, but Julia stopped him.

"Let her go," she said. "She won't freeze to death if she keeps moving. They'll find her sooner or later and get her the help she needs."

Walter leaned against her. "Hopefully, she won't get a therapist as screwed-up as yours."

"You're making fun of a woman who's holding a gun," she reminded him.

"You're not a bad Clint Eastwood yourself," he said.

She didn't want to explain the murdering force that had descended upon her and briefly possessed her. It would sound deranged, the kind of thing a defense lawyer would use for an insanity plea. Walter would call it the grace of God, but Julia could never be sure whether it was instead the will of a malevolent master whose most potent magic was served by disguise and doubt. The devil's greatest trick was in getting people to believe he didn't exist.

But maybe God's greatest trick was in granting people the free will to doubt.

"I'm no better than they are," she said, looking at the gun that was cooling in her hand.

Walter shook his head. A large purple knot was swelling above his temple. He touched it and winced. "I'm going to have a hell of a hangover tomorrow."

So would Julia. Tomorrow, she'd have to deal with the fact that she had killed someone. She had played God just as certainly as Hartley had, taking human life. Sure, she could justify it, but every sin had its price, every sinner an excuse.

"Any more of the Creeps around?" she asked. "I only saw three, plus Hartley and the doctor."

"I shot one," he said. "That's where I got the robe. But I lost Mitchell's gun climbing up the rocks to get here. It got dark so fast I couldn't look for it."

"There might be more of the 'Brothers' around, but I doubt

it. Not enough slices of the money pie."

"Money?"

"I'll tell you later. Let's get out of here."

She helped Walter toward the trail, clutching the gun in her right hand. Maybe somewhere, God and Satan were sitting in the Happy Hour of the afterlife and bickering over the nature of good and evil and which of them had won this latest dice roll of human souls.

The sun slipped behind the ridges as they staggered back up the trail, both of them weak. They had reached the granite peak of Cracker Knob when Dr. Forrest's high voice drifted up from the woods. "Oh, Jooolia. Jooolia. He *ooowns* you, Jooooolia."

Julia looked out over the dark ripples of Appalachian Mountains in the distance, at the black pockets of valleys. In a strange way, Dr. Forrest *had* healed her. Compared to a devil-worshipping lunatic who liked to play with patients' minds, Julia felt like the most sane and rational person on the planet.

They rested against the rocks, the sky in twilight. Walter fidgeted with his hand for a moment and held something out to her. "This is yours," he said. "I was keeping it for you."

The silver ring. She looked at the skull grinning in the moonlight, at the stupid empty eyes that saw nothing.

"Free will," he said.

She took a step forward and hurled the ring into the deep valley below the rocks. Judas Stone didn't exist.

She couldn't tell which of them moved first, or if they simultaneously had the same idea. They embraced, their lips meeting, body heat and the heat beyond that combining. Julia kissed desperately, afraid that each precious moment belonged to the past, was already over and never to be regained. But then Walter kissed her again, and she knew that these moments were hers for as long as she desired.

They finally parted, Julia so light-headed that she had to lean against the rocks again. Neither of them spoke, afraid to break the little magic spell the world had allowed. Walter took her hand and guided her between the boulders under the timeless night.

The wind gently pushed the last scraps of clouds away. The sky was indigo and scattered with stars. The rising moon shone down on the silver forest. They continued through the trees, pushing away the groping branches.

By the time they reached the cabin, Julia was exhausted. They found that the Jeep's tires had been slashed. The Creeps had wanted to cut off easy escape.

"Looks like we'll have to hike out," Walter said.

"Not tonight," Julia said. "I'm beat."

"No, you're not beat. They'll never beat you if you don't let them."

"I am a mountain," Julia said, with just enough strength left to laugh. She turned solemn and said, "If you let God in your heart, can you ever make him leave?"

"Free will," he said.

"You're not still trying to save me, are you?"

"Door's open when you want to talk about it."

They went inside the dark cabin, Julia's hand squeezing the gun's grip, finger ready at the trigger. No Creeps. She was finished with Creeps, real or imagined. Doors closed and deadbolts thrown. Safe house.

"Want me to build a fire?" Walter asked.

"Yes," she said, pulling him toward the loft. "Like you did up on the rocks."

Julia climbed the ladder and scrambled onto the loft. She laid the gun within reach and kicked the blankets aside while Walter hurried up alongside her. Finally, she was ready to trust.

She tore at the buttons of his shirt, burning with hunger. This hunger was deep, reaching further inside her than any fear or panic or hopelessness ever had. This surrender was of her soul, the thing that she and she alone possessed.

Nobody could steal her soul. No demon, no god, no human. It was hers to give as she chose. Of her own free will.

As she reached for the heat of his skin, she wondered how he would react to the touch of her scars.

But it didn't matter. Wounds healed, scars faded, the past always lost in the battle of forever.

"Jooolia," he whispered, arousing a last shiver of doubt.

To hell with it.

She threw herself into the fire.

THE END

Scott Nicholson is the international bestselling author of more than 20 books. He lives in the Blue Ridge Mountains of North Carolina, where he tends an organic garden, strums guitar, and practices armchair Taoism.

Visit him at www.AuthorScottNicholson.com or email him at hauntedcomputerbooks@gmail.com.

OTHER BOOKS BY SCOTT NICHOLSON
Solom #1: The Scarecrow
Solom #2: The Narrow Gate
Solom #3: The Preacher
Liquid Fear
Chronic Fear
After #1: The Shock
After #2: The Echo
After #3: Milepost 291
Disintegration
The Red Church
Drummer Boy
McFall
Kiss Me or Die
Speed Dating with the Dead
The Skull Ring
The Home
Creative Spirit
October Girls (as L.C. Glazebrook)
Scattered Ashes
Monster's Ink
Thank You for the Flowers
They Hunger
Bad Blood (Spider #1)
Cursed (with J.R. Rain)
Dirt
Grave Conditions